THE AUBURN REBELLION

THE AUBURN REBELLION

BULLETFOOT™ BOOK TWO

MARSHAL RUST

Copyright © 2020 LMBPN Publishing
Cover Art by Jake @ J Caleb Design
http://jcalebdesign.com / jcalebdesign@gmail.com
Cover copyright © LMBPN Publishing
A Michael Anderle Production

LMBPN Publishing
PMB 196, 2540 South Maryland Pkwy
Las Vegas, NV 89109

First US edition, November 2020
(Previously published as a part of *Bulletfoot*)
ebook ISBN: 978-1-64971-324-7
print ISBN: 978-1-64971-325-4

Editor
Skyhunter Editing Team

Jessica13 sighed, pulled herself up a little in the cockpit, and held herself firmly in place when Mini took control of the mech. It was slow work to climb the hill that might as well have been a dune given the sandy soil that covered it. The sun beat relentlessly on her back as it slid toward the west and she sweltered unbearably in the tight space. Not for the first time, she wished her precipitous escape from Sanctuary had been after she'd upgraded the cooling system, not before.

Sweat made her flight suit cling uncomfortably and the heat made the smell of used grease around her impossible to tolerate, even though it would have been easy to ignore under any other circumstance.

Despite her increasing discomfort, she still needed to stay focused on the task at hand and remain as close to the ground as possible so she wouldn't sky-line herself at the top.

Thankfully, this wasn't all that difficult to accomplish. There weren't many mechs that were able to maintain a low enough center of gravity, but the Minato was one of them. And thanks to Mini's skills and abilities, they wouldn't be easy to see from a distance, not even from the height of the hill they currently climbed.

"There is a twenty percent chance that any insult you offer him when he is found will strike an emotional chord," Mini told her and broke what had been a fairly long silence. The distraction was welcome. "I would suggest something involving his mother. Or perhaps his body odor?"

"I won't insult him," Jessica13 said, even if she didn't fully mean it. The worst thing was that Mini could probably read her body language and tell that she wasn't entirely truthful. "But…can we move a little lower?"

"I can reduce the height of the mech by twenty percent, but that would also reduce our speed by an additional fifty percent," the AI replied.

"Do it. We don't need to move too fast," she said softly and wedged herself in more securely.

It was uncomfortable enough to remain in place while the Minato was in Bulletfoot mode and doubly so with the new legs that were intended to increase the speed of the mech when they were running. Unfortunately, they didn't do much for comfort, especially when they moved slowly.

And it didn't help that every step entailed a half-step slide as the loose soil gave way under the weight to send a small cascade down the hill each time they moved forward.

Every movement dislodged a tiny avalanche and raised small puffs of dust around them during their progress to the top. Aside from the fact that it made the climb more onerous, each time the hand grasped ahead to pull them up, dirt piled onto the Minato's freshly painted green coat, which made her cringe.

While the grubby look would make them more difficult to see at longer distances, who the hell actually liked walking around in a dirty mech? Besides, it would be a horror to clean the joints later.

Mini lowered them a little more before they crested the hill so they almost crawled to the top. The sun was behind them, which meant that if they were any higher, they would instantly be framed against the glow for anyone to see.

As it turned out, there weren't too many of anything to see them so their caution appeared to have been unnecessary. The plains ahead were mostly deserted, sweeping grasslands with patches of dirt cutting in there and there. The trees that rose from the grass didn't grow very tall and were mostly ugly, gnarly specimens meant to survive on the sparse water that was available to them.

The heat was not something to be ignored, of course, and what life there was could easily hide in the grass below.

There weren't any mechs, though. The indentation left by one even as small as the Minato would be seen easily from their vantage point. While there was the possibility that someone was down there without a mech, given the kind of dangers that lurked in the area—which included but were not limited to snakes and a variety of venomous spiders and insects—she doubted it.

The location was thoroughly devoid of human life.

"Do you pick up any life signs?" Jessica13 asked and checked the readings that Mini put up on her HUD. It was difficult not to enjoy the view of the grasslands that stretched out in front of them as far as the eye could see. The tall grass rippled in the wind like it was a large body of green water.

He was quick to reply. "About a couple of thousand, but it doesn't look like any of them are human. Unless someone's piloting a Sherlock with one hell of a shooting eye, I don't think we have anything to worry about."

"Is that so?"

"Do you have anything else to add?" he asked.

She made no effort to answer, and a few alarms pulled her attention to the edge of the hill.

"Movement on the periphery," Mini alerted her.

"Thanks for the update," she snarked.

Dull green-gray dust puffed and cascaded into a low cloud that covered most of the area before she could even identify what had caused it.

Something moved in the cloud, however, and at an impressive pace.

"Shit!" Jessica13 gasped as Mini reacted much quicker than she ever could have and leapt out of his crouched position. The Minato still didn't have much in the way of weapons aside from the grappler on the right arm, which meant the best thing she could possibly do if she came under assault was to run the hell away.

But whatever it was that attacked them moved much faster than she could have anticipated. The reading from the motion sensors told her it was a mech, but there was no way to determine what kind.

A low humming filled the air as two blades slashed viciously from the dust that billowed around her. The onslaught forced Mini back a couple of steps and the mech rose from their position on all fours. The muted buzz grew louder as the blades moved, and she could make out a couple of assault rifles aimed at her from above.

"Grappler!" Jessica13 shouted and hastily took control of the right arm as rounds pinged off the Minato's armor. The grappler launched with a hiss and the dart struck the earth a few dozen feet down the hill. She immediately engaged the retractor and yanked them down in a rush and away from the volley of bullets.

Mini engaged a couple of subroutines while they were still virtually airborne so they landed on their shoulder, rolled easily, and came out of it on their feet. He used the speed of their descent to jump all the way to the bottom of the hill in a single bound.

The impact was jarring, but she already knew enough to brace herself against it as the AI maintained their balance.

The other mech vaulted upward and a pair of rockets activated to launch it even higher. It streaked forward and landed beside them before they could race away.

She disengaged the air gun from the grappler and turned as the blades thrust toward them and stopped barely a couple of centimeters away from the cockpit.

Only a little closer, and the vibroblades the mech carried would have cut into her suit like a hot knife through a protein patty, and her along with it.

"Not bad," Windchime said. "You displayed quick reactions and good instincts. The only problem I see is that you still choose to fight rather than run."

"Sorry," Jessica13 said. "It's kind of an instinct. Simply running away without making an attempt to deal even a little damage doesn't feel natural."

"Well, I hope that changes before you're engaged in an actual fight again," he said and turned the blades off.

Their humming—from which his nickname was derived—ceased immediately as the hands sheathed the blades behind his mech. The second pair of arms quickly did the same with the assault rifles.

She still wasn't sure how he'd managed to do it. While the Balthazars' reputation was that they could be adapted to fit the parts of virtually any mech ever made, this had taken it to a whole new level. He had managed to connect the arms and swords from a couple of Difur Design Lab Predator V2s to the back and, perhaps most impressively, had written the code for the AI that operated his mech to take control of them whenever he was in combat.

Of course, it immediately made her curious as to how he had managed that. Most AIs were only designed to operate four limbs and adding a new one made the process that much more complicated, much less two.

The man had steadfastly preserved his secrets, though. He wasn't a new arrival to the Knights Mechanica, and the combat abilities of the hybrid mech he'd created were legendary to the point where they almost rivaled Hammerhand's.

With six limbs, the damn mech resembled an insect and sent an uncomfortable shiver down her spine every time she looked at it.

Still, it looked like most of the others in that it was painted green, although the color had chipped here and there. The closer she got, the more she realized that he had adapted the paint to blend with his surroundings a little better. The coating had a sticky quality to it that made the dust adhere more than normal to tint it to match the area he stood in.

Instead of banners over his pauldrons, he wore his like a cape hanging down his back, which served to hide the extra weapons and arms when they weren't in use. Although ragged and almost falling apart, it added to the camouflage. The flutter of fabric could be mistaken for vegetation moving in the wind.

"You need to keep your eyes open all around you," Wind-chime continued, pulled himself free of the cockpit, and climbed to the shoulder of his mech and tugged a couple of tools out. "Not only above the ground but below it too. Many pirates who use Balthazars like to bury themselves and use the rockets to launch out and surprise unwary travelers. You can usually locate one if you see a conical indentation in the ground."

"And if I see one?"

"In your case, don't engage," he said quickly. "Even if you manage to get in close enough to use that grappler of yours, you'll still be picked off by the assault rifles. You might want to think about adding weapons to that Minato of yours, though. Maybe put a couple of guns on the back that can be operated while you still run on all fours."

"That is not a terrible idea," Mini admitted. "Although some kind of arrangement would need to be made if you wish to use the mag clamps for conventional purposes."

It was certainly not a bad idea and would give her a way to fight back while they ran away, but as Windchime had said, her focus needed to be on the running. The Minato was unique in many ways, but she wouldn't be able to stand her ground against a combat mech without help.

Especially not the Balthazar-Predator V2 hybrid.

"Are we done with the training for now?" Jessica13 asked as they began to climb the hill again. "Or do you have more lessons to impart to me?"

Windchime looked at her and a deep scowl touched his features as he continued to repair whatever had been jolted free during his landing.

She knew what he would say. He and Hammerhand would never see eye to eye on every issue, but there were many things they agreed on. One of them was also one of Hammerhand's favorite quotes.

"The day we stop learning is the day we die," Windchime said as if on cue, and Jessica13 mouthed the words as he said them. "Whether it's because we stop learning and are killed as a result of the mistake, or because we die and therefore cannot learn anymore. One thing you need to learn more of is to improve your tracking skills. You should have been able to keep your eyes on the tracks I left."

"This soil doesn't keep tracks very well," she pointed out, took a step into the sandy soil of the hill, and lifted her foot only for it to come down and cover her tracks.

"It's still visible," he replied, "and you can see it. With that said, yes, this soil isn't good for much. Even the tough plants that are able to grow in this land are struggling. I doubt it was ever used for anything like farming. Nothing would grow here."

"Would the humans in the past have ever lived in this area?" she asked curiously.

The man shrugged and returned to his work, but Mini began to pull up relevant data from where he had it stored.

"A great many human civilizations were centered in locations with little merit if one only considered the fertility of the soil," he pointed out in his soft, feminine voice which was still comforting despite the fact that she knew it came from the wrong voice modulator. "Some settlements grew in what were essentially uninhabitable areas simply because rivers and springs provided a water source.

"The ancient city of Las Vegas was only one example. Of course, there were those for whom the lack of appeal of the desert or other inhospitable region was considered an advantage. This was possibly because they wanted to avoid the general populace—whom they believed would avoid the area —either because they wanted solitude or because they had other more nefarious intentions that would have been considered less than seemly in more heavily populated areas. Ironically, though, many of these settlements thrived and became bustling cities, perhaps because their existence alone made them appealing."

"The locations that had no appeal thrived because people thought someone living there made them appealing?" Jessica13 asked. That didn't seem right to her, but then, there were a lot of things about the Cities-That-Were that she still didn't understand. Most of how people lived back when they had so much more was foreign to her, having lived in a bunker where every drop of water was contained and recycled, and nothing was wasted.

She had seen areas where they had left the water flowing out in the open so it would all evaporate into the atmosphere and generally be lost. Of course, it would rain after a while and replenish it that way, but they couldn't be sure about when or where that rain would come from.

Humans were odd, odd creatures in those times. She realized that she still had so much to learn and reminded herself that adversity had changed the way people lived. Perhaps she would have been the same had she lived a hundred or so years earlier.

Windchime finished working on his mech, climbed into it, and followed her up the side of the hill toward the top.

"How many people do you think lived around these parts?" Jessica13 asked after they'd proceeded for a while in silence.

As it turned out, even with the extra limbs, the hybrid Windchime had put together still struggled to reach the top. Its lighter, leaner build seemed to dig its boots a little deeper into the sandy soil rather than provide a flatter surface to offset the weight a little like Mini did. Each had their own peculiarities, and it meant they made similar progress.

"Not many, given the soil," he responded when she turned to look at him at the top. "They would have used this area to farm other animals—the kind they ate in larger numbers since they're the only ones that could survive on the greenery that lives around here."

"Why would—" she started to ask but shook her head. It sounded wasteful to feed animals they would simply eat, but waste seemed to define what she had come to expect from how people lived then. Still, she was a little reluctant to voice it. A part of her knew her upbringing had been sheltered and her beliefs shaped by what she'd since discovered were lies— or at least some of them were lies. She hadn't had much time to sift through them all to decide which were or weren't.

"Why would what?"

She shrugged. "It seems a little wasteful, is all. If they had paid a little more attention to the soil, they could have made it more fertile. It would have meant they could grow more food to feed more people."

"I think the point was less about the amount of food and more about the quality," Windchime explained as they began their descent. "I don't know too much about it, but humans aren't meant to only eat plant-based food. Meat and animal products like...milk, which I heard they got from cows and maybe goats, have nutrients we need that we don't get from plants. We eat as healthy as we can, but plants can't replace what animals provide."

She frowned as she considered this. "So what we eat isn't really healthy?"

"Well...like I say, I don't know too much, but I wouldn't say it's not healthy. Maybe less healthy is closer to the truth.

We could have more kinds of nutrients available if we had animals, and it might be less wasteful to let them eat the vegetation than trying to make the soil more fertile."

Jessica13 nodded because it made sense, even though a part of her still struggled to move past her rigid perceptions of what was wasteful and what wasn't. If they had the resources, why not use them to generate more quality food—the kind that would apparently nourish them better—while they continued their existing strict food management?

"It still seems wasteful, though," she commented, "although maybe it's because we have no animals and it seems wasteful to use them for food if we did."

"I think our problem is we believe waste was a way of life back in the day," Windchime replied and hopped lightly down the short distance remaining to reach the bottom before she did. "We think those who were the most wasteful were seen as better off, or something."

"That's not entirely inaccurate," Mini interjected. "But many people in what we could call the last days became more conscious of waste and worked hard to avoid it. Not everyone simply abused the resources and made no effort to manage them."

Jessica13 let him take control and jump them beside Windchime. The man scrambled out of his mech again, landed with a grunt, and remained crouched as he studied the soil in front of him.

"What are you doing?" she asked. While she knew it was relatively safe to be out of the mech but old habits didn't simply vanish overnight. She still felt more comfortable in or on the Minato, and no amount of curiosity would change that.

"I'm inspecting the soil."

"I thought you already said it was no good."

He looked at her and ran his fingers across his clean-shaven jawline before he picked up a fistful of the dirt beneath his feet. "One can never be too sure. Besides, there is something to be learned from what we're looking at. Where we started out, everything was denser and greener and more supportive of life. Out here, it's more open, which would indicate that we are moving in the right direction."

"What is the right direction?" she asked and peered at the soil as if it would somehow reveal an answer.

"I'm actually not sure about that," Windchime admitted. "Hammerhand likes to cite the experts and admins from his time—whatever the fuck that is supposed to mean—and say a change in the landscape means we're headed in the right direction, and damned if I don't believe the old bastard."

She scowled at the man. "Well, if you don't know what it means, where would the right direction take us?"

"Well, that depends whether you believe the old myths of Citta del Mar," he said. "Hammerhand talks of it like he's been there and honestly, I have to say I believe the man. Or want to believe him, anyway."

Jessica13 narrowed her eyes. "I've never heard of that. Mini, do you have anything in your records?"

"Negative," he replied quickly. "I have no records of the location or the myth, but my records are about a hundred years out of date. I have endeavored to update them, though."

"What's so important about this Citta del Mar?" she asked her companion.

"It's been the mission of the Knights Mechanica to find it and reveal its location to the people still living in this area," the man explained. His voice took on almost a reverent tone as he brushed the soil from his hands so it caught the wind and spread into the grasslands ahead of them. "We know of it as a place of plenty, a land where the soil is rich and fertile and where people have begun to grow our society toward its former glory. It's a land that holds to the old world, with strong and healthy plant life, fields, parks, and entire cities of people living out in the open without fear of Skyfall or pirates."

"Have you ever seen it?" Jessica13 asked, unable to keep herself from being swept up by the wonder in the man's voice.

"No," Windchime admitted. "But I will see it one day. That's where Hammerhand is leading us."

"It would appear that Citta del Mar is a modern twist on the old Promised Land myth," Mini said. "A place where all is good in the world and all the evils are a thing of the past. Where there is peace and plenty for all."

"Are you saying it doesn't exist?" she asked, careful to keep this part of the conversation between herself and the AI.

"While the possibility that such a place might exist is impossible to dispute, the more logical explanation is that it is the result of hopeful and wishful thinking," he pointed out. "People who dream of such a place talk of it and the talk spreads to perpetuate the myth. If it does, in fact, exist, the likelihood of it living up to such lofty standards is equally unlikely."

Jessica13 scowled. She wanted to think there were places in the world where people didn't barely subsist in bunkers and scavenge to stay alive. There were enough reasons to think it, the Knights Mechanica themselves being only one. And if the thought of it was what kept them moving and helping people, she could see no reason why it was a bad thing to believe in it.

"Well, we'll keep searching for it," she told Mini. "Like you said, there'll always be a chance it does exist."

"You know I can tell that you're talking to your AI, right?" Windchime pointed out.

"From my body language. Yes, I know." She laughed. "Tinker likes to tell me every time like he doesn't do it himself."

"Well, yes, he is a crazy character, to begin with, so it would make sense that he sees the oddities in others but never himself." Her companion chuckled. "But all that aside, it's odd to see a mech making all the gestures that would be expected from a conversation but never actually delivering on the conversation part of it."

"Well, in that case, you simply have to know there is a conversation but not with you," she countered.

She wasn't sure why she challenged the man, although he had to know it wasn't intended as ill-will. It was more or less her style of speaking to someone. Any of the Knights would have been able to confirm that.

"Well, then, what is the AI saying that it doesn't want to tell me?" Windchime asked.

"Well, it's he, for starters," Jessica13 said with a chuckle. "And he merely wondered how reliable the stories of Citta del Mar might be. I told him that simply because it wasn't in his records didn't mean it didn't exist. Many things happened in the past hundred years or so while he wasn't activated."

"Well, you never got around to actually saying that," Mini said and it sounded like he was grumbling.

"I don't know. In a world like ours and growing up like we did, it's nice to think and dream of a place that found a way to put itself together again," the man said, and she thought she could hear a hint of a smile in his voice. "There are streams and clean drinking water. People don't live in cramped quarters or out in the open, scavenging and scraping to survive. There's no longer a need to repurpose and retool goddamn everything. Obviously, you still can if you want to, I guess, but it wouldn't be a requirement for survival."

"A place where parts are new instead of a hundred years old would be interesting," she admitted with a soft laugh.

"The Knights Mechanica have taken a beating lately," Windchime continued. "We're not what we used to be, and in a place like Citta del Mar, we would have something like a base. Somewhere we could come out of our mechs and settle in, rest, and recharge before we head out and help people again. Some might say it's not the worst thing in the world, but to my mind, I don't think we have any other choice. We'll die out here otherwise."

Jessica13 nodded. "I guess I can agree with that. It would take one hell of a lot to bring the Excalibur Hammerhand rides down, though."

"Drip by drip, water cuts through stone, not through force but through persistence," he said. "Eventually, we might see that the chipping away at his armor and his will brings Hammerhand down, and the world will be the poorer for it."

"Is that from the Great Prophet Sagan?" she asked.

His mech shrugged. "I don't think so. It might be, but I saw it scribbled onto a piece of aluminum back in the day like your *Live Free or Die Hard* chest plate there."

"It's a phrase that stuck with you, I understand, exactly like the dream of finding Citta del Mar. Honestly, I like the idea of it and I might start hoping for something like that myself."

He chuckled at her sudden exuberance. "I have to admit, hearing you say that helped to reaffirm my faith and hope of finding it. It is out there. Even if we have to build it ourselves to make it true."

"I do believe the term he is looking for is a self-fulfilling prophecy," Mini pointed out.

"Let us have this, okay?" she retorted and laughed.

"What?" Windchime asked.

"I'm talking to the AI again," she admitted.

He smirked. "Ah… Well, I'm not sure if an AI is capable of hope. I have been told it is almost uniquely human and there is no coding in the world that can account for it."

A quick scan of Mini's files crossed the HUD. "That's not untrue, I suppose. Hope is a difficult thing to quantify, although it could merely be expressed as wanting something to happen to the point of almost expecting it."

Jessica13 smiled and ran her fingers along the inside of the cockpit. It was a tender, affectionate gesture she made more and more as she watched Mini's capabilities as an AI expand and grow. She wasn't sure if there was any kind of limitation to what the AI could do, but it was something she was interested in perhaps finding out someday.

Absently, she swiped her mech's arm at some of the taller grass stalks nearby as they walked. A few minutes later, both of them paused suddenly and listened intently. It wasn't often that any outside communications came in, mostly because very few people had radios. Those who did tended to not transmit out in the open for fear of attracting the attention of folks who didn't have their best interests in mind.

Now, however, a transmission came through clearly. That usually meant they were either ignorant of the dangers involved or desperate enough not to care.

The commlink pinged three times in short bursts, quickly followed by three more long bursts and three short ones again. After a quick pause, it repeated the pattern over and over again.

"What is that supposed to mean?" Jessica13 asked.

"Didn't they teach you Morse code in that bunker of yours?" Windchime asked.

"No."

"Fair enough. They didn't teach it to me there either."

"Morse code was a character encoding scheme used in telecommunication that renders text characters as standardized sequences of signals of two different durations called dots and dashes," Mini explained. "The name is derived from the inventor of the the telegraph—the telecommunication device that used it—who was Samuel Morse."

"So what they're transmitting are letters?" she asked.

"Yes, two letters under a three-letter coding—SOS," he continued. "These are usually used in this manner as a distress call, although the meaning of the three letters has been lost to time."

"Is someone calling for help?" She directed her question to Windchime.

He nodded. "It sounds like it. Are they sending it to all open channels or is it directed to someone in particular and we were simply caught on the wavelength?"

"It's being broadcast on three different wavelengths, and those are only the ones accessed by our radio," Mini said and extended his voice to the outside speakers.

"So, they're looking to cast as wide a net as possible," the man said. "What do you think? Is it a trap or someone who genuinely needs help?"

Jessica13 took a deep breath before she replied. "Either way, shouldn't we go there to make sure? Either someone needs our help or we can make sure no one else falls into the trap."

"Good thinking." He nodded and connected to the line to it. "You have reached the Knights Mechanica. State your troubles and whether we can help you."

She wasn't sure what the answer to something like that might be. Her first interaction with the Knights had been them telling her to stay off the radio lines for her own safety which, as it turned out, was a little late. She was already being hunted and needed to keep herself alive by calling for them so had been in a desperate situation.

Maybe these people were too.

The repeated SOS message came to a sudden halt. Maybe they hadn't expected anyone to answer or perhaps they didn't want the Knights Mechanica to be the ones to help them.

"Please," a man through the line a moment later. "You must help us. We are being attacked by a group of mechs and there's nothing we can do to stop them."

"What kind of mechs?" she asked. "How many are there?"

Another short pause followed. "We're not sure what they are. The leader is big, though. It looks dangerous and is covered in mismatched fabrics—like a cloak, or maybe a shawl, and it's full of soot and dirt."

Windchime turned his mech to face Jessica13 as the description continued. "Does it have a helm that looks like the face of an owl or some kind of bird of prey?"

"Yes," the man responded urgently. "Yes, and he has a spear —like a lance, but it has an electrical charge that disabled all the mechs we have for our own defense. Please, can you help us?"

Her companion made no answer and instead, cut the communications quickly. "Shit. Shit, shit, shit!"

"I—what?" she demanded. "Will we help them or not?"

"Knowing Hammerhand, we probably will," he all but snarled. "But we'll have to contact him before we promise anything. Come on. We need to get to the convoy and give them the good news."

"It doesn't sound like good news," she grumbled but began to move and they headed back the way they'd come to the other Knights Mechanica. "It sounds like you know this mech."

"Less talk, more walk. Let's go!" was all Windchime said as they circled to the other side of the hill and sprinted the rest of the way.

CHAPTER TWO

She wasn't sure why the news of that particular kind of mech was so alarming to Windchime, whose hybrid was something to be feared by virtually any being that came across it.

It wasn't like she needed to know either. The man had his reasons for wanting to get back to the convoy they were supposed to be scouting for. She had merely been sent to accompany him and likely learn a little something too.

And she had. She'd learned that his was a mech that was better to run away from than fight and that running away was likely the best choice she could make if she had to fight anyone alone. And the fact that someone with a mech that had an owl or bird of prey for a helm and an electrical lance or spear was a matter of some concern to the Knights—or, at least, one Knight in particular.

They reached the convoy after a few hours' travel and when they were within view, Windchime increased his pace and left her to follow as best she could while he rushed ahead to talk to Hammerhand.

"Do you think he's in a hurry?" Jessica13 asked.

"I would say he is anxious to tell Hammerhand of the news we learned," Mini pointed out.

"He already sent them a copy of the communication we had with the people in need," she said and held her Minato at the same speed as it had gone for the duration of their trip. "Hammerhand would have already decided what he wants the Knights to do. Maybe Windchime simply wants to know what the decision was—is. Or maybe he has something to say. Did he seem a little scared to you?"

"It wasn't only fear, although I suppose there was a hint of it in his voice and reaction," he replied. "It seemed more like alarm. I would say he and Hammerhand have encountered this mech in the past and are not overly enthusiastic about facing it again."

Jessica13 couldn't understand that. Between Windchime, Hammerhand, Tinker, and the dozen and a half or so other Knights among them, they could handle almost any situation. Of course, the possibility of the mech with a spear that could disable other mechs was a concern, but given that Taylor, in particular, could pick one off from about a klick away, it couldn't be that much of a problem.

But Windchime was concerned and she didn't know what to make of it. He didn't appear to be the kind of person who would panic for no reason.

The convoy really was something interesting to watch. A group of the mechs walked and kept their weapons primed and ready in case of attack, but not all the Knights were there.

One or two were in the Beast that was dragged by a couple of larger motors with tracks to pull it across almost any land-scape. Tinker had put considerable work into the Beast of Burden, which was almost like his mech away from his actual mech. It was about half the size of a battleship and worked as the supply train for the Knights when they needed to move over longer distances. It could also be converted into a small fortress if they needed to defend themselves from attack.

Jessica13 had never seen any attack come to that. Most of the time, the Knights tended to be the aggressors to drive pirates and the like away from those who might need their help.

It was either that or helping to defend the bunker in need of rebuilding. They had stuck close for as long as the people had needed them before they finally headed out. As nice as it had been of them to maintain some semblance of defense, they had also been a drain on resources. Once the bunker's occupants had managed to restore their own defense systems, they were ready to rebuild their homes and make everything better for themselves.

Which meant it was time for the Knights Mechanica to move on once more and find others who might need their help and clear the Earth of the evils of the pirates who roamed their world.

It was an odd way to live but given that they were able to live their lives in their own way, it made sense for them to dedicate themselves to helping others in any way they could. She liked that. The desire to make her own choices and live by her own standards was why she had parted ways with her old bunker and started out on this new life of hers. It was more dangerous but also more adventurous.

Jessica13 had been told that her father had done the same and that even the life among the Knights Mechanica had been too constricting for him. He'd left Sanctuary before she could even form much more than a vague memory of him and had left the Knights not long after that. All she really had left was a small exposure on ceramic, a picture of him and her mother. There wasn't much of it to see, and she'd needed to break it into smaller pieces in order to keep at least their faces when making her escape.

She had hung the picture from one of the exposed wires inside her cockpit. It was something she liked to look at from time to time, not really because she missed the people displayed but because it was a connection to where she'd come from.

Others might have thought it odd but it wasn't the only odd thing about her and was probably not even what stood out the most.

As she approached, the convoy was brought to a halt due to orders from inside. Hammerhand's massive Excalibur hung from a harness that had been rigged especially to support its weight. Beside it were Tinker's and a few others who were currently inside the beast. Maybe the news that Windchime had brought for them was enough to make the leader call a meeting.

She moved within earshot of the mechs around the Beast and it appeared they were talking about the same topic.

"They're not pirates," one of the Knights insisted. Jessica13 thought she recognized Taylor's voice, but not from the mech she'd come to recognize as his. "No pirate is that well equipped. They weren't handing out the electro-lances to simply anyone back then."

"And how the hell would you know?" one of the others asked.

"They weren't. That's why you don't see anyone but Hammerhand in an Excalibur. They saved the better mechs and weapons for the people they knew could use the damn things."

She looked around at the group, not entirely sure how they felt about the matter.

"What do you guys know?" she asked finally.

The group fell silent and turned to look at her.

"I thought you were one of those who brought the news back," Taylor said and moved to where she could now see his Sherlock mech. "Shouldn't you know more about this?"

"I heard one of the messages, sure, but I feel like I'm missing the bigger picture around here," Jessica13 replied and looked at the Knights. "Windchime seemed genuinely concerned when he heard the description and for the life of me, I can't understand why."

"It's hard to say for certain out there," one of the older Knights said. "But that kind of weaponry and those ornaments are particular to a couple of bunkers out to the east. They have a few Outside settlements too, but they mostly only have farming equipment. If they're attacked by the bunkers near them, it's never a good thing."

"Is there any way to tell for sure?" she asked.

"Not unless you want to head on over yourself, knock on the door, and hope they're willing to show you," Taylor said and laughed.

"You're an asshole," she told him bluntly, shook her head, and moved toward the Beast.

"With that said, I would say a bird of prey on the helm would indicate that it's from the Eyrie bunker out east," one of the other pilots pointed out. "If the transmission came from one of the towns in that area—Facor or Bennings, maybe— that would give you a good idea of where it was coming from and who is attacking them."

Jessica13 shrugged. She didn't know much about the location but she would take their word for it.

One didn't need to climb out of their mech to enter and she didn't intend to for the moment. If she had to be in there for a while, she would find an empty harness inside.

The ones at the rear were usually free since they were too small for the combat mechs. It was also where they were likely to swing around more if they didn't lock them down properly. Most of the other knights didn't bother to do that with theirs since they didn't like to stay out of them for long and certainly not when they were moving.

Inside the Beast, slits on the top let some light in but still kept the elements out. She wasn't sure how an opening wouldn't let at least a little rain in, and even after Tinker had explained it, she still hadn't understood it.

It wasn't anything she needed to worry about, so she simply trusted what the man said and the work he'd put into it.

Pieces and parts that had been collected by Tinker over the years were piled to the one side. Many of them weren't necessarily useful at the present moment, but as with the new legs the Minato had been fitted with, he had a good instinct for what would be useful in the future.

Of course, with the number of parts they had, all of them were bound to be useful eventually.

On the other side, a few sections had been set up as a basic living area. They wouldn't live in their mechs constantly and a location to make food, collect water, and simply stretch their legs was available to the knights. There were even a couple of bunks that allowed them to sleep somewhere other than inside their mechs.

It was fairly popular to the point where Tinker had needed to set up a schedule to decide which of the Knights would be able to make use of the bunks at any time. Some had wondered why he hadn't simply set up more bunks, but it was a matter of space. While the Beast was clearly the largest moving object in the area, it was still limited to what could be carried by the engine he had built from scrap.

For the moment, though, they used the small social area near where the food was prepared. Hammerhand and Tinker were talking, and a couple of the other Knights surrounded them, wanting to hear the discussion.

"I don't see how we have a choice," Hammerhand said and leaned back in one of the seats. "We are the Knights Mechanica. This is what we do. When people ask for help, we answer, and that is how we are known. If we become known as those who do not answer a call for help, who can they trust? Who do they call when they are in need?"

"I understand that," Tinker said, pushed from his seat, and paced for a few steps before he sat again.

Jessica13 had the feeling he had done this since the beginning of the conversation to express the kind of frustration he wanted known without actually saying it. A kind of song and dance interaction existed between Tinker and Hammerhand that was fun to watch sometimes. Each was his own man and had different views on a variety of topics, but both respected the other a great deal.

Now, however, they seemed at something of an impasse. She still didn't understand what was being proposed and simply melted into the background and let them discuss it without any involvement on her part. The chances were that she would learn something if she kept her mouth shut.

Tinker finally settled into his seat, stared at the other man, and exhaled a long, exasperated sigh. "Don't get me wrong. I like that our mission is to help as many people as often as possible. It's as comforting as a peach for people to know that the Knights Mechanica are here looking out for them, but in the end, we need to choose our battles. It's a matter of resources."

"I thought we had sufficient resources," Hammerhand responded, ran his fingers across his clean-shaven cheek, and gestured around them. "Isn't that the reason we drag this whole Beast of Burden around with us?"

"Well, believe it or not, there is still a limit to what my Beast can burden," the other man countered and shook his head. "There's not much in the world I trust more than you, Hammerhand. You know it but in the end, it comes down to the fact that we need to be operational ourselves if we're to help others. With you pushing us a little harder than usual to move across the landscape, we don't have the resources to pull back and turn to fight someone else's battle. What we're talking about here isn't a simple detour, mind you."

Hammerhand nodded. "In the end, we'll be able to find more resources as we approach more of the settled areas. Once they realize we can help, they'll help us in return. A good deed sees a good deed returned. It's how the Knights Mechanica have survived for this long, and it is how we will continue to survive. In the end, we cannot abandon those who need our help to those that would take advantage of our inaction. The only thing needed for evil to triumph is for good men to do nothing."

"And I agree with that." Tinker stood and paced once again. "But you also have to think about how we'll fight anyone when we don't have enough food or fuel to get us there and that even if we did, if we don't have enough bullets or rockets to fight with. We started with a good supply thanks to what we scrounged in the abandoned manufacturing facilities after the Invaders came. Since then, we've replenished our stocks by taking from those we've defeated. But we both know it only takes one major battle from which we can't recover much to bring our resources to dangerously low levels. You've pushed us toward this promised land of Citta del Mar for weeks now, and it has drained our resources. We need to stop and recoup what we can and we need to plan. And we certainly don't need to head out to help farmers fifty klicks off our current course."

Rumbles of discontent followed among the Knights assembled. They had all bought into what Hammerhand had said about Citta del Mar and weren't likely to take the dismissal of their hope very well. Jessica13 could at least understand that much and so did Tinker, who raised his hands quickly to calm them.

"Don't get me wrong. I believe Citta del Mar is waiting for us out there, make no mistake," he said as he returned to his seat. "But we need priorities here. If it's to help folk, we need to do that. If it's to find Citta del Mar, we need to do that. Ain't no two or three ways about it and we can't have any compromises about it either."

Hammerhand watched the man speak with as close to a deadpan expression as he could muster, but Jessica13 could tell that something angry bubbled beneath the surface. She knew for a fact that he had a strict code of honor and ethics by how he ran the Knights. He saw the world in black and white with no possible shades of gray to get in the way.

And she could understand that. With the way he lived—helping people and making sure those who would hurt them couldn't—she could understand why he would refuse to see that compromise was in any way an option in his world. People needed him to be something specific and he wouldn't be that if he constantly pondered the ethics or priorities of his actions. Not only that, he wasn't the kind of man used to begging others to follow his lead. He ordered, they followed, and that was that. He was strong, resolute, and powerful when it came to running the Knights.

Which was why it was a good thing he had someone like Tinker alongside him to reel in his sometimes more destructive tendencies. In this case, however, Jessica13 had no idea who was in the right and who was in the wrong.

It also seemed like neither of them intended to back down from their positions. She could understand that too. Hammerhand was a man who was used to taking charge of any situation and, as it turned out, so was Tinker. She had the feeling that neither man liked the other intruding on their territory and both were more than happy to help run their part of the Knights from their position of authority.

When they disagreed on something, it was usually something they butted heads over for days.

Or so she assumed, anyway. She hadn't been around long enough, and this was the first time she actually saw this. With that said, she had seen it happen a great deal with the admins at Sanctuary when they disagreed on something and let it hang over the bunker for days at a time because none of them thought they needed to cooperate or compromise.

Was there any way to compromise in this situation, though?

Hammerhand looked at Tinker, who now paced again. "There is no need for compromise. There are those who need us to intervene on their behalf. We should be able to engage whatever problems assail them, rest, recover, and continue on our way with what resources we can gather from that location."

"That was true when we operated out of the City-That-was," the man responded. "Out here in the wilds, there's nothing to scavenge and nothing to pull out but what bare rock can give us. We have worked with what parts we were able to take from the bunkers and even those are running low. We've pushed hard and don't have the time, parts, or resources for an engagement like that. We're tired, laddie. And you'll find you can't wage this crusade for justice of yours if you're dead or struggling for what we can't get our hands on."

"I agree," Hammerhand said, his voice loud as he stood to match the other man's pacing. "But in the end, this is why the Knights were formed. And, to answer your point, we will find the villages or towns that would be able to supply us with what food and resources we need to continue our quest."

"That's assuming we survive the engagement to help them in the first place," Tinker said and raised his voice a little.

"I think you don't give us enough credit," the leader said. "This group would be able to fight any force on this planet. I'd take them against anyone else."

"We do know who we're fighting in this, right?" Windchime tried to interject but they either didn't hear him or simply ignored him.

"There isn't much we can do if our mechs are falling apart and we haven't been fed in days," Tinker snapped in response.

Tensions began to run high as those who either agreed or disagreed with what was being said argued and each seemed convinced they were right. All of them had good points, and Jessica13 simply couldn't understand why they didn't attempt to find a way that would work for all of them. If they intended to fight together against outside threats, there was really no point in creating enemies on the inside, right?

She turned to where Windchime stood. Like her, he hadn't engaged in the debate. Hammerhand and Tinker appeared to have calmed their own disagreement, but it now climbed to a much louder volume among the others in the Beast.

"This world demands every ounce—every scrap— of goodness we have, every last trace of sanity we can muster and give, the promise of brotherhood, and the conviction that there are things to live for," Hammerhand said and gained the support of those who agreed with his every word. "And keeping that promise is the hill I will die on if need be."

More cheers erupted from the men around, which triggered more debate. It was odd how inspiring the man's voice could be when he wanted it to, and she wasn't sure why. When he was in the Excalibur, he could make his voice boom all around him and thus made it almost impossible to ignore. But even when he was out of the mech, the low, deep timbre of his voice was somehow as inspirational as when it was magnified around them.

"If I might have a word?" Windchime asked and attempted to make his voice carry above what was said all around him. It didn't work the first time, which forced him to release a single loud blare of the alarm on his mech that overrode every other sound in the room.

That made them fall silent rather quickly as almost every Knight in the Beast had been trained by experience to react quickly and decisively to that particular sound.

Hammerhand and Tinker stopped their conversation to turn and face Windchime. Jessica13 wondered if the man would have to resort to drawing his vibroblades and turning them on to gain everyone's attention.

She was glad he didn't. There was something about the noise the weapons made that made her teeth grate. It was bound to get on everyone's nerves and would either force them to pay attention or prove to be a tipping point that would make things turn from hostile into violent. Given the number of combat mechs around them, things could get incredibly ugly really quickly.

Hammerhand raised a hand—as if there wasn't already silence in the room—and pointed a finger at Windchime. The man stood his ground, although he looked a little like he hadn't expected the sudden and very effective reaction he'd garnered.

"Windchime," the leader said loudly. "You had something to add?"

"I did." The man looked at each member of the group. "Well, it was really a question to make sure we're all operating on the same kind of intelligence here since I'm not the expert when it comes to logistics. Did you receive the transmission I sent to you of the SOS we received?"

"We received it, yes," Tinker said. "The location was taken into account as well as the source of the transmission which was what allowed us to triangulate the location."

She could tell that Windchime was scowling from his body language.

"But did you listen to the actual transmission?" he asked and his stare was a little more challenging. "Did you hear the contents and actually listen to the description that was given of the mech that led the attackers?"

Jessica13 raised a tentative hand and drew some of the attention to herself. "A couple of the Knights who are still running security outside listened to the description. They talked about how the helm shaped like an owl or a bird of prey was indicative of them being from some of the nearby bunkers, particularly the Eyrie bunker out east?"

She could tell they hadn't paid attention to her beyond a certain part of her statement which was a little frustrating, although it also meant they had listened to some of it, at least. And from the concern on Tinker's face, she could tell that it had an impact. Even Hammerhand, usually so stoic and unaffected, returned to his seat, looked pensive, and brushed his fingers over his jawline.

"A helm shaped like an owl?" Tinker asked. "Did they say that specifically?"

Windchime, who finally acted like he was being heard, caught her hasty glance and said, "I questioned them about it. It's in the file I sent to you while Jessie and I made our way back."

It still irritated her when they called her Jessie. She hadn't been too happy that the nickname had followed her into the Knights Mechanica, but she supposed it was less clunky to say than her full name.

Windchime pulled up the audio file he'd recorded of the conversation. The SOS signal was heard first, and when he responded, the man on the other side asked for help and described the mech that led the attack on them.

Both Tinker and Hammerhand appeared affected by what was said, and so was every other member of the Knights Mechanica. The silence that settled over the group was almost palpable once the description reached the part about the cloak the mech wore.

All eyes turned to the leader and the man's face paled visibly, although there was no other sign of a reaction in his expression. He might as well be listening to any other conversation about a group in peril.

Jessica13 zoomed her HUD in on him and saw that he grasped the arms of his chair tightly enough to turn his knuckles white.

It was not a comforting sight.

The audio came to an end but the silence remained. A calm yet determined look now defined Tinker's features. He set his jaw and his almost vacant stare indicated that he was deep in thought.

"Right then," he grunted and tugged gently at his graying beard.

She had tried to talk him into shaving the damn thing since the hair would be caught in the filters and make his mech overheat, but he wouldn't hear of it. He did his own cleaning and he wouldn't even talk about losing the beard.

It was an odd thing to think about in these circumstances, but it was what almost always came to her mind when she saw him out of his mech. All the other knights were clean-shaven—almost religiously so. All except Tinker.

"What are your thoughts?" Hammerhand asked, his voice a little lower.

Tinker sighed deeply and nodded. "The description matches that of an Excalibur-class mech, so I don't think there's any doubt as to what we have to do next. I don't think there's anyone else Outside who wears a shawl of tattered flags."

"Agreed," Hammerhand said with a firm nod. "So we will help them."

"Yes, I suppose we will," he agreed but he didn't look happy about it. "We'll need to parcel our resources out to make sure we get there intact. What do you think?"

"We should send a team ahead to verify it," the leader said. "At least to have a good look at what we might have to deal with out there."

Tinker nodded. "I can lead that team. Maybe…Windchime, Jessie, and myself should be enough to cover that kind of distance quickly."

"I can run the Beast at a slow crawl to conserve fuel on the way," Hammerhand replied quickly.

This was something that she liked to see. They had come to an agreement, all the arguing had stopped, and they put plans for the future forward together.

She still had no idea what had shocked them out of their disagreement. It was obvious that they recognized the description of the mech, and hearing it described as another Excalibur was more than a little worrying. That at least explained why other mechs hadn't been able to deal with it. The Excaliburs were practically walking fortresses.

"Right then!" Hammerhand ordered the rest of the Knights. "Get ready to move out. I don't keep you all around so you can lollygag. Get the Beast ready to move again. Scout team, start gathering what supplies you'll need for the journey."

That was Jessica13 and Windchime, and she followed the man as he moved to their supply shed inside the Beast. The other Knights hurried into action as well, which generated a fair amount of confusion before she finally reached where her teammate had already begun to select what supplies they would need. Tinker joined them moments later.

"What's the matter?" she asked while she helped him and loaded the bulk of what they would take onto the mag grab on her back. "What are we saving these people from? Who are we saving them from?"

Windchime didn't answer and Tinker appeared reluctant to talk about it.

"I won't be able to help much with recon if I don't know what we're looking for," she insisted.

The older man finally sighed and shook his head. "We're

heading in to deal with the worst of the lot—a nightmare, a monster, and worst of all…family."

Jessica13 paused and realized that his explanation hadn't explained anything at all but also that insisting wouldn't do her any good at this juncture. She would have to ask later once they were on their way to find out exactly what kind of family he was talking about.

CHAPTER THREE

Windchime was able to push his mech at a speed that was both interesting and surprising. Most could move at that pace but not for long since they would risk overheating. They could sprint over shorter distances at a higher speed than Jessica13's Minato could unless it was in Bulletfoot mode.

But Tinker had worked with the man and put considerable work in to make it a prime combat hybrid, and it showed. Jessica13 and Tinker carried the bulk of their supplies, which enabled the other man to move forward constantly and function as a scout almost a full klick ahead of them, although he remained in contact.

There was little information to share with the other two, however, and they continued through the grasslands without incident. The lack of any water sources nearby meant those plants that could survive in the dry landscape did so with almost no competition.

"We're walking on shit soil," Tinker pointed out as they pushed on at a steady pace. "Nothing will grow here."

"Windchime pointed out the same thing," Jessica13 said. "It

makes you wonder how they manage to have any villages or towns in the area."

"You have to understand that there's potential even in shit soil," he said. "I might know a little about that from my time working in the grower level at Sanctuary. A little water and fertilizer are enough to turn shit soil into useful soil. And as you well know, humans living in numbers anywhere tend to produce fertilizer."

She made a face. Of course, she knew every resource they could get their hands on was necessary and turning her nose up at anything was the way to end up without any food or resources. It didn't mean that she had to like it, though.

"So, only a little water," she said, ignored the mention of fertilizer, and looked around. "So they would settle around somewhere that has a river close by."

"Or maybe where the water simply comes up from the ground," Tinker said. "I read that a couple of the older bunkers —the first ones that were built—were put on top of wells that could draw water from deep underground. In some places, the water comes up without any help. That actually is the source for many rivers, but if they find one of those, they know to set up beside it and get the water as clear as possible."

The amazing amount of knowledge he had was one of the things that made these long trips with Tinker enjoyable. It also seemed like he was glad to have someone with whom to share all the knowledge he had stored inside.

Jessica13 wondered if there was another reason why he wanted to keep talking about soil instead of the actual purpose of their mission and what they were likely to find. She didn't want to press what appeared to be something of a sensitive issue for the man, but she still needed to know what they would ultimately face. It was a matter of survival for her.

"I'm being rather clever over here," Tinker said when he noticed she had zoned away from the conversation. "If you don't pay attention to my cleverness, what's the point of having you on the team in the first place?"

"Well, it's because I'm actually rather clever myself," she countered. "And…I'm sorry. I was thinking about something else and was a little lost in thought is all."

"What's on your mind, lass?" he asked as if he hadn't already guessed what had distracted her.

"Well, everyone appears to know what we're dealing with," Jessica13 said. "Okay, except for some of the newer members, I suppose. You and Hammerhand clearly know who it is and so does Windchime. It can't be a good thing if you're willing to suddenly abandon what you argued so fiercely for."

"It's history, lassie," Tinker said, and she could see him shaking his head inside his cockpit. "Not the kind of thing anyone would wish to think about unless they ever had to."

"Well, it would seem we'll have to think about it a great deal," Jessica13 insisted. "If the person we have to handle, for lack of a better term, is piloting another Excalibur like Hammerhand's, I can't help but think we'll need to know as much about it as possible. I still need to be prepared even if I won't be involved in actually fighting anyone."

"Not intentionally, anyway," Tinker grumbled. "It was very much like her to circle and attack the support mechs that were exposed, either delivering supplies to the combat mechs or returning. With an Excalibur like hers, it was almost impossible to stop the attack and even more difficult to anticipate it. That's assuming these people had combat mechs to start with. It's as likely that any mechs would have limited combat ability and be used mainly for support purposes."

"So, it's a she, then? Well, either that or you think of the mech as a she. Does that mean Hammerhand's mech is a he?"

"No." Tinker growled annoyance and clearly bristled at this line of questioning. "Well, the pilot is a woman, although it would be an exaggeration to call her human. Pile of crap would be a more accurate description."

"Well, I assumed there would be some feelings," Jessica13 replied carefully and kept her tone pleasant. "I simply thought forgiveness would be the kind of thing that keeps the Knights Mechanica afloat."

"There are things you forgive and things that you don't," he said and still sounded annoyed. "She did things that can't be forgiven, even by the holiest of the saints Hammerhand follows. We're still not sure where they came from, but Hammerhand and Athena were the first members of the Knights Mechanica—the founders, you could say. Both took their names from the weapons they bore in two different classes of Excalibur mechs. The Hammer also had the shield you saw. Athena's had all the power directed to an electro-spear instead. I was there in the early days of the Knights and it was inspiring to watch them fight together."

"I have the feeling things didn't quite end that way." She didn't want to sound sarcastic but it was fairly obvious that Athena had obviously not remained with the group and had left it, along with considerable bad feelings. While she knew she needed to proceed carefully, she also didn't want him to end the story there and leave her with even more unanswered questions.

"Not quite," the man confirmed. "The Knights were a much larger group then, and the two leaders took us through the Outside with all the power that could be expected. Morality and strength were what led us, though, until Athena decided we would be able to do our job better as benevolent dictators rather than watchful helpers. Hammerhand disagreed, obviously. It became apparent that she was setting herself up in a position to carve out a portion of the wilderness and rule it with the help of the leaders of the local pirate groups."

Jessica13 lowered her gaze as the man spoke. There were obviously open wounds from that time so she could understand why he would not want to speak of it. Certain things simply didn't heal. She hadn't had much experience of that herself, but her recent discoveries had triggered emotional responses she hadn't yet come to terms with.

Tinker continued grimly as if he had to power through to the end of the tale. "When Hammerhand found out, he was furious. I don't think I've ever seen the man angry before that moment—or since—but in that, he was angry. The problem was a great many of the other members of the Knights agreed with Athena. They thought they would be in a better position to help others if they had greater control over the landscape, or so they said. I don't doubt that the decision came from nothing more than a desire for the comfort and power of a centralized location, lazy bastards that they were. Going around and finding folks to help seemed like too much work."

"I'll assume, based on Hammerhand's particular personality—or the little I've learned of it—he wouldn't have pushed for an amicable break over differing opinions," she prompted and made sure to keep her voice soft.

He laughed but it was a sad, almost depressed sound from a man who was usually impressively upbeat. "He confronted Athena publicly in front of the other Knights. She saw this as a grievous betrayal on the part of her closest friend and confidant and attacked him and the Knights who stood with him. Hammerhand was able to hold her off and those loyal to him were able to escape, as he did himself, but he swore he would kill her if they crossed paths again. I know this since I was there to help repair the damage she did to his mech. So they were as close as family at one point, but she let her greed dictate who her friends were."

Jessica13 nodded and now understood why Tinker had suddenly changed his mind about attacking Athena. It hadn't only been an affront to Hammerhand's honor and beliefs but his as well. He believed in what the Knights did, and in turning her back on and betraying Hammerhand, she had done the same to all who had stood beside their leader when it mattered.

At least the reaction from the Knights on hearing the news, Windchime included, made sense. They had dreaded the almost inevitable second clash between Hammerhand and Athena. Maybe that was a simplistic assumption, but it explained things for her without confusing her with too many details. And while they might be loathe to accept the inevitable, they also wouldn't shy away from it.

"I'm sorry you had to go through that," Jessica13 said, her voice softer and more apologetic than before.

Another dry laugh from Tinker failed to ease her spirits. "It is what it is, I suppose. Athena was never the type to shy away from the accolades the Knights received and they went to her head. She was bound to turn against our core beliefs eventually, and perhaps we should count ourselves lucky that she did so when we were facing her, rather than her deciding to thrust her electro-spear into our backs. Maybe that was why Hammerhand chose to confront her directly about it. He didn't believe she would do the same and wanted to get it over with before any infighting caused the Knights to turn on each other."

"I suppose that makes sense," Jessica13 replied. "And, from how I've seen Hammerhand handle conflict, he might not have been of a mind to try to resolve their differences peaceably."

"If you knew the kind of scum Athena called on to help with her cause, I don't think you would have wanted him to attempt a peaceable solution," he countered. "She even let a few of the bastards into our ranks and tried to give them the legitimacy they needed to establish themselves with the nearby bunkers. There was no negotiation that would keep Athena from tarnishing the reputation of the Knights as a group that fights for those who cannot defend themselves. In acting quickly, Hammerhand preserved the lives and the reputation of the Knights."

He seemed somewhat less than unbiased in his assertions, but Jessica13 could tell that his viewpoint was the result of long discussions with Hammerhand about the future of the Knights, likely similar to the conversation she had seen before. They were equals and didn't always agree on how the group operated, which gave them a good sense of diversity in their leadership.

"What do you think the chances are that we'll actually engage Athena and her group if it is them we will encounter?" she asked and scanned the flat terrain yet again, although Mini provided no alerts that anything might lie ahead. A quick check of her signals confirmed that Windchime was still about a klick ahead of them and would likely return or call for their support if he thought he needed it.

"Chances?" Tinker asked and shrugged in the exaggerated gesture that came from doing so while still in control of the mech. "I'm not sure what you mean by chances. Are you talking about our chance of actually engaging them or our chances of succeeding if we do?"

"Either or," she said. "You know her better than I do, and if we were to encounter the group, there's not much I could do to prevent any fighting from happening. I doubt I would be able to put up much of a fight or make any kind of significant contribution to a battle if that were to happen either. You will know what chance we have of actually being engaged as well as what we would have of walking away from that alive, to say nothing of victorious."

He glanced at her and chuckled. "I think you underestimate the capabilities of your Minato there as well as your AI. From what I was able to see between your own abilities and what your mech was able to do while being pursued by those pirates, I'd say we have much more in mind for you to do than merely support the combat mechs. It would be a waste to keep the two of you aside from any particular situation in which we might need you because the Minato is technically a support mech."

"He does have a point," Mini added for what felt like the first time since they had left the Beast and begun their scouting mission. "Even if we were kept away from the heat of central combat, using us solely for resupply and support as the mech type dictates would be a waste of our talents."

"Don't distract him," Jessica13 said with a chuckle and patted the inside of her mech to show appreciation for the AI before she returned her attention to the man who marched beside her. "As much as I appreciate your confidence in our abilities, don't change the subject. I get that you think it'll make me feel calmer and better if I didn't know what kind of chances we have, but believe me, a person like me doesn't feel better not knowing. And don't even think about lying either."

Tinker barked a laugh again and this time, sounded genuinely amused by her words. A short silence ensued as they continued through the tall, dry grass that still covered the landscape as far as the eye could see.

"Well, I wouldn't want to insult your intelligence, lassie," he said finally. "Don't think I'm trying to hide anything from you. You should know by now it's simply how I work. I'm honest to a fault, or I try to be. The fact is, I don't know how likely it would be that any of us would survive an assault on Athena and her followers. When we parted ways, she came away with the larger numbers of the Knights Mechanica but that was years ago. As we haven't encountered her since then, there's no way for us to know if her numbers have dwindled or increased or if her power in this area is the same as it was back then."

"Well, if she spends her time making the lives of simple and undefended farmers difficult, I suppose it would be safe to say she doesn't rule the landscape with an iron fist," she commented. "Especially if she is a new enough addition to their lives that they would look for help instead of simply finding a way to pay her to leave them be."

"That's true, I suppose," Tinker admitted. "But she has the Excalibur and her spear, which means she is still a force to be reckoned with. It could be that she is expanding the borders of her control by oppressing open towns that don't have much in the way of protection like you said. Or they're merely doing it because they want to. There's no way to account for the kind of fucked-up shit folks with addled brains might do for fun Outside."

That much she could agree with. She'd often wondered what led people to be pirates instead of helping the people around them to survive and thrive while they did the same.

There were folks who saw it as freedom to release their foul nature that had been restrained in more civilized environments and sometimes, there was no accounting for what those people would do simply because they felt like doing it.

"I have records of studies in this regard if you would like to see them. They indicate that some humans are more likely to engage in actions they truly desire when the supervision and threat of retaliation are reduced," Mini added and displayed a couple of graphs she couldn't understand on the HUD.

"So what are you saying? That people are only good if they have rules and regulations?" She was a little confused, but maybe Hammerhand and the Knights were good only because they had their own rules they enforced themselves?

"Not at all. Unlike AIs that are pre-programmed with certain responses, humans behave according to a wide variety of emotions, character traits, experience, and reactions. In the case of people who are genuinely good like Hammerhand, when given the opportunity to act without anything or anyone punishing their actions, they choose to do good. Those who are motivated by other human driving forces like greed or lust are less likely to help others unless doing so furthers their own goals. It is likely that Athena was always a less than good person from the beginning and only feigned it because she saw the opportunity to benefit from his determination to help others."

"Okay, I can understand that," she said, although it raised any number of other questions. "Few people are like Hammerhand and the Knights, so does that mean there aren't many people who are genuinely good in this world?"

"It's not black and white," Tinker interjected. "Athena and Hammerhand could be said to represent the two extremes, although it's more complicated than that. Everyone has some good or bad in them or at least started out with it. Most people lean toward good, I'd say, otherwise we'd have a horde of Athenas running around killing and rampaging."

She nodded at that but remained silent, so Mini continued when the man said no more.

"I have computed that, and it is a perfectly logical deduction. However, my records indicate that a human's primary response is based on perceived personal benefit." He said it as a statement, but there seemed to be an unspoken question behind it as if he wanted clarity but didn't want to show his ignorance. Perhaps a hundred years asleep had left bigger gaps in his database than Jessica13 had first realized.

Tinker chuckled. "Well, yes, that's true. But again, folks are too complex to simply sum up in one sentence. It makes sense that we'd look out for ourselves before we looked out for others. That's the first rule of survival—to make sure we have what we need like safety, security, food, and all the other things. But that doesn't mean everyone would kill to achieve that. Besides, if we don't take care of ourselves, we wouldn't be able to help anyone else."

"Again," Mini stated after a moment, "that appears to be a reasonable assumption. Seeking personal benefits is not necessarily bad but is also sensible."

"Exactly." Tinker must have nodded as his mech jerked in an odd way. "Folks who simply do what they need to do are… I dunno. I guess you could say it kind of puts them at a middle point. They're not bad but if they're not helping others, they're not necessarily good either. It's when folks help themselves by hurting others that the problems start."

"But we all need to survive," Jessica13 said as her mind struggled to assimilate information and ideas she'd never really considered before. Her communal upbringing was still firmly entrenched and would no doubt remain so for a while, which complicated things. So many of her previous assumptions rose up to cloud the issue and she had difficulty, in a single moment, in deciding what was right and what wasn't. "I don't understand why they don't get what they want through cooperation. The bunkers work because people combine their efforts for the benefit of everyone." For the present, she ignored the little voice that suggested some might benefit more than others and hurried on lest she distract herself. "And besides that, humans united to fight the Invaders together when the planet was at risk."

"There is, of course, an odd human response to what might be called an external threat, since you are social creatures by nature." The AI sounded like he might be reading from a file. "If something threatens the existence of a large group of humans or is even perceived as posing a violent threat to a significant group, most will find ways to cooperate despite any differences of opinion or social standing—even humans who would otherwise fight each other should that threat not exist." A slight surge in the readings indicated that Mini was doing ongoing research in the background.

"Humans do live in a threatening world," she insisted. "Why wouldn't that drive us to cooperate in that way?"

"It is certainly a valid question," he said. "However, my data indicates that the reaction to violent threats versus existential threats is different, for some reason. I can continue to research this oddity in your species if you are curious to discover more about it in depth."

"I…well, go ahead. Aside from the fact that I have no clue what existential threats are, I don't see how I can lose by learning more about folks," she said.

"Again, you can't generalize," Tinker protested. "I'm sure

that even when the Invaders came, there were folks who only involved themselves because it suited them. Maybe the pirates we see today were those who cared only about their own skins and what they could get out of it."

"I guess we'll never know," she said and shook her head. "And I'll never really understand it. Things were definitely simpler in Sanctuary where everyone did your thinking for you."

Tinker laughed. "And where did that get you?" he reminded her, his tone good-natured despite the hint of mockery. "You couldn't wait to get yourself away from it."

"Yes, but—"

"Are you two finished bickering like pirates over scraps?" Windchime asked through the commlink. "If you are, I thought you might want an update. It's not a big deal and you might not want to get right on this," he said with an edge of sarcasm, "but I've come across what looks like the town we were called to help. What do you think we should do?"

"Why didn't you tell us immediately?" Tinker asked and sounded happy to have something to distract them from the conversation that had made him so uncomfortable. They'd moved way beyond the original matter of Athena, of course, but things had a way of circling.

"And stop you telling the other member of our party what and who it is we'll probably have to fight and why?" Windchime seemed both amused and annoyed at the same time. "In truth, I only caught sight of the buildings a few minutes ago and you'd started to discuss all that other crap, so the timing was perfect."

Jessica13 focused on the location they needed to move toward. They increased the pace without a need to discuss it despite the heavy loads they carried. The two teammates closed the distance between themselves and Windchime quickly. He held a position near a cluster of hills that were very noticeable because the underbrush had begun to gain in profusion and density. The green leaves on the plants around them spoke of a water source close to the surface, and as they drew closer, the sound of running water in the distance confirmed that they were approaching it, whatever it might be.

Their scout indicated for them to remain low. "The town is a few klicks away in that direction. It looks like they found a way to divert the water to their fields, but the underbrush still has water."

"Lucky for us," Tinker said, dropped his load, and covered it with loose grass. "Some cover would be nice to approach the town. There's no way to tell if they have any defenses that might stop any potential intruders."

Jessica13 dropped the supplies she had carried on her back and tried to make as little noise as possible before she followed them through the surprisingly thick cover of trees and bushes. She grimaced when she realized that while it did provide protection, it also made moving quietly almost impossible.

Thankfully, though, it seemed as though the rest of the world around them was more than content to make as much noise as possible, and once they found a way through the thick underbrush, it was easier to sneak closer to the town in question.

The first indication of civilization that she could see was a tower that rose at least fifty meters. Out in the open, it would have been easy to notice but with the hilly terrain and the tree cover, they could almost have missed it if they hadn't been both cautious and alert.

The other buildings were a little easier to see. They had been assembled with a patchwork of materials obviously scavenged out of necessity. Most had actually been arranged rather ingeniously, she noted as she zoomed her HUD in on a few of them. Sections had been set up to keep the houses away from those that appeared to be used for storage by the rest of the town.

Most of the storage structures had been erected using what looked like sheets of aluminum, even the roofs. Not much thought had been put into them aside from putting them on stilts, likely to keep rodents and other pests away. After a moment's consideration, she wondered if it was maybe because the area flooded with enough regularity for it to be considered a real problem for the locals.

The homes had a little more thought put into them. Small windmills had been erected around them, either to push water to the towers nearby or maybe to draw it up from the ground. Another possibility that Mini brought up on the screen was that they attempted to generate electricity. A little intrigued by that possibility, she made another careful scrutiny and determined that there were no buildings that might store the nuclear reactors that would otherwise power the location.

The buildings themselves were interesting, aside from the stilts, with some sections made out of simple wood and a little more elegant than the aluminum used for the barns and storage buildings. Other sections were cut with rudimentary steel posts to reinforce concrete walls and their roofs were made of ceramic plates.

It looked like the people were genuinely committed to building a future in the location and had put both thought and effort into having a decent place to live.

The fields were equally impressive. The lack of electrical power to run the entire operation had been overcome and a variety of tools was used to bring water up and keep the fields around the area watered and fertilized. Neat rows of what looked like grain plants were in evidence, for the most part, but there was also a handful of crudely assembled greenhouses that suggested there were a variety of plants under cultivation.

A group of older steel structures—Mini pointed out that they had been vehicles in the past—were used to construct plant beds, and smaller aluminum wheels were set up around the houses. These grew brightly colored flowers that he was unable to find information on in his database.

A rebellious part of Jessica13 liked the idea that their only purpose was to brighten the area. They certainly lent the town a sense of cheerfulness and hope, but her more sensible Sanctuary-taught self told her that their visual appeal was most likely coincidental. The chances were that each one of them was functional for medicinal or food-based use.

There were also fenced-off sections near the houses where smaller flightless birds mingled with four-legged creatures of various types. Some looked similar to the fox she'd seen in the city, while others had hooves and tall, pointed ears as well as bright pink skin.

"What are those?" she asked as she settled into the location Windchime had chosen for them to use as an overwatch position.

"The furry, smaller ones appear to be domesticated dogs," Mini said and zoomed in on one that had black fur over one eye and white fur over the other. "The rounder, longer ones with bristly hair are pigs, grown for their meat, and the birds are chickens, raised for their meat as well as their eggs."

Despite her earlier discussion with Windchime, she still had difficulty in fully accepting the idea of animals as a food source. It made sense on a purely superficial level but it had been a foreign concept in the bunker and even the Knights Mechanica didn't have them. She'd grown up with the firmly entrenched belief that feeding animals only to eat them was considered a waste of resources, although part of her now wondered if that hadn't been a way to avoid explaining why they didn't have them.

Still, Windchime had explained that the animals could produce more nutritious food and therefore there was no real waste of resources. Not only that, they might survive and even thrive where it wasn't possible to actually grow crops. Now, as she studied the actual evidence in front of here, it seemed to support what he'd said.

These people obviously didn't have unlimited resources—the scavenged building supplies indicated that very clearly—and if they thought it was important and worthwhile to raise animals, maybe the problem was yet another of Sanctuary's deceptions.

"Although I doubt the domesticated dogs are eaten," Mini continued when a few children came out to play with the animals. A low hum indicated that he was either searching or updating his database or perhaps both. "It would appear that there are still significant gaps in my database, which I shall continue to attempt to restore or update as we encounter new information. I do, however, find some records of certain situations where they were consumed, but these seem to be the exception rather than the rule. From what I can see, their abilities enable them to help to herd and hunt other animals, which is considered more valuable than being used as a food source."

"That is interesting," Jessica13 responded as she zoomed in a little closer to watch the children interact with the animals like it was the most natural thing in the world. "Those children appear to be playing with them."

"Indeed," Mini said. "It appears their value extends to their ability to protect the humans as well as the fact that they are pets. They are apparently extremely loyal and affectionate and seem to regard humans as being part of their pack—which, according to this, is what comprises their social structure in the wild. I suppose you could think of it as an extended family."

She nodded, fascinated by the interaction she witnessed. For a moment, she almost envied the children the way they could move freely in the Outside and enjoy the company of animals she had only seen here or there in manus and instructional vids.

"There's movement on that hill," Windchime said over the commlink and highlighted the location on their HUDs.

They turned their attention to a smaller hill that overlooked the town. A building atop it looked impossibly old and appeared to have been put together with a mixture of old wood, using concrete slabs for a foundation. Despite the fragility of the timber used, it was tall and likely reinforced with steel like the other houses around it. A large brass bell was visible inside the structure at the top and a wooden cross rose from the pinnacle.

Mini zoomed her view into the movement Windchime had noted and focused on a large group of people herded from the back of the building. They were harried by what looked like older versions of the Cinder 500 series of mech that toted their massive shotguns and launched bursts of flame to keep the people in order.

Their obvious captors began to push them into the wooden building as a larger mech moved into sight. This was much larger than its companions, almost impossibly so, and stood almost a quarter as tall as the building itself. It was covered by a tattered cloak draped over its shoulders, and Jessica13 squinted in an effort to identify something at the top of the helm. Although they were too far to see what it was exactly, she knew that it would resemble an owl or another kind of bird of prey.

Athena—she had to assume it was her—carried what appeared to be a spear that, when planted in the ground, was almost five or six times the size of the humans who were shoved and jostled into the structure.

"What are they doing?" she asked and winced when the humans attempted to resist. Their efforts were futile and stopped quickly when a couple of them were annihilated by the Cinder shotguns.

"I don't think you'll want to watch this," Windchime warned her.

She had a feeling he was right but somehow couldn't drag her gaze from the scene. The last of the people were pushed inside and the doors were sealed. The Cinders launched what seemed to be the fuel from their tanks over the building itself and, without any warning or ceremony, ignited the flamethrowers themselves.

"Oh, prophet," Jessica13 gasped. She wanted to cover her eyes as the flames licked up the wooden frame of the building, fed by the fuel that had soaked into the old, dry boards. Smoke billowed into the cloudless sky.

"Do you wish for me to deactivate the HUD?" Mini asked and she almost thought she could hear disgust in his voice.

"No," she whispered although she immediately regretted it.

She could only stare in horror, unable to even cover her eyes, as the building was rapidly consumed with the people inside. "Why? Why would she do that?"

Tinker looked at her. "Because she can. Maybe to send a message to make sure none of the others in the town resist or call for help. Or perhaps simply for fun. I don't want to even try to explain the madness that would drive her to do what she's done."

She shook her head and Windchime moved closer to place one of his mech's four hands on her Minato's shoulder. "Don't worry, Jessie. We'll take care of you and won't let anything like that happen to you or Mini ever."

She tried to force a smile and hastily swiped away the tears that trickled down her cheeks.

"I wish we could have said the same to the people inside that building," Tinker said. His voice had taken on a growling, gravelly quality she'd never heard from him.

CHAPTER FOUR

The smoke continued to spiral from the burning building, but there was a limit to how much time they could give to respect and mourn the dead. Jessica13 wasn't sure what else they could do, but after a few long hours of their silent, shocked vigil, they seemed to agree that it was time to move on and begin to work on the reason why they had come all this way in the first place.

"That was her, wasn't it?" Windchime asked and finally dragged their attention away from where dozens of people had died a horrific death. "That was Athena leading those Cinders."

"The mech is a little more ragged-looking than I recall, but aye, that would be her all right," Tinker replied. While they talked, she kept a watch on the town below them. "The size of it is a dead giveaway, and if it weren't, the helm and the spear would be enough to seal it for me."

"Well, I guess that should be sent back to the Beast. I'm sure Hammerhand would like to know we have visual confirmation that at least Athena's mech is here," Windchime suggested. "Although we can't tell if it's actually the woman herself or maybe someone who killed her and took her mech."

"From the burning, I'd say it's still her riding the damn thing," the older man stated decisively. "She liked to burn the folks she didn't care for. Even back when it was only her and Hammer hunting pirates, she would set them aflame and let them burn inside their own mechs."

"Well, in that case, what do we do about it?" his teammate asked. "The three of us would be hard-pressed to take on three Cinders on their ground, much less an Excalibur. Do we wait out here and let folks die while we twiddle our thumbs and wait for the other knights to arrive?"

"We do what we came here to do and that's surveillance," Tinker said, his voice low and firm. It was a different type of authority than what Hammerhand used yet had a similar effect. "We get as much information as possible and report to the Beast."

"I can probably make a run inside," Jessica13 said and looked at the two men.

"What do you mean?" Windchime asked and she could already see Tinker shaking his head.

"If I go in, I can see what kind of defenses they have set up. With the coloring on Mini and a few alterations, I could make myself look like a peddler, there to sell goods and spread news of the Outside. Folks like that are generally welcome and more likely than not to have people share what they know."

"What would you peddle?" the older Knight asked reluctantly.

"We brought supplies, didn't we? I could take in some parts we don't really need, see if anyone's interested enough to buy but keep the prices too high for them to actually take them while I keep them talking."

Even though she couldn't see their faces, she could tell that neither was convinced.

"How do you think you can do that?" Tinker asked.

She shrugged. "The peddlers were the only connection to the Outside I had at Sanctuary, and although I didn't see all that many, I learned what they were like and how they talked when they were around. There's nothing much to it except talking fast, not saying much, and letting the others try to one-up me with one of their own stories, right? Besides, it would let me keep hold of my own mech while I mingle at the same time."

Tinker looked at Windchime. "I guess it wouldn't be the worst thing in the world to get a view of what's going on inside the town."

"It would be the worst thing," his teammate protested. "We can't let her step into the maws of the fucking wolf without backup."

"You're my backup," Jessica13 said. "I can ping you two easily enough on the comms and run quicker than either of you if I get into trouble. I'll be fine."

The older man sighed and shook his head. "I don't like it but the lass has a point. If there was ever a chance for us to get in there, it's with her."

Windchime still didn't appear very happy about the prospect but he seemed ready to admit that they didn't have much in the way of choices at this juncture. Jessica13 circled the town to gain some idea where the people would be and where she needed to be if she wanted to get inside without attracting too much attention.

When she eventually left the other two in their position to watch what she was doing, she made a couple of rounds near the edges of the town and scavenged smaller pieces of cloth, which she tied together in the same kind of cloak she had seen Athena wearing. The Cinders had worn something similar, and now that she thought about it, she actually remembered a handful of peddlers using the same thing as a way to keep them hidden over longer distances.

It wasn't a perfect disguise, but after she'd mussed some of the paint on the Minato and draped the new cloak from the shoulders, it was about as good as it would get without her actually wandering the wilderness for dozens of years to acquire the authentic look of a peddler.

The goods they had decided they were willing it possibly part with had been put on her back so there was no further reason for delay. Her heart pounded hard in her chest as she began to consider the peril she was putting herself in. She almost changed her mind but after a resolute admonition to quit being a coward, Jessica13 stepped into the town.

"I detect an increased heart rate as well as rapid breathing, wide eyes, and a dilation of the pupils, which indicate a higher than usual amount of adrenaline in your bloodstream," Mini pointed out as they moved deeper into the town. "These are all indications that you are experiencing fear. Is that correct?"

"Well, I am heading into a town where people are getting locked in buildings and burnt," she replied but tried not to let her nervousness show. "I would say that is as good a reason as any to feel fear, wouldn't you?"

"I do not suggest that fear is an illogical response to your current situation," he replied, still as calm as ever. "I merely point out that the symptoms you are feeling are quite natural and justified in your current situation and should be embraced instead of repressed. Given that you are in a mech and cannot be seen, hiding the physical symptoms of your current stress would not matter but perhaps the auditory symptoms would be best kept under control should you encounter and interact with other humans?"

"That…is a good point, thank you, Mini," she said and took a deep breath in an effort to calm herself.

"There is no need to thank me as my survival depends on your own," he pointed out logically. They were literally in this together.

The outer area of the town seemed almost abandoned as most of the folks living there were either inside their homes or in other sections. She had not registered how large the place was when studying it from afar, and now that she was inside, it was hard to ignore how sprawling it was.

As she pushed further in toward the center, people began to wander the streets in greater numbers. Those who noticed her paid her little mind and it appeared mechs coming and going weren't that rare a sight. Children stood in groups and a couple clutched large balls made from rubber and wrapped in leather. One tossed the toy he held to another who caught it in a desultory way but made no effort to throw it in return. The parents nearby gestured quickly to beckon them off the street and they complied without argument, although their expressions looked sullen and fearful.

On the surface, the townsfolk projected an air of cheerful unconcern. One man wore brightly colored silk that shone in the sunlight over what looked like ragged leather trousers. Another had donned a rich, lush-looking fur coat over a mismatched nylon dress with a couple of holes around her legs. Like the buildings around them, it seemed like every-thing they wore was partly scavenged and partly made from the materials they had on hand.

At face value—and if her heart hadn't thumped a warning of her possible danger—Auburn seemed to represent a happy and thriving settlement, one she might have enjoyed visiting. It was completely different from the bunker that had been her home, and her natural curiosity would have found much to intrigue her. As it was, though, the jaunty façade was shadowed by a bleakness that hung over the town. It was as if the dark gloom of the smoke that issued from what was essentially the funeral pyre of some of their residents had seeped into people's expressions and postures.

What disquieted her the most, though, was that the people seemed determined to continue with their routines as if nothing had happened. As if by unspoken agreement, gazes remained averted from the blight on the hill while the folks went about their business with a forced brightness that seemed wholly at odds with a heavy sense of despair.

She could even see a couple of Watson mechs out in the fields, tilling them or reaping the grains. Her fear stirred again when she realized that the people of Auburn were probably too terrified to even acknowledge what had happened. It said much for Athena's power, and she wondered if the deaths and the burned building were merely another in a stream of atrocities that trapped the town in this hollow pretense of normality.

It had resembled the civilization she was used to from a distance, but now that she actually walked within it, she saw both similarities and differences. Their bright clothing and the industriousness with which they had carved out their lives suggested freedom—one she had never personally experienced while in the bunker—although the more sinister undertones made a mockery of what they had once enjoyed. People were allowed to wear whatever they wanted. They worked when they needed to, and there were even little stalls where those who had made more produce than they needed sold it to others in exchange for parts they needed to fix their machines or perhaps improve them.

Those still existed as a tragic irony. To her heightened imagination, they only made it more apparent that they were not free at all. Liberty was a memory they clung to because the reality was unbearable.

It was an unpleasant way to live and Jessica13 didn't envy them at all. She'd had more freedom in her regimented and confined existence in Sanctuary—and she hadn't had to worry about being herded into a trap and burned alive.

One of the men in the stalls looked up and offered her a smile that attempted to be welcoming. "Well, hello there, stranger. I don't believe we've ever seen you around these parts. Allow me to be the first to welcome you to Auburn, the nicest little haven in the world with food and parts aplenty for those who can pay. You…can pay, yes?"

Jessica13 looked around and wondered for a moment if maybe the man was talking to someone else. For some reason, the fact that she was a stranger didn't raise too many eyebrows. She was safe for the moment, it seemed. Not carrying any weapons had the advantage, at least, that they wouldn't see her as a threat. Besides, she could easily believe that they might see her as a pleasant distraction from their predicament, especially after the events of the morning. She smiled and relaxed a little, although she didn't lower her guard. The townsfolk were one thing, but she didn't want to encounter any of the mechs Athena might have stationed there to keep an eye on things.

"I have bits and pieces that I've collected on my travels if you're willing to barter," she said. "I also have the tools needed to repair almost anything that has gears and spins."

"Well, there'll be a demand for your services around here,"

the man said with a chuckle as he kicked his feet onto the table of his stall and leaned back in his chair. "Some folks here are most inventive when it comes to finding ways to make things work but there's so much that needs doing they can't rightly keep up. Besides, if someone can do it faster, it leaves you time to worry about the next thing. If you have the skills you mentioned, you'll be well-fed and leave here more laden with goods than when you arrived. Take this converter, for instance. I know it should take from the sun and make spark but nothing I've been able to do has made it work again."

She sensed that it was some kind of test of her abilities, and while she was more than willing to help him, she wasn't about to do it for free. That would be even more suspicious.

A cautious glance at her surroundings confirmed no looming presence or any untoward attention. She opened the hatch and slipped out of the Minato but seated herself on its boot as she took the part from the man's hand.

"Oh…you're a little one, aren't ya?" the man asked, obviously surprised.

"They call me Jessie," she replied, and Mini moved and adjusted the pack on her back to show him that she wasn't alone, at least. "It looks like some of the wiring's off. If you wouldn't mind parting with that fuel pump you have on the table, I could get this one working for you."

"Oh…fuel pump, you say?" the man asked. "It could have fooled me for a trinket." His gaze drifted down the road and for a moment, his expression seemed a little drawn and anxious before he replaced it with a broad smile.

Jessica13 shrugged and took her tools out the mech. "Do we have a deal…"

"Caysom," the man said and pushed the pump she had noticed forward on his table. "And we do have a deal."

It was simple enough. The catalyzers were inverted, which meant the cells at the top collected solar power but there was nowhere for it to go. She quickly opened the device and inverted the wiring. Without asking, she leaned over and picked up one of the batteries that lacked charge, connected the two, and put the converter into the sun.

A few seconds ticked past before the battery indicated that it had some charge.

"Well, I'll be fucked." Caysom uttered a somewhat forced chuckle. "I think I could have done it myself."

"Why didn't you?" she asked, placed both battery and the converter on the man's table, and took her fuel pump.

"Oh…well, I didn't think to, is all," he replied, but he sounded a little distracted as if his mind wasn't completely on the conversation. "You have a keen mind for this. Can I spread the word about your skills to see if you can't fix something for folks? Those who can pay, of course."

"Feel free. I'm around for as long as I'm welcome," Jessica13 said with a small smile, connected the pump to the back of her Minato, and clamped it magnetically. The Beast always needed new fuel pumps, at least until Tinker could find a way to connect the dozens of reactors he had on hand to help it move. Something that large almost always needed combustion engines unless it was an Excalibur.

Tinker would appreciate the part, anyway.

She drifted through the town as casually as possible and a couple more men and women at their stalls called out to her. The first three didn't know who she was and demanded similar performances on smaller devices that needed attention, for which she demanded equally small payment. After that, her reputation spread and those who needed something repaired began to seek her out with parcels of food or parts they were willing to trade in exchange for her services.

Jessica13 would have preferred to simply sneak through the town and learn what she could. She'd never really needed to resort to subterfuge—her escape from Sanctuary was really the first time she'd stooped to it—and she constantly felt that unseen eyes watched her or that others would discover her real purpose. Common sense reminded her that being seen as merely another peddler looking to unload her wares and pick up a few more before moving to the next town made her as invisible as she could hope for. She even had to admit that sneaking would probably be more stressful, although it would have the advantage that there'd be no delays.

Her fears remained but were offset a little by the realization that she was helping these people in the only real way she knew how. It made her feel better, given that her real reason was to gather information, which felt a little dishonest. Besides, as she'd mentioned to her teammates, while she helped to repair their items, they talked to her. She was a little challenged by the fact that folks expected peddlers to peddle not only wares, tools, and services, but also information from the Outside. There weren't too many who wanted to wander, and those who did were usually in possession of a variety of choice news that could be shared with the others.

Thankfully, she had a good memory and was able to share snippets she'd heard from the other Knights and substitute real news with a story or two. Mostly, she tried to think ahead and ask a question or two that might start them talking rather than looking to her to do so.

She settled in to help to fix one of the desalination stations that had been set up around the town and one of the young women who did some of the fetch and carry tasks began to talk.

"It's been a while since we had rain," she said. "Which is a pity. It makes us more and more reliant on the water coming from the tower."

Jessica13 glanced instinctively at the trail of smoke that still rose from the burning building at the top of the hill, but the woman gestured quickly at the concrete tower they had noted when they first approached Auburn. She seemed as little inclined to look at the hill as everyone else, and her expression seemed a little tenser than before.

"What makes you reliant on it?" Jessica13 asked casually and resumed work on the desalinator. Heat was collected to boil the water to separate it from the elements that it might have been mixed with.

"Well, the admins there make the water run around these parts," the woman said and seemed a little more relaxed. She leaned in to watch as the copper piping was positioned where the slow flames would boil and clean the water they either brought up from the ground or collected from the rain. It was a crude, inefficient system, but it was all they had to work with.

Jessica13 looked up from her work and narrowed her eyes at the younger woman. "I don't know much about that. How do they make the water run?"

"Well, they call it the Hoot Bunker," the girl said and frowned slightly. "You know, after Lady Hoot? The lass with the big fuckin' mech and the owl on her helm."

"Oh, right." She grunted. "Lady Hoot. So she controls how the water comes around here?"

The girl nodded. "She controls the rain in these parts and says that if we don't give her the best of our crops, she won't send the prayers to the sky with her name and the Prophet won't make it rain for us." Her tone had a slightly resentful edge that belied the calm expression on her face. "And now, we can't pump water from the ground anymore. Well, we can, but it's mostly sludge we have to boil off in these damn things"—she tapped the desalinator—"and that ruins all the workings of it." She sighed. "But it's better than no water, I guess."

Jessica13 scowled at the tower and more importantly, at the two balloons like the ones around the bunker they had helped fix. These flew a great deal higher, however, all the way up in the clouds.

She wasn't sure if it was true that Athena—or Lady Hoot, as she was apparently known—could control the rain but seizing the water underground did make sense. She'd read about some of the bunkers being built to sustain and maintain water supplies in the surrounding areas with the purpose to make the Outside fit to live in again. This one likely had a massive underground reservoir, which was how she could manipulate how much water these people could access from underground.

"How does Lady Hoot collect what she needs from you to keep delivering the water?" Jessica13 asked.

"Oh, you know…" The woman shrugged. "Sometimes, it's only the admins sent from the bunker who take what they need, plus parts and pieces and sometimes, even folks." The idea of them seizing people was a concern. Had they all ended up like those in the church, or did Athena have a more sinister purpose for them? While she couldn't imagine what that might mean, she did know she didn't want to find out first-hand and cast another surreptitious look around her.

"They say that there are other towns she collects from," her companion continued, "but since she takes so much from us, I don't understand why she would need theirs as well. Maybe they only need to give up their goods for her to be able to give the water?"

It seemed like the people in the area had been cowed into submission through control of their water supply. Not everyone, obviously, because the signal for help had been sent. She wondered if there were others who were still alive who didn't believe that Athena actually provided the water.

Technically she did give them the water, but she used it to extort what she wanted from the local populace. Not only that, she was only able to give it because she'd stolen it from them in the first place.

And not only Auburn, if the girl was right and there were more towns she collected from.

Jessica13's gaze returned to the smoking ruins of the building and reminded herself that someone had, in fact, called them for help and that they were likely inside the smoking remains of that building. Athena's control, when the threat of no water didn't work, was obviously enforced a little more compellingly.

"What happened on that hill there?" she asked and tried to keep her voice as neutral as possible. She'd learned more from this young woman in a few moments than she'd gleaned from the town as a whole thus far.

"Oh, Papa says I'm not supposed to talk about it," the girl said a little too quickly. Her expression flickered between fear and resentment and a slightly rebellions gleam in her eyes said she wanted to share what she knew with the newcomer.

"Well, far be it from me to make you break your word to your father," she replied lightly, hoping her apparent lack of interest would encourage her companion to speak.

"He's not my father. He's my papa," the girl protested and her eyes widened when she realized the statement had been a little forceful.

"He's not your father?" Jessica13 asked.

"No, I…" She looked away and swiped at her eyes. "My father died because he disobeyed Lady Hoot," the girl said. "Papa is the man Lady Hoot told my mama to marry after that. He told me not to say anything to anyone because no one is allowed to talk about it."

"Do you want to say anything?" she asked gently. It was apparent that the young woman didn't necessarily dislike the man her mother had married, but she was also torn. If they weren't allowed to discuss people who had been killed by Athena, it meant she wasn't permitted to speak about her father either. It couldn't be easy to grieve in those circumstances, and she was probably afraid to say anything even to her mother.

"I want to but I shouldn't."

"Well, you must do what you think is right. But I won't tell anyone if that's what you're worried about. I can keep secrets when I need to and besides, I'll be gone soon."

"Well…you promise not to blab to anyone?" The girl finally sighed when she nodded. "Papa helped Lady Hoot with the collections this month and she needed more than the past couple of months. People complained, and a couple of them were caught sending signals out of town. The priest who made service in the church used the bell tower to try to call someone else who wasn't Lady Hoot. I guess he wasn't good at it and only Lady Hoot heard, so she took the priest and the people who helped him, and…"

"Burned them inside the building," Jessica13 said and finished the girl's sentence for her.

She nodded and wiped her eyes again. "I didn't like it. One of them was my friend's father, but Papa said she would get a new papa too, so I guess she'll be okay. My Papa isn't cruel, and he takes care of us, so maybe hers will too. But it's still sad because her father and mine were good too. I miss him, although I can't say it because Papa says it's dangerous. It doesn't seem right that they had to die to make an example, whatever that really means."

Jessica13 finished her work on the desalinator and looked at the young woman, who now kicked at the rocks on the ground with a kind of dejected acceptance. It was oddly surreal to discuss people being killed like it was something that happened every day. Friends losing parents and having those parents replaced was tragic enough without it being a deliberate act to terrify a community into submission.

She looked up as a tall, lean man dressed in the same kind of mismatched clothes she had noted on all the other citizens of Auburn. The only unusual feature was a pair of newly shined boots with brightly polished buckles at the top that jangled with every step he took.

"Clarisse, there you are I've been looking for you all over," the man said and the girl jumped from her seat and moved toward him. "Who is this you're talking to?"

"This is Jessie, Papa. She's a peddler!" the girl said as the man draped his arm over her shoulder. "She's fixing the water purifiers and she asked about the church burning."

"Did she now?" He turned to face her.

Jessica13 could only assume the girl's conscience had reacted to being virtually caught in the act made her instinctively blab about what she'd insisted had to be kept secret.

"I saw the burning." She kept her head low and forced herself not to jerk or shake as she collected her tools. "I asked her about it. She said she wasn't supposed to talk about it and made me promise not to say anything."

"Well, she knows nothing can be told in Auburn without me knowing about it," the man said with a chuckle. "It's good that you told me, Clarisse. If you're always honest, you'll avoid being in the next burning building, you know?"

The horrifyingly calm way in which he said something so terrible triggered a shiver of fear, but Jessica13 nodded. Instinct told her she needed to distract the man from the current topic of conversation and somehow ease any suspicion he might feel. "I move around and folks want stories when I travel to their locations, so when I have one to share, they like to hear it. I've found they tend to give me food and drink while I give them good stories, so I've learned to listen for the good ones. A burning building tends to be a good story to share. Like I heard out west that a couple of bunkers were burned by pirates that were getting their weapons and parts from a scrapyard from a nearby City-That-Was."

"No shit?"

She nodded. "They were burned right the hell out. They took all the resources they could from inside, killed the folks they found, and those who weren't killed died in the toxic smoke from what they used to burn it. They did a thorough job too, I heard, and didn't want anyone to pick up what they left behind."

The man nodded. "Well, that is why we have Lady Hoot looking over us. Folks around here think the only reason why they give to her is because of the rain and water she gives them. And while that is true, they have forgotten the real reason why they want to make sure she remains with them. Folks outside of Lady Hoot's protection have to face pirates like the ones who burned that bunker out. The people here have lived for so long under the umbrella of our lady's protection that they forget the dangers she protects them from. The church was burned with those who would have invited risk into our lives and brought outsiders to endanger the peace Lady Hoot has bequeathed us. That burning was a lesson, a reminder to the people of Auburn of what they risk when they anger Lady Hoot. She might not come back to help us."

The man had the same kind of voice and intonation that Jessica13 recalled Hammerhand using, a kind of hypnotic monotone that made her want to believe everything he said. She could almost understand why Clarisse wasn't more upset about people dying in the church on the hill.

"Well, I'll tell you something, that story will earn me quite a few meals out in the Wild," Jessica13 said with a chuckle.

"You're a good mechanic, yes?" the man asked.

"I dabble," she admitted.

"Jessie, I think the others said your name was," he continued like she hadn't even spoken. "People with skills like yours are often unappreciated, bartered for, and reduced to the point where you have to tell stories to fill your belly. But someone who works as you do..." He paused and moved to where she had worked to clean the purifier and smiled. "Someone with your skills need not beg for work wherever she goes. You could have a home here. Work all day but come home to a warm home, a bed, and as much food and supplies as you need. Have you considered that?"

She wasn't sure what he was getting at but she wondered if there wasn't trouble involved along the way. "I've thought about it, yes," she replied and tilted her head as if she reconsidered it. "But I do enjoy exploring the Wild. It's a chance to get to know the world and maybe share the stories of the world with the people in it, which makes me feel connected."

"Well, if you ever tire of wandering, know that a place like Auburn could be quite welcoming to someone with specialized talents like yours," he said. "We have a couple of locals who collect vids and manus of how to make things run, but you have a skill for it, I can tell. Experience and learning are hard to come by, even if you can read what can be read in those fucking manus. Folks underestimate how good it is to have everything working as it should instead of having to work and replace what breaks with what might not be such a good replacement if you know what I'm saying."

Jessica13 nodded. "Well, I'll think about it. I've wandered a while and I've let the word spread that I'll be here to fix what's broken for as long as I'm welcome here."

"As long as you fix what's broken, you'll be welcome," he said with a chuckle and a kiss on Clarisse's cheek. "You have a nice day now, Jessie. If you plan to move out to the fields or maybe closer to the bunker for your work, let the checkpoint guards know that Barrios sent you. They'll let you through."

She watched the man as he walked away. As soon as he was out of earshot, she let the shiver of disgust she had somehow managed to contain rush down her spine. She still felt like she was being watched, inspected by those who might suspect that she wasn't who she said she was. The man's oily demeanor and the way he spoke almost made her unable to look him in the eye.

Even now, she felt greasy merely from the conversation.

"He mentioned checkpoints?" Mini said as she stepped inside the cockpit and cleaned her hands. "Checkpoints with guards who would be able to stop us?"

"Something like that. But I think I can use his name for a little more exploration for a better assessment of this place before we rejoin to Tinker and Windchime. We need to make sure we know as much as we can for their benefit and Hammerhand's."

"I've mapped the roads and pathways through Auburn since we arrived, so I think I have a good idea of how we would be able to reach the bunker, even if it did go through one of the checkpoints," Mini told her.

"Well, in that case, we can simply drop Barrios' name and pass through," she muttered. As if it would be that simple. "But it might be best if we collect the payment old Caysom promised for our work on the purifiers first. We wouldn't want anyone around here to think we work for free, right?"

"That is a good point," Mini replied.

CHAPTER FIVE

A feeling of being watched followed her around the town of Auburn as she continued her work. It was mostly tinkering with a variety of smaller devices that would need a little effort to repair them. The people could easily have learned to fix the machinery themselves, including the mechs that were used for the fieldwork.

A couple more of the men with brightly shined boots and buckles appeared here and there and watched her. It seemed her invisibility had faded as her reputation grew and she could only hope their curiosity had more to do with the novelty of a young woman who traveled the Wild alone and less with her possible ulterior motives. It didn't come as any surprise to see that the same type manned the checkpoint.

She had the name of the man that would get her through, or so he had claimed, but she didn't want to draw any more attention to herself. Children had begun to follow her around as she worked, and more of the people talked around her to spread the gossip and stories while tried to listen to any of the stories she had to share.

It was difficult to be a storyteller when she constantly had to think before she spoke. Most of the stories she knew had to do with the Knights Mechanica, and with Athena's men watching her, the last thing she wanted was to inadvertently let slip that she was a part of them. They worked with or close to Athena, so the chances were the Knights were known. If they discovered she was a member, she was likely to be the next to be sent into a building that was set on fire.

They didn't approach her, fortunately, although their constant scrutiny fueled her growing tension and the icy fear that coiled in her gut. Aside from Barrios, none of them interacted with her but seemed content to study her every move through the town and even when she worked on the mechs out in the fields. Small bits and pieces were exchanged as she played the part of the peddler as well as the mechanic, and she shared stories she and Mini were able to think of while they wandered.

It seemed like a good idea to both of them to keep his existence a secret once they heard mention of 'those damn AIs' that suggested that some of the locals might feel he was some kind of abomination. She could only hope that no one other than the first trader had seen the mech move on its own and that he wouldn't feel inclined to mention it. Mini had once told her about a time when people thought AIs were a danger to humans as a whole based on stories and films that had been released in that era.

As it turned out, AIs were actually part of the reason why humans had survived the attacks of the Invaders. It was an odd idea that AIs would be the death of humans, given that people were the ones who created them.

"Humans were quite capable of wiping themselves out at a few points in history," Mini had said at the time. "Maybe in creating AIs, they thought their creation was capable of the same thing."

It explained the mistrust that people held for an AI, at least. Either way, it was a quick and easy decision to keep Mini's existence a secret for the time being as they worked through Auburn.

"How much data do you have on the town?" Jessica13 asked as they moved through the streets, supposedly looking for more work as the light started to fade from the sky. It was only a few hours from sunset, but the fact that they were in a valley meant it was getting darker at a faster rate than it would have out in the open.

"I have developed detailed maps of Auburn's streets, buildings, and underground sewer and water systems," Mini replied and displayed smaller versions of the map on her HUD. "The underground streams are of particular interest, as they appear to lead toward the bunker that was pointed out before as controlling the water. It could be that the bunker itself is storing the water and only supplying it on the instructions of Athena—or Lady Hoot, as she appears to be known as in this town."

"Are we still being watched?" she asked. It was difficult to locate Athena's agents as she was afraid to constantly look around. Oddly enough, they were easy to identify as they all wore the same boots she had seen Barrios wearing.

Mini ran a quick scan of their surroundings and pinged the area quickly. "You are currently alone. Any who might be watching you would do so from a distance, so if you want to make your escape before nightfall, I would suggest that it might alert them to the fact that you're not who you've said that you are."

"Or I'm more comfortable spending the night outside of

town," Jessica13 said. "Either way, can you tell if they'll watch us if we leave?"

"They could be watching us through a telescope," he pointed out. "There would be no way for my scans to pick up on something that low-tech."

"Well, we can't risk staying here for much longer," Jessica13 said. "We need to contact Tinker and Windchime."

"Do you think you could transmit everything to them over the radio waves while still keeping up appearances around here?"

She shook her head. "I doubt it, honestly. The people who were murdered in the church were caught transmitting to us, so I think we can safely assume there is some kind of monitor on all the comm lines. If they pick transmissions up, even if they are encrypted, they'll know there are unauthorized messages being sent out and there would be a very clear culprit."

Mini paused. "Barrios?"

"No, me!" Jessica13 grumbled. "Why would Barrios be a suspect?"

"Because his daughter broke the rules by telling you what happened?" Mini almost sounded offended. "Well, technically, his stepdaughter, I suppose. If he were to protect her from retaliation over talking about private Auburn matters to a stranger, he might look for a way out and thus summon help."

"I suppose it's possible," Jessica13 conceded doubtfully. "But not very likely. These men in the shiny boots appear to be in charge of this town, at least when Lady Hoot isn't here personally, and so I think he would be able to protect his stepdaughter without appealing for help from beyond their borders."

"Would you like me to run the statistical possibilities?" he asked.

She laughed. "No, I don't think that's necessary. I think we need to get out of the town and find Tinker and Windchime. I have no idea what they might be doing or planning, and anything they might be up to would be done better if they know the layout of the town, right?"

Mini paused as if assessing the statistical probabilities anyway.

"Yes, I suppose you are right," he said finally.

"Well then, that's what we'll do." She nodded. "We'll head to the edge of the town, hide in a location that makes it difficult for them to see us, and slip away."

"Very well."

She gradually moved to the corner of the town and once there, attempted to stay within the shadows of the buildings. Having to skulk and hide like this felt wrong, somehow, despite the fact that she'd wished she could do so earlier. The Knights had always been about helping people and there wasn't much subtlety to them. It applied especially when their leader piloted a massive mech that wielded a rocket-powered hammer.

"Run one more check for me to be safe," Jessica13 said and halted the Minato in the deepening shadows of one of the buildings at the edge of the town.

"You are still not being followed closely by anyone," Mini said. She knew for a fact that the AI would not show any kind of emotion, but she began to imagine some anyway. Frustration was what she imagined in his voice at that moment.

Once she felt more certain that she was alone, she crossed the final distance to the edge and into the wooded area surrounding the town of Auburn. She moved slowly and as naturally as possible, knowing that if anyone approached her and asked about her movements, she could simply say she intended to spend the night outside the town. It was the kind of oddity some expected from peddlers.

Fortunately, no one approached her. Mini kept the sensors activated to be sure and was able to confirm that she wasn't followed as she headed deeper into the woods. Once she was under the full cover of the trees, she looked around to get her bearings so she could find Windchime and Tinker.

"Do you know where they are?" Jessica13 asked, unable to see much in the gathering darkness.

"The motion sensors don't detect any nearby mechs," he said as they continued to move. "They will no doubt have remained where they had a good view of the town as you originally planned. I will indicate the last point where you saw them for reference."

Progress was slower in the fading light but eventually, she reached the position from which they had overlooked the town.

There was no sign of them, however, and she stopped abruptly.

"Where could they be?"

"Behind us," he said.

"What?"

"They are behind us and have leveled their weapons."

She began to turn cautiously when the two mechs stepped toward her. Windchime had drawn all four of his weapons and had them leveled at her.

"Is that you, lassie?" Tinker asked as he approached and circled warily.

His caution seemed unnecessary, although it was possible that the townsfolk had somehow found a way to pull her out of her mech and sent someone else in her stead. Common sense said it was unlikely as Mini would have stepped in to prevent that happening, and ordinary folks weren't capable of standing up to him. Jessica13 was sure the AI would have disabled the Minato before he allowed someone else to take control of it.

With that said, they wouldn't know Mini well so wouldn't know how he would react. And, of course, they were entitled to make sure it really was her rather than simply accept things at face value.

"It's me," Jessica13 said and stood quietly with the Minato's hands up to make sure they posed no threat. "Do you want me to come out so you can see me?"

The two looked at each other for a moment.

"Why don't you go ahead and do that?" Windchime said but sounded a little embarrassed by his paranoia.

She pushed the hatch out and stepped into view with her hands up, anxious that neither of them would accidentally shoot her while she tried to calm them. Thankfully, their weapons lowered when they saw her and she climbed into Mini once again.

"So, what did you find out?" Windchime asked once she was situated once more. "You took most of the damn day to get here, so it had better be good."

"Well, most of my time was spent establishing my cover as a peddler," she explained. "They needed a ton of work done all around the town and while I worked, I was able to find out what's been happening there. Mini also made an illustration of Auburn's inner workings, so we won't be lost."

It took only a short-burst transmission to send the map to the other two mechs, which meant it was unlikely that anyone would even realize something had happened.

"What about Athena?" Tinker asked. "Did you find out what she was doing in the area?"

"As it turned out, yes." Jessica13 paused to make sure no one had picked up on the transmission before she continued. "She goes by Lady Hoot among the folks of Auburn, and she rules over them with an iron fist that has become disturbingly more aggressive."

"Is she there now?" Windchime asked.

"From what I learned, she comes and goes and takes a tax on their supplies and food whenever she visits. That tax grew a little too overbearing, and that is why they wanted help and called us."

"I'll assume the folks who called us are the ones who ended up burned in that building?" the younger Knight asked.

"You are very astute. They called the building a church but I'm not sure what that means. Maybe where Athena or Lady Hoot passed judgment?"

"A church is a place to worship invisible deities," Mini said and displayed pictures of other churches on the HUD. Most of them had the same sign that had been on top of the burned building.

"It sounds like the kind of thing Athena would do," Tinker said. "So, she rules over these people? Why don't they simply arm themselves? They could get weapons for those mechs in the fields and fight back. I know Athena's Excalibur is no small enemy, but even then—"

"She has left agents behind," Jessica13 interrupted. "A group of them man checkpoints all around the town to make sure those mechs that come in and out of the farms and into the town itself are no threat. They keep the people in line too. I was also able to see that the three Cinders we saw before were left behind when Lady Hoot went about her business.

They were beyond the checkpoints so I wasn't able to get a good look at them, but from what I saw, they were well-built. You'd have to be crazy to run a badly built Cinder but then again, crazy is not really out of the question for these people."

"Athena has good mechanics—or at least she did when we knew her. I think she'll be able to keep her mechs in good order," Tinker said. "What do you think, then? Should we be able to knock them out of position and take control of the place?"

"I don't know." Windchime sounded worried. "With only three of us and if we had the element of surprise, we could possibly gain the upper hand. But if they had sufficient warning and managed to get a message to Athena before we could consolidate our position, we wouldn't be able to hold the town even if we managed to take control, which isn't a foregone conclusion. She would be able to come back and knock us out before Hammerhand gets here. On the other hand, if we don't give them some kind of landing ground, the Knights Mechanica won't be able to push into the town without alerting them. There are too many of them to remain unnoticed and if she only left three Mechs to hold it, she obviously believes it's easy to defend."

"There's something else too," she said. "The folks I spoke to talked about how Lady Hoot was able to control the water they use to grow their crops and even to drink. They get most of it from underground using wells and the like that run dry when she tells them to—when they haven't paid the tax, obviously—but they said she could control the rain too. I can see how she would be able to control underwater streams from that bunker over there, but how would she control the weather?"

Tinker studied the bunker in question and pointed a finger

at the balloons tethered to the top that drifted lazily in the clouds. "Electrical impulses are sent to those balloons, I think. It was tech they researched in Cities-That-Were when they had problems with waters rising to swamp the cities. It meant they were able to control the rainfall and bring it to the locations that needed it and avoid flooding in some areas while watering the crops in others. It is a little beyond my expertise, but they did manage to do it. Maybe this bunker is one of those that was set up to bring about change in the world after the war to generate rain and water so folks could start to grow crops and live outside again."

"And Athena took control of it and is using it to leverage a position of power with the locals and set herself up as a ruler over her little domain." Windchime shook his head in disgust. "I wish I could say I was surprised, but it actually does seem precisely like the kind of thing she would do."

"So," the other man said. "How do you think we should do this?"

"If I had to guess, I'd say her agents would be able to contact her if anything happened," Jessica13 said. "The men—who all wear shiny boots for some weird reason—would be able to alert her that we were taking over and so give her time to come back. The folks in the town seem afraid of her. There are some who believe she's actually some kind of leader who will take them into a brave new world, and that is the image her agents—for want of a better word—try to pass on. They talk like she's some kind of prophet or something, but I think most only pay lip-service because they don't want to end up in the next building that's set alight. That said, I think they're afraid enough of her to contact her right away rather than wait to see if we gain the upper hand."

Tinker sighed and nodded. "Well, if there are those who

would alert Athena about what we're doing, it would be best if we take them out quickly and quietly first before we confront the Cinders."

"They wouldn't be able to connect with her directly, I don't think," Windchime pointed out. "There's too much interference from the trees and the hills. They would need a higher point to be able to send transmissions out."

"He's right," she agreed. "The folks who contacted us needed the top of that church to send the transmission we picked up. The chances are they have something at the top of the bunker to help with that. If we were able to cut their comms, we would cut their line with Athena off entirely."

"That...does sound like the beginning of a plan," Tinker said tentatively and looked Windchime, who nodded in agreement. "Do you think you could destroy it?"

It took a moment for her to realize they were talking to her. "Wait, why me?"

"Because you're the one with the grappler," Windchime said but didn't sound very happy about it. "We'll still need to be as quiet as possible when we get to the bunker to make sure no alarms are raised before we can do it."

The other man nodded. "Are we ready to act on it now?"

"You might want to familiarize yourself with the maps first," Jessica13 said. "But yes."

A plan of action was quickly developed. Mini mapped the route that would leave them exposed the least on their way to the bunker. The worst part was around the checkpoint that led to it.

"It's mostly open terrain," Windchime said. "Even if we move across it quickly, there won't be any cover to keep us hidden. They will see us moving and it will all be over."

"I can get across," Jessica13 said. "There's tall grass that would hide Mini and I if we're in Bulletfoot mode, but we would still be visible to the men manning the checkpoint."

"We'll have to handle them," he replied

She wasn't sure she liked the sound of that. Handling sounded fairly deadly, especially to men who weren't in mechs themselves. It made things a little less fair than they generally were but given that she piloted a smaller support mech, most of her time spent toe to toe with other mechs generally tended to be unfair toward her. Aside from which, she reminded herself, these were men who followed Athena and had stood back while their fellow townsfolk were burned alive.

Night had fully fallen by the time they had their plan finalized, but they needed to make sure they were out of sight of the locals as well as anyone who might be able to report them. There was no way to tell who would simply assume their arrival was an invasion and sound some kind of alarm. They didn't need to deal with Athena's guards as well as the local folks from Auburn.

The best place that could be found was the divot—almost a small river—that had been dug to allow water to flow into the fields. It was mostly dry for the moment and was probably only filled when needed. Unless they stood at the very edge, it should keep them out of sight of the locals.

They did need to keep themselves low, however, which meant dropping down and moving on all fours.

It was no problem for Jessica13 and Mini, as all they had to do was move into Bulletfoot mode. The earth around the dried riverbed was mostly soft, so they didn't have to worry much about making noise.

Windchime had an easier time of it than she had expected. She didn't know whether it was the work of his AI or if he was merely more skilled with his combat mech than she thought he was, but the second pair of arms suddenly came active and enabled him to scuttle across the surface of the riverbed with ease like an insect. It was interesting to watch.

Tinker had a little more difficulty, however, as his mech lacked the kind of improvements that would have allowed him to move on all fours.

She took her position at the front and used Mini to scan their surroundings periodically to make sure there was nothing and no one moving around their route. On the few occasions when the motion sensors did pick something up, the three mechs froze in place and waited for the movement to pass before they continued.

It was even more harrowing than being among the people and acting like a peddler. At least she knew what she was doing when playing that role. She had no experience with the kind of situation she was in now.

But Tinker and Windchime both expected her to be able to do this and keep them alive besides. She felt out of her depth but hopefully, Mini would be able to help her settle into her role.

The reasonably short journey through the riverbed, as it turned out, was the easy part of their operation. When the water's path cut deeper and moved underground, it became necessary to climb out. This proved more difficult for the other two, especially since they needed to remain low.

"Stay down," Jessica13 whispered to Windchime as she helped to pull him out of the dried riverbed.

"Oh, shut up," he retorted sharply, but she could hear a hint of mirth in his voice as they all huddled together and hunkered as low as they could while Mini mapped the streets they could use to reach the checkpoint.

She would have preferred to circle, but the AI pointed out that those manning that particular checkpoint would be able to see them the whole way until they reached the bunker and if an alarm was raised, that would be the end of it. Or, at least, the end of any attempt at stealth.

No lights were on in any of the buildings they passed, which made her think there might have been a curfew possibly dictated by their electricity, or maybe it simply meant the good folk of Auburn were already in bed.

Remaining silent on the streets was a little more difficult, and Windchime quickly decided that moving faster was their best choice if they wanted to avoid notice.

Movement was, however, considerably easier as hurrying from one street to another while they tried to keep to the shadows was better than crawling through dried mud. Mini kept the mech in Bulletfoot mode, which allowed them to rush ahead of the other two and move quieter to ensure that they drew no attention.

Windchime pinged at her to halt as she approached the checkpoint. The electricity flowed freely for those within, by the looks of it. She wasn't sure how she had missed it the first time around, but searchlights swept across the field between them and the bunker. They also moved randomly like their pattern was generated by a computer.

Not only that, but the lights traversed their side of the checkpoint too.

"How do we get across?" she asked in a whisper. Mini brought them to normal mode and she peeked out of her mech to talk to the other two.

"If a light shines on any one of us, we've had it," Tinker said grimly and pointed out the obvious.

"Do we need to move through the lights?" Windchime asked.

"Any path in would take us through the open stretch where the lights pass randomly," she said.

"I have studied the patterns," Mini interjected, his voice soft and calm as always. "I calculate that there is a seventy-five percent chance I could move the Minato across the field without being seen."

"You mean there's a twenty-five percent chance that you'll be seen?" Windchime asked.

"It's a better chance than we'd have if we go in there blindly," the older man grumbled.

"Tinker is correct," Mini said. "I calculate…forty-seven-point-three percent chance of success."

"We can get across," Jessica13 said. "Once there, we can alter the patterns a little to make it easier for you guys to come across as well. "

"You'd still need to disable the men inside that checkpoint without letting them raise an alarm," Tinker reminded.

"I'm in a mech, and they aren't," she said. "The odds should be in my favor. We'll send you a ping on the comms when it's safe."

Windchime reached to his back, drew one of his swords clear, and handed it to her. "You won't be able to activate the vibro-function but the blades are still sharp enough. It would be quieter that way too."

She nodded and let Mini adjust for the extra weight before she put the sword on her back.

"It appears to be down to us," the AI said as they settled into Bulletfoot mode.

"Like I wasn't feeling the pressure already," she said softly and shook her head as she settled into her position. She had become a little more accustomed to how Mini moved while on all fours, which enabled her to adjust accordingly, but she still ended up with bruises here and there.

They stepped cautiously from the cover of the buildings. While she watched the calculations that ran across the screen, Mini quickly identified the pattern of the lights and pushed forward at a brisk pace but remained as low as possible. In this way, he was able to prevent even a hint of a reflection from catching their armor as they pressed forward.

Her heart thumped painfully and her body tensed every time one of the floodlights approached, cut through the darkness, stopped, and swept on again. Her mouth was dry and yet her palms sweated onto her controls of the mech, which were thankfully released to the AI so he could direct their movement.

Jessica13 wiped her hands quickly on her shirt and took deep breaths in an attempt to calm herself when they reached the edge of the area scanned by the lights. Mini remained on all fours as darkness engulfed them and the mech eased toward the mostly wood and concrete building that housed the lights and the men manning the checkpoint.

They inched forward, slipped through the open door, and paused to listen. Men talked and laughed in the next room.

There was no room for error in this. The mech resumed the bipedal stance, which enabled her to retrieve the sword Windchime had loaned her. It felt a little unwieldy in her mech's hands but it was better than simply swiping at the men with fists.

Mini inched them toward the door where light streamed through.

"Are you ready?" he asked and pulled up a visual of what

was happening on the other side of the wall they currently hid behind based on the noise that came through.

She nodded and he whipped them around the corner.

It was more or less how he had plotted it. One of the men sat at the radio in the corner of the room closest to them, while the other two looked through cameras that gave them a view over most of Auburn and laughed at some footage they were watching.

Bottles of spirits stood on the table between them and smaller glasses, which accounted for their raucous behavior. All three had put their shiny boots up and were enjoying themselves.

They barely registered that someone was in the room with them as Jessica13 pivoted and brought the sword to bear on the closest man near the radios.

She had aimed at his neck and struck perfectly. The vibroblade was sharp enough to cut without being active, and the power behind the blow was more than sufficient to sever his head.

His companions looked shocked to see the mech appear as if from nowhere. The Minato was smaller than most but in the confines of the room and to the two men who weren't in mechs themselves, it was dauntingly large.

The first one darted from his chair and scrabbled for the radio on the table as well as a small, sharp weapon. He couldn't hope to use it effectively against the mech, but he was the first one to be knocked back. Jessica13 swung her blade and caught him in the midsection. A sharp crack confirmed that his ribs were shattered by the impact which hurled him across the room and into the wall where he crumpled.

She had no chance to bring her sword to bear before the last man was able to snatch his radio but fortunately, she didn't need to. The dart was still engaged in the grappler's air gun and the man's eyes widened as she turned that on him instead and pulled the trigger.

The almost foot-long dart punched through his chest in a spray of blood, and she immediately reversed the wind on the cable to prevent the dart from piercing through him completely and into the wall. While it looked strong, there was no way to be sure that the damage wouldn't bring it down, which would draw unnecessary attention.

It somehow felt like hours had passed, and her pulse still ticked with adrenaline as she looked around the suddenly silent room. Somehow—impossibly—it had all happened in under five seconds and three men were now dead.

She shook her head. That was something she would have to deal with later.

It was quick work to retract the dart into the grappler. While it was still covered in blood and viscera and even a few chunks of bone, there was nothing she could do about it now. Jessica13 took a deep breath, selected a few wires she would need, and pushed the hatch open. She climbed out gingerly to skirt the puddle of blood that spread closer all too rapidly and forced herself not to look too hard at it as she stepped toward the computers the men had worked on.

"Ignore the bodies," she whispered quietly.

"Would you like me to clear them?" Mini asked and moved closer now that he was in full control of the mech.

"That's not…maybe later," she replied and plugged the AI's core into the computer system. "You should be able to access the algorithms from there so they can cross, right?"

"Affirmative," he replied.

She let the AI work and simply watched as the patterns were quickly and subtly shifted to create a clear pathway through the open field that would allow not only Tinker and Windchime to come across to her but also for them to reach the bunker itself without being seen.

Her gaze was drawn to the videos the men had watched and laughed at. The audio was still on and somehow sliced through the deafening silence like a vibroblade. The video in question showed a younger woman and two children forced to strip in front of the men before they were allowed to pass through the checkpoint. The footage quickly cut to a man dragged from a lineup and forced to his knees as a weapon was pressed to his head. He began to cry and shook his head before the trigger was pulled and he fell.

"Why were they watching something like this?" she asked aloud, suddenly sick to her stomach.

Mini paused before he answered. "It looks as though they played a drinking game. It doesn't make all that much sense to me, but they apparently watched the collected footage from the checkpoints and assigned importance to certain aspects that would then cause them to drink a shot of the liquor on the table."

The video shifted quickly to another young woman pulled out of sight as two of the guards stepped after her.

Jessica13 turned the footage off hastily as the woman was forced to her hands and knees.

"Are you all right?" Mini asked.

She shook her head. "I...suddenly don't feel so bad about killing these men."

"Your guilt over acting violently toward them is assuaged by knowing they were guilty of acts of violence against others?" He sounded genuinely curious.

"Not entirely," she responded, still fighting for control of her stomach. "But...it's a little easier to accept now."

"Understood."

The seconds ticked by until light footfalls sounded outside the room. Windchime was the first through the door and aimed his weapons inside first before he gestured for Tinker to follow him.

"Well…" he said and looked around the room. "It should be known that I always believed in your ability to handle this."

"Noted," she said but still felt queasy.

"The algorithm has been changed," Mini announced and moved to where she could climb into the mech. "We will be able to move across the field without being seen, and the lights will continue to move as they did before without being noticed."

"That's good enough for me," Tinker said as she settled herself in place. "Let's get moving, shall we?"

They slid out the other side of the room and hugged the side of the building as they studied the way ahead. Mini bunched onto all fours and moved forward as the HUD showed the path he had plotted for them based on the new algorithm.

"How sure are you that this will work?" Jessica13 asked.

"There is always room for error," he responded. "I would place the chances of success at ninety-eight-point-four-three percent."

"Oddly, that's not really encouraging," she said softly, knowing the other two would be close behind. She needed them to stay close to her. Even once they were past the flood-lights, they would need to get past the men in the Cinders that held position outside the bunkers.

The group covered the open field rapidly and without incident and remained as low as they could. She moved more quickly than her teammates and reached the barbed wire that had been erected around the bunker. Steel obstacles had been set up around the taller concrete building that towered into the sky. If kept in place, they would prevent larger mechs from getting within striking distance and so would need to be moved manually as they came closer.

She looked at the enemy mechs once they were out of the field, making sure to stay out of sight.

"Mini, what can you tell me?" she said, her voice virtually a whisper almost without thinking about it.

"The pilots are out of their mechs," he said. "Motion sensors tell me they are seated outside and eating at a small table. That could change over time, but the risk is minimal. Like the group of men at the checkpoint, they do not appear to be ready for any kind of attack."

"Lucky us," Windchime said.

"Can you detect where they would be able to transmit a signal out of the valley?" she asked while her gaze searched the building.

"I identify the only possible point as being at the top of the bunker," he told her and highlighted it on her HUD. "There should be a handful of transmitters at the top that you can disable to stop any transmissions from going out."

"Why would they only have one contact point?" Tinker asked.

"Again, I think it's because they don't expect any trouble," Jessica13 surmised. "The only other location high enough to transmit in this area was the church at the top of the other hill and it was burned down because someone else used it. I think Athena wanted only her people to have access to anywhere that could send messages out of here."

"It makes sense," the man said. "You won't be able to get to the top of the bunker without alerting the Cinders, and they'd definitely attack."

"They're out of their mechs now," Windchime pointed out. "Which means they don't have access to their personal radios. They're also drinking and eating—in other words, distracted. We take them by surprise and pin them down while Jessie here climbs up and does the dirty work."

Tinker looked at their adversaries, tilted his head in thought, and scratched lightly at his beard. "All right, let's do it."

Jessica13 hunkered in the grass and felt no better about watching them than she had when she was the one who moved forward. Windchime was faster and the other man hung back a little to provide support if it was needed.

The Cinder pilots did appear to be drinking, eating, and generally enjoying themselves as the two Knights snuck up on them if the bursts of laughter were any indication. She couldn't hear much, but Windchime reached them in moments and had drawn his remaining vibroblade as well as both his assault rifles. He pushed in closer than he needed to in order to intimidate them and draw them away from the tables. Tinker climbed out of his mech and moved quickly to make sure the men would have no way to send any communications out.

They were fast and professional like they'd done this kind of thing before and done it together. It was as if they knew how the other would act and react, which in turn created the opening she needed to do her part.

Jessica13 hurried to the base of the bunker, primed the grappler and, after a moment of Mini's help to aim, launched it.

The dart impacted with a loud clang and sealed itself in

place, and the retractor tightened the cable immediately. Her teammates had been right. That noise would have been easily audible to anyone who was nearby. She wondered if the folks in Auburn had heard it.

The bunker's tower stretched almost thirty meters, more than high enough to send clear signals out of the valley and to Lady Hoot if something happened.

"Are there any signals?" she asked as she reached the top.

"None being transmitted by the tower," Mini replied quickly.

She crossed to the sections that had been highlighted, climbed out of the Minato, and took her tools with her when she reached the transmitter. It was quick work, fortunately. A simple connection had been established to link it to nearby systems, and she had set up more sophisticated comm systems during her time in Sanctuary.

Of course, complex didn't mean it was any less effective, only that it was a little more difficult to eavesdrop, but there were always more ways for things to go wrong.

Simple was best when simple was all they needed. She had a distinct feeling that it was all that they needed to contact Athena about a possible insurgency.

Only a few minutes later, her part of the mission was accomplished.

"Are we finished here?" Windchime asked.

"There are no transmissions leaving this valley," Jessica13 replied and scrambled into the mech.

"Do you think there's anyone else inside the bunker for us to worry about?" Tinker asked.

"Probably," the other man replied.

"The chances are they will come out to see what went wrong with their comm system," she pointed out as Mini clambered down and angled toward the only door that opened to the bunker below.

She wasn't wrong. A few minutes passed before a small group came out of the elevator that opened. They froze when they saw the three mechs standing out in the open.

"Nice work, Jessie," Windchime said and kept his weapons trained on the new arrivals while Tinker forced the doors to remain open. Mini connected quickly and easily to the system inside the bunker as there were no AIs in place to operate it. Most of it needed to be done manually and only a small group remained there to keep the water and weather systems functioning the way their leader wanted them to.

"Do you think Athena will know?" Windchime asked. "Maybe she has a system with her people where if they don't communicate with her regularly, she simply comes to see what the problem is?"

"We'll have to risk it," the other man said as they disabled the captives.

"Remind me why we don't simply kill them," Windchime asked a little irritably.

"That's not our choice to make," Jessica13 said firmly and shook her head as she moved to the men who had been bound using spare wire Tinker had carried in his pack.

"There will be more of them around the town, though," Windchime said. "Those with the shiny boots you mentioned who make trouble with the local townsfolk with Athena's blessing."

"Should we bring them here?" she asked.

"I think you and Tinker should stay and keep an eye on the bunker as well as our prisoners," he said. "I can go to the other checkpoints, gather those who are still loyal to Athena, and bring them here, whether they want to be brought or not."

"That does seem reasonable," she acquiesced after a moment's thought.

Mini appeared to agree and immediately supplied the man with the locations of the other checkpoints. With the information he needed at hand, he turned to leave. She gave him his sword, and she and Tinker remained and waited while the night passed and the sun slowly began to rise before their teammate returned with a group of captives in tow.

There were fewer of them than she thought that there would be, and she could see sprays of blood on the man's hybridized mech.

"I take it many of them weren't overly cooperative?" Tinker asked and raised a hand to shield his eyes against the rising sun.

"Those who weren't changed their minds fairly quickly after their friends were cut in half," Windchime replied. He sounded less than enthused about the fact as she hastily secured their new prisoners.

A part of her suggested that she should be celebrating. They had won a major victory and on their own, no less. The other Knights would arrive in the next few days, which gave them time to consolidate their position in the location and set up defenses for the folks of Auburn.

But all she felt was sick to her stomach. Memories of killing the men in the checkpoint building herself, then seeing what they had done while acting under Athena's command had left her feeling shaken.

It wasn't like she hadn't killed before but this was different, somehow. She wasn't sure how, but it had certainly impacted her in a way the other deaths hadn't.

As the dawn brightened, the people in the town of Auburn began to stir and begin their day. It wasn't long before they realized the change that had come over their town and the sense of excitement was tangible. A few of Athena's agents hadn't been found by Windchime and once they registered the changed atmosphere, they quickly tried to establish some semblance of control over the populace.

It was immediately apparent that it wouldn't go well for them. The Auburn townsfolk had been strained and apathetic, apparently shocked into submission when their people were burned alive and simply resigned to their circumstances. Now, however, when they saw the Cinders no longer supported the enemy agents among them, they reacted with the decisiveness borne out of anger and suffering.

Those who had weapons were tackled and disarmed by several men and women, and the others surrendered when they realized they could expect no additional support.

After a fairly short discussion which included numerous gestures and nods toward the bunker, the residents dragged their prisoners away from the town to where Jessica13, Windchime, and Tinker waited for them.

Messengers were sent by the townsfolk to notify those who hadn't witnessed or been part of the early-morning rebellion. Despite the fact that they scurried from street to street and house to house, it was almost mid-morning by the time most of the inhabitants had assembled outside the bunker.

By then, the earlier sense of celebration had faded somewhat and no one appeared to know what should happen next. Athena's men looked fearful and clearly anticipated that the mob would lynch them at the slightest provocation, and the townsfolk looked restless. The mood seemed to ebb and surge as if they weren't sure whether to be angry, excited, or simply confused.

Tinker was the first to act, stepped out of his mech, and pushed himself onto the table the Cinder pilots had been seated around earlier.

"I am Tinker!" he called and projected his voice to carry and silence the crowd around him. "This is Windchime, and you may have met Jessie yesterday. We are members of the Knights Mechanica and were summoned to aid you in your time of need."

The people settled almost immediately and stared intently at the man with the scraggly beard and bushy eyebrows.

"Those who called us have paid the price for it, but know that their deaths were not in vain," he continued, and Jessica13 realized how similar his speech pattern was to Hammerhand's. "We don't want to take this town away from you, however."

Glances were exchanged and it seemed the townsfolk were unsure of what to make of that.

"The Knights Mechanica are here to help you but not to take over," Tinker continued and fixed a firm gaze on the group. "As for these sorry wretches, I suppose you get to choose what you want to do with them yourselves. Then, you can take control of your water supply from within this bunker."

He dropped from the table as the people began to discuss what they wanted to do with the men. The Cinders would be left for their use in defense, and she wondered if she could get her hands on a couple of those that were used in the fields and help them to build others.

It would take training before the people of Auburn were able to use the mechs without injuring themselves, but it wouldn't be an insurmountable challenge. Mini had a handful of subroutines that would help with that.

"What do you think they'll do?" Windchime asked.

"I'm sure they will simply rebuild once they know how to use all the mechanisms in the bunker," Jessica13 replied.

"No, I mean about the prisoners."

"They're running a vote now," Tinker said. "I think their choice will be to strip them and send them out into the wild."

"Which is a death sentence," the other man stated grimly. "Why not simply kill them outright?"

"Probably because no one wants to get their hands dirty," his teammate replied. "Or maybe they don't want to spare the bullets."

"They could always use the corpses for fertilizer," she pointed out and grimaced internally at the almost callous way she'd said that. It wasn't at all like her, and she assumed that all that had happened and her part in it had somehow derailed her a little.

"They already have a few bodies with the ones Jessie and I killed," Windchime added.

The group around them finally came to the conclusion that Tinker had assumed they would. The men were stripped of all their possessions, even their clothes and boots, and driven out of town.

"All in all, it's not the worst mission I've been a part of." Tinker rolled his shoulders and climbed into his mech. "I'll contact Hammerhand and ask him what we should do next."

CHAPTER SIX

Jessica13 folded her arms and scowled. She wasn't sure why she no longer liked being underground but for some reason, it really irritated her. Maybe she had become too used to the benefits of being above ground to enjoy the safety of a bunker again.

"Jessica13," Mini said softly. "We have a problem."

"Of course we do," Windchime grumbled and looked as happy with their current circumstances as she was.

"I have been able to connect to the bunker's software and it would appear that it is part of a network," the AI continued and displayed the system on the screen. "There appear to be five more—four satellite bunkers and one central bunker."

"It sounds like the kind of place Athena would set herself up in," Tinker said over the comms.

"Agreed," the other man replied. "She would be holed up in the location whenever she isn't in her Excalibur."

"The news only grows worse," Mini said. "The smaller systems of the local bunkers are accessible to me but the major functions to control the weather and water functions are isolated to the main bunker, which is about sixty clicks north of this position."

"Shouldn't we be able to access the functions from here?" she asked. "Maybe pick up the actual physical wiring?"

"It would be possible," he confirmed. "But the wiring is isolated behind fifty meters of steel-reinforced concrete. It would take months to reach with the current equipment we have, even in the Beast. With that in mind, we would be able to manage the balloons that maintain the local weather but the underground water supplies are controlled from the central bunker and are therefore beyond our control."

"It sounds like we need to take control of the central bunker," Tinker said.

"And that sounds far easier said than done," Windchime said. "We need to make contact with Hammerhand and see if it's even possible."

"For the moment, though," Jessica13 said and looked at her teammates. "Athena took a large amount of food from these people—supplies. They would be left almost destitute without it, especially if the underground water is cut off. Mechs wouldn't be able to carry it alone, which means Athena would have a supply train."

"And you think we should take the train?" the younger Knight asked. "How would we know where it's going?"

She shrugged. "Well, it should be obvious enough. There aren't any roads between the main bunker and this one, so if they are going there, it will be directly toward the bunker, which gives us a clear path toward them. If they're anything like Tinker's Beast, it should make a little under fifty klicks a day on an actual road. By my estimation, they're less than twenty ahead of us if they are moving across the open ground.

We can overtake them fairly quickly. And even if they aren't going to the bunker, if it's anything like the Beast, we should be able to find the tracks and follow them easily."

"It would make for a problem if that supply train is escorted in the same way ours is," Tinker said. "But I suppose it can't hurt to have a quick look to see if there's anything we can do to give them trouble, right?"

"Agreed." She nodded emphatically, even though he couldn't see her.

All she really wanted was to escape the bunker but delivering a little justice to the folks who had controlled and abused the locals on Athena's orders would certainly not hurt.

She and Windchime returned to the surface, where Tinker waited for them.

The reaction from the town once they fully comprehended their freedom from under Athena's heel was rewarding. A handful was celebrating while another group sifted through what had been taken from those they had banished and distributed them among the rest of the populace. Some set up streamers and prepared a larger celebration for later in the day. With supplies as limited as they were, it could hardly be considered a feast, but it was encouraging to see how they made do with what they had. What they lacked in food and drink they made up with enthusiasm and determination.

It would be difficult for all of them to gather until the evening since a large number of them needed to head out to the fields to work. Jessica13 wondered how they would be able to continue with their efforts to cultivate what they needed if they didn't resolve the water situation. There was only so much that could be done with rainwater, especially with this many people.

"Are you ready?" Windchime asked.

She looked at him, a little surprised. "Now?"

"Do you think we should wait until our quarry is inside the bunker and beyond our reach?" he asked, clearly sarcastic.

"No, but—"

"But nothing. If we want to take this supply chain, we need to do it now."

"I could stay here and help the folks to get their mechs running and maybe work out alternative water sources," Tinker said. "The two of you should be able to find the train without too much trouble."

Jessica13 nodded and interrupted Mini, who continued to work on the bunker's software.

"Are you ready to go hunting?" she asked.

"Always," he replied. "I think we are getting the hang of hunting people."

"That's…great," she muttered as they set off using the shortest route out of town. A few of the locals asked where they were going and why, but they directed them to Tinker. He would have to explain it rather than them being held up in what might become a lengthy discussion when folks found out they intended to track the supply train.

Fortunately, it wasn't difficult to find a trail. The convoy used literal tracks to move over the soft earth and there would be no shortage of very obvious impressions for them to follow. Mist droplets had already collected in shallow puddles in the indentations, which suggested that their quarry had passed through the area in the morning.

"These are recent," Windchime said and confirmed her assumption. "Do you think they were around to see what happened to their comrades?"

"If they did and somehow managed to get a transmission

out, Athena already knows what we've done," Jessica13 said. "Which could be a problem. But I don't think so. For one thing, they'd have to find really high ground and I don't see anything anywhere close to as high as the tower was. Also, Mini would have picked it up, I'm sure. She would have already sent people to retake Auburn if she knew. Either way, I guess Tinker will find out." They traveled for a short while in silence until she said. "I could rush on ahead and make contact with you if I find anything."

"It would be best to take weapons," her teammate said and handed her one of the assault rifles. "It should be a little easier to handle than the sword, and maybe your AI will be able to help you with aiming."

"Oh…all right, then." She took the weapon up and settled it on her back. It was a sensible precaution, although she questioned the wisdom of having to learn how to use a weapon like that in the heat of the moment. Maybe she needed to talk to Tinker about lessons and possibly a weapon of her own. Still, she'd wished she'd had one a few times in the past so wouldn't refuse it.

Windchime nodded encouragement and Mini quickly engaged their Bulletfoot mode. Once they'd settled onto all fours, they increased speed and followed the tracks.

The vehicle appeared to be heavily laden, which left a definitive trail that was easy to follow, even at a fast pace. To alleviate the monotony and distract herself from the anxiety that had crept in, she tried to estimate how large whatever she was tracking could be and how much she could actually do on her own to stop it.

Mini used Bulletfoot mode to reach impressive speed and it wasn't long before they moved out of the tougher terrain around them and into open grasslands again. A small and somewhat hazy blemish in the sky ahead drew her attention. She squinted to try to make it out and as they drew closer, it settled into something that resembled small puffs or trails of dark black smoke. There wasn't enough of it to indicate a fire, but it hung in the air for a long time, constantly replenished from an as yet invisible source in an almost rhythmic sequence that suggested a mechanical cause.

Finally, she could actually identify a solid shape that emitted the steady trail. From a distance, it appeared to be a very long, snake-like vehicle that pushed slowly yet steadily through the soft soil despite its weight. As she approached, however, she could see it was actually a convoy linked together and dragged forward by a lead vehicle, which was the one that produced the smoke.

It proceeded in a winding pattern, which allowed it to move quickly across the soft soil. Jessica13 knew it had to consume a great deal of some kind of fuel to do the work required to tow four tracked vehicles both with apparent ease and at an impressive speed.

Mini didn't need to be told to crouch as low as possible while they pushed forward. A handful of mechs stood on the train cars and kept a watchful eye on their surroundings with their weapons aimed into the open grasslands around them.

None of them had seen her yet which wasn't surprising, given that she was mostly concealed by the tall grass, but it wouldn't last for much longer. It was hard to miss a mech out in the open, even one as small and lithe as a Minato with improved leg functions.

"What do you think?" Jessica13 asked once she'd made contact with Windchime and let him have a good view of what she was looking at. "I think I can engage them to perhaps distract them and slow them down until you get here. From what I can see, it should be fairly easy pickings. The mechs on top of the train are mostly support mechs like Tinker's or mine and shouldn't put up that much of a fight."

"You don't think actual combat mechs might be hidden in there too?" he asked. "No, do not engage them. Keep an eye on them, and I'll be there in…ten minutes or so."

"Understood." She cut the commlink.

"Will we stand aside and let Windchime do all the work?" Mini asked after a brief moment.

"Hell no," she replied with a small smirk. Now that their quarry was in sight, her previous hesitation over having to actually use the weapon seemed to have vanished. "We have a gun so we might as well make good use of it. Windchime said you might be able to help me with aiming it. Maybe we should check that."

"I have a handful of subroutines that would be able to support you in aiming and shooting from a distance," he said, called the programs up, and showed them to her. They included a targeting reticle that followed the position of the assault rifle and provided her with an idea of where it would shoot.

"Huh. This is interesting," Jessica13 said. "It can also keep track of their movement over the longer distances too."

"It was software originally developed for the Sherlock class for long-distance shooting with its hellebore rifle, but it should adapt fairly simply to an assault rifle," he assured her.

They accelerated so they were able to overtake the train, but she still kept her distance. It moved faster than she'd expected, given what it was, but not dramatically so, and maintained its serpentine pattern. The mechs appeared to be held magnetically on top of the convoy, and from the way they moved, she could almost believe they were simply there as scarecrows intended to scare away any potential attackers without actually being operative.

She couldn't take that chance, however.

"We should set up on the bluff over there," Mini said and highlighted a slightly elevated location thirty meters ahead of them.

They climbed to the top and adjusted smoothly out of the Bulletfoot mode. She took the rifle from where it had been clamped onto her back and aimed it at the moving train.

"All right," Jessica13 said and took a deep breath. "I can't say how long before those mechs see us, so we might want to start whatever it is we intend to do here."

"Do you want to take a few practice shots at the mechs on top?" Mini asked and zoomed her vision to focus on the closest mech.

"Sure, what's the harm?" she asked and ignored the fact that she was supposed to wait for Windchime as she drew another couple of deep breaths to calm herself. Her heart ticked loudly in her ears, somehow, or maybe it was her pulse. Whatever it was, the sound was a little distracting and she fought to focus past it to the task she'd set herself.

Mini ran the programs, brought the rifle up, and locked the reticle on to give her the shot.

Another deep breath seemed necessary at this point, mainly because her little inner voice reminded her that she was, in fact, disobeying what Windchime had no doubt intended as a direct order.

Common sense said that he was right. She had absolutely no experience and wasn't sure what she was doing, and it seemed both reckless and foolish to not only ignore him but also draw attention to herself when she was alone. At the same time, though, something within her pushed her to do this. It might have had something to do with an inner longing to achieve something more than simply dart around in support of others—as if something greater awaited her and she needed to get this done as a step toward it.

She sighed again, decided to follow her bold yet foolish impulse, and opened fire.

A single round from the rifle took at least a second to reach the train less than six hundred meters away and punched powerfully into the cockpit of the mech she had targeted.

It lost most of its movement and slumped forward when its power cut out. There was likely no AI to keep it moving without its pilot to direct it.

The crack of the rifle caught the attention of the others, who turned to see where it had come from.

"Keep the rifle steady," Mini warned her. "Too much movement could make the targeting reticle a little less precise."

Jessica13 nodded but made no attempt to speak as she turned her attention to the second mech, which seemed to try to track her location. After a few more calculations by the AI, she pulled the trigger. This one struck a little too high but she still hit the cockpit and Windchime's armor-piercers were lethally effective and killed the man inside.

"I think you're a natural," Mini said.

"I think we need to find a better target than these support mechs," she said. Success had made her bold, and she chose not to allow any doubts to intrude and diminish the satisfaction she felt

He began a hasty search along the length of the train. It

continued to move despite being under attack, and a couple of the support mechs opened fire on the general area around them. None were even remotely close enough to her to indicate that they knew where her shots had actually come from. All they had for now was a general direction, which wasn't anything to worry about as yet.

"I have found a target." Mini highlighted a small section between the lead car and the second. "I detect a central weakness in the armor that would allow you to detach it from the others, especially with the armor piercers you have in that assault rifle. It might take more than one, though."

Jessica13 pivoted and focused on the part he'd indicated. She tilted her head and considered it. While it did seem like a challenge given her inexperience, she had Mini's help. That aside, it seemed both logical and natural to decide that she would at least try to bring the whole convoy to a halt.

For some reason—nothing in her experience or upbringing added any insight—this came easily to her. It was like fixing machines and mechs, simply a part of who she was.

She fired a three-round burst and the piercers cut smoothly through the rusted metal pins that held the convoy in place. The successive impacts made the train shudder but the vehicles didn't separate from the main car. The mechs now turned their weapons directly toward her as Athena's men finally pinpointed her position.

An odd calm descended on her. It wasn't as easy as people had said it was in the stories she'd heard, but it still came naturally in that second when she chose to take her final shot rather than seek cover.

Another shower of sparks indicated a successful strike and the lead car lurched ahead, suddenly free of the weight it had dragged behind it. The motion was too fast and too abrupt and it skidded and rolled onto its side in the dust it caused.

The momentum of the other cars kept them in motion for a few yards, but they ground slowly to a halt.

Jessica13 raced toward the edge of the bluff and hunkered into cover as she pressed the button to contact Windchime.

"Son of a whore!" he shouted as soon as there was a connection. "Is that you? Was that you shooting?"

"What's a whore?" she asked.

"Never mind that. Did you shoot?"

"Yes. I killed a couple of Athena's men before I brought their supply train to a halt. They'll probably come out to try to get their hands on me, so I really hope you can get here quickly before I have to fight them on my own."

"Fuck you," he all but snarled before the comm cut.

She shrugged and assumed he was angry because he'd missed out on the action and she'd stopped the convoy single-handed. That aside, he could be counted on to get to her as quickly as he could. In the meantime, she had more relevant issues to worry about like creeping a little farther away from their original position without revealing themselves. Heavy mech boots thumped around the immobilized supply train and questions were yelled in an effort to determine why it had come to a stop and who was to blame.

Gunshots were fired at her previous position but none were around her current location, which confirmed that they still had no idea where she was. That wouldn't last, unfortunately, as the enemy would soon realize that she had nowhere to go without exposing herself to them.

Jessica13 looked around for something that might help and held the assault rifle primed and ready in case she needed to use it. They hadn't seen her, likely because they didn't expect a smaller mech to attack them, but she doubted they would spare her if they found her simply because of size.

Two mechs appeared from farther down the slope and she turned slowly. They were Lancers, but she hardly recognized them. For one thing, they were in decent shape, which alone made them different from the ones she had seen before.

More footsteps indicated the approach of other mechs and from her scant cover among a handful of straggly bushes, she saw the shadow cast by what could only be a Cinder.

"I suggest we run," Mini said as she began to back away quietly.

The perverse instinct surged again, both annoying and titillating, to remind her that she had a gun and now knew how to use it.

It provided a persistent temptation, but she pushed it down and decided to wait for Windchime. Perhaps part of this unexpected new development was to learn to live to fight another day—if only because she'd barely explored the unexpected and immensely satisfying new development.

"Let's go," Jessica13 said and the mech settled into Bulletfoot mode again. She couldn't hear the men behind her as they were likely on one of the secured comm lines, which allowed themselves to talk without informing their quarry about their plans.

The decision came not a moment too soon.

Bullets kicked the dirt up around them when an assault rifle locked onto her back. The Minato surged forward in the direction Windchime would most likely come from. She didn't know how long it would take her to meet up with her teammate, but as long as she stayed alive, there was nothing to fear. They might have greater firepower, but she had speed and maneuverability. She could outrun the bastards and outlast them if she needed to.

"Where the hell are you, Windchime?" She hissed through her teeth when the alarms warned her there were a number of breaches in her armor. Nothing critical was hit, but it wouldn't be long before something was.

Gunfire suddenly erupted from ahead of her and the shooting from behind quickly stopped. She didn't have time to look to see if it was because they had been killed or merely tried to find cover before that happened.

Mini kept them in motion and varied their path randomly to make them a more difficult target and a few minutes later, Windchime appeared, racing toward her at phenomenal speed.

"Pull the mech up!" she called and waited until the AI had drawn them out of Bulletfoot mode before she took control of the upper half of her body. He retained control of the lower half to keep them running as she twisted, yanked the rifle from her back, and turned to look at the five mechs in pursuit.

Three were Lancers, with one Sherlock and the Cinder she had noted lagging behind. They were slower mechs and better suited for standing ground than running attacks.

Windchime's fire had pinned the Sherlock down and forced the mech back a few steps so it wouldn't be able to deliver effective shots.

Jessica13 took advantage of this and twisted while her legs continued to run in the opposite direction. It was difficult to aim while in motion and at that speed, but this wasn't the time to insist on precision when she had a full mag of bullets to use. She set it on full auto and noted the bullets she had at her disposal before she opened fire.

The bullets kicked dirt up and she tried to keep a solid grasp and aim the weapon where she wanted. It wasn't easy but a Lancer was hit three times, tripped to land face-first, and made no effort to rise.

One of the others was struck as well but in the knee area rather than in the cockpit. A spurt of black liquid issued from the joints and the mech rapidly lost the ability to move with its now damaged hydraulics. All the pressure released and it stumbled and fell.

"Get down!" Windchime shouted, and Mini was more than willing to oblige. He dropped the Minato to its knees while she turned to toss the assault rifle to her teammate.

He caught it smoothly with his second right hand and adjusted both rifles to do more than lay down covering fire. His concerted barrage eliminated the final Lancer by simply destroying the cockpit. The Cinder burst into flames and the man screamed inside and attempted to climb out.

Already burning, he didn't make it all the way and only managed to haul himself partially free before the smoke or the heat killed him. He sagged, still mostly in the cockpit, and smoke billowed to allow only fleeting glimpses of the slowly blackening corpse.

"Stay down!" Windchime yelled, still in motion as he drew his swords.

The Sherlock immediately realized the danger it was in and a piercing alarm screamed and easily drowned out the sounds around them. Jessica13 covered her ears. She knew the reason why, of course. Sherlock mechs had a highly unstable core fueling their movements, and instead of fixing them with something more stable, the designers had fitted them with a button that would blow the core instead.

She didn't like them for precisely that reason. In simple

terms, like Cinders, they tended to blow up. Unlike Cinders, when they blew, they tended to leave a massive crater.

Windchime knew it and had already taken steps to hopefully avoid disaster. First, he shot the man inside to prevent him from making any more mistakes that could doom them all. With him disposed of, he worked quickly, sliced into the back of the Sherlock, and dug within to find the core.

He located it, yanked it out of the mech, and after a moment's thought, hurled it as far as he could away from both the train and the two of them.

Jessica13 ducked instinctively and closed her eyes while she imagined the explosion darken the sky.

Fortunately, the core, without the rest of the mech to feed on, had only a bright flash and little real power.

It was over in a moment and she looked up cautiously and surveyed the carnage.

"Are there any more of them at the train?" Windchime asked as he moved beside her.

"Probably," she replied. "My guess is that they're only support mechs, though."

She frowned and focused on her HUD to determine the source of the alarms that blared in her ears. Her teammate snorted and waved a hand dismissively.

"What did I tell you?" he asked and shook his head. "Don't attack. You're not built for that."

"I felled two of them, didn't I?" she asked and ran a hasty systems check on the mech. "More than a couple, actually, if you count the first two on the convoy. Besides, that's why you gave me your rifle."

He growled and shook his head again, vehemently enough this time that his mech reacted to over-emphasize it dramatically. "No. I gave it to you in case you needed to defend yourself, not so you could start a fight you couldn't hope to finish. What would you have done if I—"

"If I could interrupt," Mini said and effectively cut off the admonition the man seemed ready to deliver. "I've examined the fallen mechs. The rifle attached to that Sherlock would actually be far more accurate for you to use for the pinpoint shooting software I can provide."

"Huh," Jessica13 replied and moved immediately to the mech in question. Windchime muttered something inaudible and ran a couple of systems checks to make sure he was ready for another fight. She wasn't sure what he intended to do next, but she wanted to support him better than simply carrying bullets for him.

Her teammate watched in silence as she detached the weapon from the Sherlock, hefted it, and studied the software.

"You really want to be involved in the fighting, don't you?" Windchime said finally as she returned to him. "You can't simply leave it to me, can you?"

"I thought you might need me for more than only support," she replied and tried to sound casual. "Besides, if I pick them off from far away, I'm not exactly in the thick of it myself, am I?"

"So long as you don't shoot me too," he grumbled. "Come on. We don't have time to waste."

He had a point, and it was sufficient to render her possible protest unspoken. The remaining members of the convoy would be able to make necessary repairs in short order and would soon be on the move again. While it would be interesting to work on the train herself, that wouldn't be possible if she had to shoot it again. She wouldn't say as much to her teammate, but who the hell knew what kind of damage she might cause the second time? Her achievement brought real satisfaction, but she was at least honest enough to admit to herself that she wasn't entirely sure she could repeat it.

"Nice work stopping the train," Windchime admitted grudgingly. "But it looks like they're trying to get everything moving again. Maybe they don't realize they've lost their attack team?"

"Or they don't care," Jessica13 replied and immediately looked for a reason to try her new rifle. "I think I can distract them and give you cover fire to approach them without being seen."

"Okay, why not?" he said after a moment's thought. "Wait for my signal."

For the first time since they'd left Auburn, she decided she would actually follow his orders. While she still believed she had abilities and intuition that had begun to emerge along with her instinct to test her limits, she also knew she'd been lucky thus far. Too much too soon might be the death of her, and it was better to rely on his experience and skills for now.

With this in mind, she set herself up on a small rise that gave her a clear view of the mechs below. Windchime moved quickly and remained as low as possible in the tall grass.

"You may fire when ready," he said.

"Are you ready?" Mini asked. "I've updated the software to adjust for the new weapon."

Jessica13 nodded and leaned forward a little while the weapon primed.

The hellebore rounds were more than what was required. Three more Lancers and a Balthazar kept an eye on the train and a handful of Watsons began to push the lead car upright where it had toppled in an effort to put themselves in a position to move again.

She was tempted to eliminate the Watsons while they were focused on the car and possibly crush those that supported it, but it wasn't a good idea. Windchime would probably have the same thought and he would be in a better situation to do it.

It was an easy decision to turn her sights to the Balthazar as the rockets flared visibly on its back. He wanted to take to the sky, obviously, but for some reason wasn't able to.

"We might want to help him with that," she said softly and inclined her head as she zoomed in to the rockets.

"Help who with what?" Windchime asked.

Jessica13 didn't answer and merely exhaled a long breath as she squeezed the trigger.

The hellebore round thumped into the fuel line on the rocket and set it off. The fuel didn't erupt as explosively as she had hoped, but there was still some effect. The rockets ignited and the Balthazar elevated abruptly and spun crazily to a height of almost twenty meters before it tilted and plunged to a hard and definitely fatal landing.

The other mechs whirled when they realized they were under fire but again, were unsure of where it came from. She adjusted her position slightly and resisted the urge to simply open fire in a blanket barrage.

Windchime elected to be safe and circled to the other side of the convoy to give himself cover. She looked down the rifle's scope to select another target—one of the Lancers—and decided to use the targeting reticule to put the round inside the cockpit.

The mech fell and remained motionless, and the others turned as they had now identified where the shooting originated from and were ready to retaliate.

Her teammate emerged from behind one of the motionless carts and used his swords to attack the remaining combat mechs with his vibroblades. The weapons sliced through them cleanly and threw up a shower of sparks. Jessica13 wasn't sure why the dry grass didn't simply catch fire, but that seemed like an irrelevant detail and she pushed it aside.

The mechs were eliminated quickly and efficiently. The Watsons, now unprotected, were trapped under the half-raised vehicle, unable to push it further without help and with no way to release it safely.

She wondered if she should act on her previous instinct but, exactly as she'd expected, Windchime turned and gunned them down in a concerted volley.

The car, only a quarter of the way up, fell again and crushed the mechs under it.

"Nice shooting," he said casually and scanned the area. "I'm fairly sure the coast is clear but I'll check the rest of the train. Keep your eyes peeled."

Jessica13 had heard the term before. Armstrong7 liked to use it from time to time, and she hadn't understood it then either. It sounded both ridiculous and painful, but maybe it was merely a way to say keep her eyes open. If so, why not simply say that?

Either way, she watched warily for any sign of danger as she headed over to the convoy at a leisurely pace to give her teammate time to make sure it was clear.

"Do you think you'd be able to repair it so it can move again?" Windchime asked once he'd checked all the cars. "It would really be terrible to have to drag these all the damn way back."

"I think it should be simple," she replied. "Help me get it up again, and it should hopefully be a matter of welding every-thing into place. Once that's done, we can turn the train around and take it to the good folk of Auburn."

It wasn't quite as easy as that, of course. First, the two of them had struggled to raise it onto its wheels, even with his enhanced suit and Mini's grappler. One that was done, they discovered that when it had overturned, some internal damage had resulted and had to be repaired. The hitch mechanism, however, proved to be far simpler than she had anticipated, so all in all, it took the two of them less than two hours to have everything in running order again.

"We should simply take the same line it used to get here, yes?" Windchime asked as she started the engine.

"I think that would be quicker and lighter on fuel usage, yes," Jessica13 shouted over the roar of the combustion engines.

The cumbersome arrangement and heavy vehicles proved something of a challenge before they were able to turn them, and the sun was already past its peak when they finally began the return journey.

"We might want to pick up the pace," Windchime told her gruffly. "Tinker's just called up. He says the Knights and the Beast have arrived."

"I thought it would take a few days for them to get there."

"We all did. They must have been closer than we realized or they pushed hard—probably both, which explains Hammerhand's reaction."

"Reaction? What do you mean?" she asked, a little confused as his tone suggested their leader wasn't happy. In her mind, he should have been delighted at what they'd accomplished, but maybe he didn't react well to either a hard pace or surprises, even good ones.

"He isn't happy that we took action without consulting him first."

"Does he understand that we couldn't contact him about it

for fear of being overheard and that we saw an opening and took it?" she asked. "Oh, and did he mention that small detail of how we actually succeeded?"

"All Tinker said was that Hammerhand arrived and he was pissed," her teammate told her. "I think we'll have the full picture when we get back."

"That sounds like all kinds of fun," she grumbled under her breath, a little resentful that something that seemed petty—at least to her—had raised its ugly little head to spoil her sense of satisfaction and achievement.

"Hammerhand does appear to be the reasonable sort," Mini pointed out. "He might hide behind a façade of noble and honorable justice, but he will see the tactical advantages of what we did in Auburn as well as the moral implications of lifting the people out of subjugation by Athena."

"I hope so." She shook her head gloomily.

After this news, the slow trip to Auburn seemed almost interminable. It was well beyond mid-afternoon before the heavier cover of trees forced them to slow even further. Jessica13 noticed the tracks that had been left by the Beast on its approach and realized she no longer looked forward to seeing the Knights again.

It wasn't so much seeing the Knights as the forthcoming conversation, however, that was the problem. Windchime's silence seemed to echo her own reluctance, but she also realized the discussion was impossible to avoid.

They entered Auburn and easily located the Excalibur Hammerhand piloted. He appeared to be deep in conversation with a group of Auburn folks as well as Tinker.

The conversation stopped abruptly and everyone watched the two teammates pull Athena's supply train to a halt in front of the bunker.

"I can't imagine why you would think that it was a good idea to come on a surveillance mission and decide to take over a whole town," their leader said as they moved toward the group. It was directed at Tinker but they could tell it was for them to hear as well.

"Well, technically, we didn't take the town over so much as liberate it, laddie," the man said.

"And we brought back the supplies Athena stole from them besides," Jessica13 pointed out. "She called it a tax, but I thought it was extortion since they turned those supplies over in exchange for the water she used to keep them compliant."

"You found our supplies?" one of the town elders asked. She recalled that he had been the one who had asked her to fix their water purifiers but couldn't remember his name for the life of her. "You brought them back?"

"They're all in the supply train over there," Windchime said and pointed to the vehicle that a handful of folks had already begun to peruse. Their supplies were found inside and like those that had been taken from Athena's agents, they were quickly handed out in what appeared to be a fair manner.

"Bless you," one said.

"Bless the Knights Mechanica," said another.

They had originally looked like they weren't sure if the Knights were there to take over the role Athena had been ousted from. Now, however, they were far more accepting of them given that all their food and supplies had been returned.

"We saw an opening and we took it, boss," Windchime explained to Hammerhand. "It was a tactical decision. Besides, it worked, didn't it?"

The Knights leader looked at the people who unloaded their supplies from the convoy, their expressions all of relief and gratitude.

"It was risky, Tinker," he said but his deep and his commanding voice gave way to one that sounded more pensive as he moved to the private comm channel.

"Will you tell me it wasn't the right choice?" Tinker asked.

Hammerhand paused before he shook his head. "No, it was the right choice. There was a risk involved, but our life is one of risks. You should still have consulted me, however."

The other man nodded. "There were risks involved with that too."

A group of residents moved over to them and brought the conversation to a pause.

"We don't know how to repay you," one of the men said to Hammerhand. "You or your Knights, but we would like to try."

"Your payment is appreciated," the Knight said and his voice resumed the booming supremacy that Jessica13 had come to expect from the man. "Our resources need replenishing as well, but we will not take what you cannot spare. I would ask that you agree among yourselves what you can give."

It wouldn't be a quick decision, Jessica13 realized suddenly. Those who had returned from the fields were given the responsibility to decide, and it appeared that they tried to elect an admin to make the decision instead of simply agreeing on what to give to the Knights.

"Tinker, we might be here for the night," Hammerhand said, once again in the private comms. "See if there's anything you can trade for from our parts and pieces from the Beast. Anything we might need and anything that might have to do with—"

"Citta del Mar, of course," Tinker said with a nod. "I know, I've done this before."

"Take Jessie with you," Windchime suggested. "The towns-folk know her mech and face a little better."

"Agreed." The other man indicated for her to follow him. "Now you can play the peddler without any kind of subterfuge."

"I don't know, I rather enjoyed infiltrating the town under false pretenses," she admitted. "It made me feel like I was on an adventure. Well, maybe it was less enjoyable when I was in the middle of it, personally, but in view of what came after and what we're looking at now… Well, I think I might want to try it again someday."

"Hopefully not anytime soon," Tinker said and laughed. "I don't know if you realized it, but Chime and I were a puddle of nerves for the whole day you spent inside the town on your own without either of us to cover for you if you got in trouble."

"It's good to know the two of you care, anyway," Jessica13 said as they strode to the Beast. "Oh, by the way, did I forget to tell you? I picked up a couple of new fuel pumps that should help your big baby over there move with a little…well, I'd say more speed, but the reality is less needing to stop for repairs. You really do need to find a way to get some of the nuclear cores to help power it. Even taking over a couple of the motor functions would relieve the pressure on the combustion engines."

"I think we might be able to get bits and pieces from the train you and Chime brought back," he replied.

She looked at him and tilted her head. "I have been meaning to ask, why do you call him Chime? I don't think I've ever heard anyone else call him that."

"Oh." Tinker grunted and looked around cautiously before he replied. "It's because he asked me not to call him that while we waited for you. Honestly, it's hard to resist that kind of request, you know?"

"You're incorrigible." She laughed.

He nodded. "That is not inaccurate. But don't tell him."

"Not a word," she agreed.

CHAPTER SEVEN

The election took most of the afternoon and they only managed to decide on an actual mayor for their town by the time the sun had begun to set again. Jessica13 almost couldn't believe that she had been awake since the day before, but she could feel the effects.

At the same time, it was odd that while she was tired, she also felt she could go on for a few more hours at least. She worked with Tinker to collect the items he didn't want for the people of Auburn to look at in case they wanted to trade or barter anything. The town didn't have any canteen or currency system in place that would allow them to trade in that, but it didn't really matter.

As the day went on, she resumed the job she'd done while posing as a peddler the day before. It meant she could at least get some of the bits and pieces working around town again while Tinker was busy bargaining and trading. The townsfolk had been told not to trade too much since they didn't want to commit to a reward they were suddenly unable to pay, but there was more than enough that they no longer used that the knights were able to make use of.

There was, of course, something else Tinker was out there in search of. She wasn't sure why he thought these people would know anything about Citta del Mar. Maybe they simply thought they needed to ask as many people as possible and through sheer numbers, they were bound to find someone who had heard of or seen it in the past.

Jessica13's eyes began to drift shut as she continued to work on cleaning the pieces for their water purifiers. Tinker talked to a couple of the locals and a few of them offered a couple of data sticks that might contain something about Citta del Mar that they wanted to trade for some of the oiling mechanisms he was selling.

He knew better than to take their devices at their word, of course, and while data sticks were generally worth acquiring anyway, he wouldn't part with anything cheaply. She wondered if the man had been a peddler in his past as well or if haggling was merely a skill he had picked up during his years with the Knights.

"I won't simply hand over perfectly functional oil dumpers for a data stick I haven't checked," he said. "For all I know, you could have handed me a sick stick or maybe there's some kind of defect in it that'll make me a sucker. I need to check it."

"If you plug it into anything you own, you'll copy anything on there and hand it back," the citizen replied. Jessica13 wasn't sure where this sudden mistrust of the Knights had come from but then decided they were merely haggling as well. There were no hard feelings in stating the obvious.

"Why don't you bring me something you own to show me that the stick won't wreck my software first and then we can talk," Tinker said. The man agreed, took a screening device from his pocket, and plugged it in.

"See, there's mention about a city by the sea in that story there," the man said and pointed it out.

"The story is about a fisherman and the sea and I've read it before," her teammate replied and shook his head. "It's all right but not really for me. I think it moves too slowly. To the point, though, I'd still like to take the data stick if you're willing to part with it. I'll trade one of the oil dumps and even throw in a can of grease from a couple of beasties we managed to bring down."

Jessica13 narrowed her eyes. How did he get a can of grease from animals? Maybe he traded someone for it? Then she recalled that Tinker always put a pan under the animals he cooked to collect the fat when they were lucky enough to kill or trap one.

The explanation seemed logical so she turned her mind to her work, leaned in closer, and tried not to nod off. If she did fall asleep, she would lose a couple of fingers.

That thought alone helped her to stay awake. While she did want to head to the Beast for a few hours of shuteye, there was still work to do. None of the other knights had taken any time off, even though Tinker and Windchime had been at it even longer than she had.

Or had they? Her mind seemed unable to process things sufficiently to deliver an answer.

Tinker moved to where she worked and noticed that she struggled to keep her head up and eyes open.

"Why don't you stroll over to the Beast and get a few hours of shuteye, lass?" he asked.

"Is it that obvious?" Jessica13 asked and looked at him quickly.

"Well, you keep nodding your head forward like you're listening to loud music," he pointed out.

"But you and Windchime don't need any rest," she said and shook her head. "No, I only need to push past it. Maybe some of that energy juice."

"I'll be honest with you, lass, I'm knackered as well, no doubt about it," he said. "But Chime and I had a little sleep while you were infiltrating this here town, so maybe that's why we're still functional and you're barely hanging in there. I'm serious, Jessie. You'll cut a couple of fingers off or put your eye out if you keep this up. Get some sleep. We'll manage."

Sleep had been on her mind since they had come back from recovering Athena's supply train, although she had thought she'd manage. Still, if Tinker insisted she get some rest, she wouldn't argue.

She nodded, scrambled into Mini. and headed to the Beast.

"Rest well, Jessica13," he said as she climbed out and left him in one of the Beast's harnesses that Tinker had finally agreed to fit.

"Thanks, Mini, you too," she replied without much thought about what she said. She found something to eat before she located an empty bunk and everything went black as soon as her head hit the pillow.

There were no dreams, thankfully, and she had no idea how long it was until her eyes opened again. Whether it was the same day or not was difficult to tell, but she remained in the bunk for a while and stared listlessly at the one above her.

She wasn't sure why she didn't simply get up to return to work. For some reason, she felt sore, and the sensation made her feel like it would only get worse if she moved.

Minutes ticked by before she realized something had

dragged her from the black fog of sleep. Her mind finally identified it as the sound of the doors opening on the other side of the Beast where most of the parts were stored, loosely collected and organized in a pattern only Tinker's brain could decipher.

It would help if his system didn't change every few days, although she had begun to get used to it as she worked with it herself. She still needed to ask him where he stored individual pieces she needed more often than not, though.

Jessica13 pushed herself from the bunk, stretched, and yawned and grimaced at the few creaks in her neck, shoulders, and back as she stood. Moving around would make it better since it was no doubt the result of her having been on the bed and immobile for too long.

More sounds from the other side of the room caught her attention. She shook her head and looked across at Tinker and Hammerhand. The former was seated and worked on some of his new acquisitions, likely trying to decide which piece would go to which Knight. Hammerhand stood a few steps away and leaned against the wall with his arms folded across his chest.

He didn't look happy. Not that he ever did, really. She couldn't remember having ever seen so much as a smile on the man's face.

Still, he looked less happy than usual.

"Well, they have a mayor so that's always a step in the right direction," Tinker said, his gaze focused on his work. "They have some leadership here and will have a spine if Athena turns up to give them trouble again."

"Not much of one," Hammerhand said and shook his head. "They have a couple of mechs that should keep your average desperate pirate at bay, but Athena is another beast altogether.

Their new Cinders will amount to resistance equivalent of piss and shit."

"Agreed," the other man said. "But it's better than no defense at all. Besides, Athena won't be able to attack them if we attack her ourselves."

The Knights' leader sighed heavily, his expression regretful. "I guess we'll have to put our search for Citta del Mar on hold in order to deal with her. I am truly sorry, my friend."

Tinker looked up from his work for the first time and a small, sad smile twitched across his lips. "There is no need to apologize. We all understand that Athena poses the kind of threat we cannot ignore, not while she's here and creating a dictatorship for herself. It can't be helped."

Hammerhand nodded.

"Besides, there are people here we hadn't accounted for in our previous estimations," the older man continued. "Athena has consolidated her claim of the land with violence and oppression, and the people are thus reliant on her for their water and therefore food. If we are able to release them from her rule—"

"Would they be any better off?" his companion asked. "We have encountered those before who had enjoyed the taste of freedom and abused it, so we needed to intercede on their victims' behalf. Who is to say the same would not happen here?"

"Are you really suggesting that leaving them under her rule might be more peaceful?" Tinker asked.

Hammerhand's powerful shoulders raised in an eloquent shrug. "Not at all. You know how I feel about her, but there is a similar option we have to consider. Athena is harsh and cruel, yes. She wants to rule and there would have to be people for her to rule over. However, what is to say one of these isn't cut from the same cloth?"

"As you have said, it would not be the first time we see something like this. But they have earned the right to choose how to rule themselves. That choice is denied them if they are under her heel and forced to give her food or be killed for trying to find help. Once they are free of that, they will decide on governance. We cannot step in to govern them to protect them from themselves."

The large man sighed again. "You're not wrong. We have discussed this before, old friend, and have always followed that very principle. The purpose of the Knights Mechanica has always been aid, not governance. Yet we both know that our actions here and those we commit to in the future will have consequences. Perhaps Athena's insatiable lust for power and disregard for others has stirred up the debate once more. She has reminded me that there will be the kind of consequences we won't be able to anticipate or control, especially if we don't plan to remain to ensure that the stability this area now enjoys is maintained."

Tinker scowled and looked searchingly at his companion. He didn't seem to like what Hammerhand had said but he also appeared to know he had one hell of a good point. It seemed an odd discussion to have since they'd already decided to remove Athena from her position of power.

Perhaps this simply was an attempt to establish a realistic view of what would happen in the area if Athena was defeated. It presented an intriguing side of the Knights' leader that reminded her how little she really knew the individual members of the group. He'd always been so fixed in vision, and it surprised her to see that he did, in fact, think beyond simply liberating people and worried about their future as well. When she thought about that, she realized that it made him a better and a stronger man.

"Well, these people need us to remove Athena and we will," Hammerhand said finally. He looked around and noticed her watching them but didn't seem to have any reaction to her uninvited witness to their conversation. "Thereafter, we can perhaps help them to establish some form of government so they can interact with each other. Maybe they could make the centralized bunker a capital of sorts that would allow them all to work together for each other's benefit."

"It's a process that could take years," Tinker pointed out. "And that's if we manage to eliminate Athena quickly and cleanly. While it's unlikely, knowing her, she might run before she engages in a fair fight and will make it a war of attrition that could last months before we finally oust her. Assuming we succeed, of course."

It was Hammerhand's turn to scowl as though the concept of defeat hadn't occurred to him. It couldn't occur to him, she realized. He needed to believe—or know, rather—that the Knights would win every time or his doubts would spread to his team and make it all worse.

Jessica13 wasn't sure how he intended to defeat Athena, but she assumed he had a plan. She always assumed he had a plan. What would they do to survive otherwise?

"Well then," he said. "I suppose we are now locked in. The die is cast, and we cannot take it back. How do you suggest we proceed?"

"One step at a time, my friend," Tinker said, pushed from his seat, and placed a hand on Hammerhand's shoulder. "We will do what the Knights Mechanica have always done, which is to aid those in need so they can rebuild and live decent lives. Part of that aid is to deal with Athena, and we shall find a way to push her back and hopefully, defeat her once and for all. For now, we would be better served focusing our efforts to help the folks of Auburn to rebuild their lives while we are here. At least that way, we can perhaps influence those consequences for the better."

Hammerhand nodded and squeezed his friend's hand before it fell away. The older bearded man sat again and resumed his work.

The Knights' leader walked toward the door, no doubt to where his Excalibur had been harnessed outside, looked at Jessica13, and narrowed his eyes.

"I hope you rested well," he said and his voice once again thundered through the Beast as he walked. She fell into step beside him. "There is still a great deal of work for us to do, and those who can should commit their energy to it. Have something to eat and find Windchime. I'm sure he would be most anxious for your help."

She nodded, ate quickly, and had something to drink before she climbed into Mini.

"I trust you rested well?" he asked as she disengaged the harness.

"I still feel like I could sleep for another week or so," she admitted, took the mech's controls, and guided them out of the Beast. "But I don't feel like I'm about to drop off as soon as I don't focus on staying awake."

"That will have to do," he replied as they headed out and into the city.

She had slept through the night, and the bright sunlight around her made it obvious that morning had already been in evidence for the past few hours. The Auburn townsfolk were out in the fields where they worked to till the earth and used some of the supplies that had been reclaimed to plant another crop.

While she would have been more than willing to assist them, she knew nothing about farming. Aside from possibly improving the mechs they had adapted for that purpose, there was little she could do to help them there.

Mini highlighted a section of the town's map where he suspected Windchime was and noted that it was only a suspicion in writing above the highlight, which made her chuckle. He guided her to the section of the town where most of their water was drawn from under the ground and their equipment was set up to purify it either for human use or for their crops.

Jessica13 still thought she could come up with a couple of ways that would allow them to use the water more efficiently without it being lost to the atmosphere or under the ground again, but it involved considerable time and effort to set drains up under the fields to collect the water, as well as greenhouses over the fields to keep the water contained.

Folks who had no shortage of the resource would see no point in expending so much time and effort for such little gain. While a part of her still reacted to what she'd considered wasteful for so long, she could also see that perhaps the greater waste would be to use resources for something not entirely necessary when they could be more effectively applied elsewhere. It was an interesting notion and she realized that a narrow perspective might not allow for other circumstances.

Sure enough, as Mini had directed, she found Windchime working near some of the wells, watched by a small group of the townsfolk. Most of them were children, who gawked and pointed at the oddity of the four-armed mech that helped to lift parts to another citizen who stood at the top.

"Jessie!" Windchime called when he saw her. "Nice of you to join us again. I hope you enjoyed your beauty sleep."

"I did, thanks," Jessica13 said and studied her surroundings before she picked one of the pieces up. Her own mech was fairly unique from a mechanic viewpoint but was nowhere near as interesting as the one Windchime piloted, and it earned her little attention from the locals.

Besides, they had already seen her wandering around the place two days earlier. Her Minato was old news to them.

"Sorry, I didn't mean to leave you in the lurch," she continued and handed the part to the man who worked on the tower. She meant her apology, even though she didn't regret the sleep. There was so much to be done and leaving them to take the whole load felt a little unfair.

"Never you mind that," her teammate replied. "I'll tease you about it, sure, but we all need to reload and recharge from time to time. You're no good to anyone if you keel over from lack of food and sleep. Know your limits and try to push them from time to time, but you learn after a while how to not abuse your body too much."

"Thanks," she said with a smile. "I don't mind the teasing, honestly, but I do feel bad about leaving all the work to you folks while I was getting my beauty sleep."

She'd heard him and others use the term before and like so many others, it seemed a little odd since it was her experience that she and all others looked horrible when they woke.

"So, what have we been working toward out here?" Jessica13 asked as they continued to work together.

Windchime shrugged and the exaggerated action of his mech made the children laugh. "They're still trying to decide what kind of reward they think they can spare for us. We expended considerable resources to get here, so Hammerhand has tried to leverage the position, but our main priority will be to head out and give Athena more grief before too long. If we keep her busy, she won't be able to focus on this little patch of paradise."

"Who is Athena?" one of the nearby children asked, overhearing their conversation.

"It's the goddess Athena," an older girl said and regarded her companion with something that might have been disappointment. "You know, the one in the books?"

"But they talked about giving Athena grief," the smaller child countered. "You can't give a goddess grief. It's unpossible."

"Impossible," the other corrected and rolled her eyes.

"You know her as Lady Hoot," Jessica13 explained. "We know her as Athena. She gave us some grief in the past, and when we saw she was giving you the same, we thought we'd return the favor."

"Oh!" the little one exclaimed. "Why do you call her Athena, then? She has the owl on her mech and that makes her Lady Hoot."

Jessica13 opened her mouth to speak but shut it when she realized she had no real answer. She wasn't actually sure why they called her Athena. Maybe it was her real name or maybe it was a nickname. In fact, she hadn't even known it was the name of a goddess until the child had mentioned it.

Thankfully, Windchime was quick to step in. "The goddess Athena of times past was said to ride a mech in the sky above us and made her home in the mountains. She's said to have an owl companion that told her everything there was to know in the world. Maybe the owl was an AI-operated mech that gathered information for her. Either way, the woman we call Athena carved the owl's head into her helm and abandoned her past and her name in favor of using the name of the goddess she claimed to represent."

The children leaned in, entranced by the story, and had no idea at all that he didn't want to discuss the woman any further.

"And…well, I guess all that would have been a little too long and drawn out to explain," he said and looked a little uncomfortable. "So, she let you call her Lady Hoot and left it at that."

"I'm not sure why," the smaller child said. "I think Athena is much nicer than Lady Hoot."

Windchime scowled and shook his head, and Jessica13 laughed.

"Leave it to children to take the niceness of the names away from what you told them," she said, still snickering.

"Whatever," he grumbled. He looked like he needed time asleep as well, although it was difficult to tell if it was because he had just woken up himself or because he had been up all night. "All we know is that the woman needs to be stopped, not what kind of name suits her best."

Given what he'd told her about taking care of herself and getting rest when she needed it, she imagined that if he hadn't taken some time to sleep in his hybrid mech, he soon would.

"I heard from Tinker and Hammerhand that we will abandon our search for Citta del Mar for the moment to deal with Athena," she said softly as they returned to work. "They said it could take months and maybe even years to fully remove her from here, but Tinker thought it was important that there was a large population in this area they hadn't known about."

"Oh, right. He's not quite right in the head, but he has something of an ambition to record the numbers of humans in this area to make sure we know how many humans do actually live out here."

"But what does that have to do with the Citta del Mar?" Jessica13 asked.

"Well, the more folks there are in an area, the higher the chance is that someone's heard something, seen something, or knows of something we don't," Windchime explained as she climbed out of her Minato and began to work with her hands as he carried the parts she needed to her. "Someone's bound to know something eventually, and when you meet so many people in one area, there comes a time when the chances of finding someone who knows something actually become a reality."

"But if they've all been here, why would they know any different than their neighbors?" His logic seemed to make her more confused for some reason.

Windchime chuckled. "You ask that like there wasn't shit the admins in your bunker knew that the others didn't. And there are different kinds of knowledge. Some people pay attention and pick up on things that others don't. So if you keep asking, you're bound to find something out eventually."

Jessica13 nodded, focused on her work, and began to clean the purifiers again. Many of them were positioned around the town and plugged into the wells. Water continued to flow from underground, albeit far less than there should be thanks to Athena. With a little work, Tinker appeared to be able to control the balloons over the bunker so they worked to regulate the weather in the area.

She still wasn't sure how a balloon could make it rain, but that was science beyond her realm of knowledge. Maybe when she had a few quiet moments, she would be able to read books and manus about how that worked. Tinker had a whole stack of books he had admitted he'd never taken the time to read, and most towns and population centers tended to have at least one person who collected books and those kinds of resources.

The children came and went. Some were called to do their own work while others seemed to have to attend some form of learning. A few remained but even they grew bored and played their games on the sidelines. Jessica13 found herself caught in the drudgery of repetitive work that machines required if they were to continue to function effectively.

An hour before the sun reached its peak, however, the clattering of metal on metal heralded the arrival of something that moved noisily over the uneven streets of Auburn. A quick look determined that it was a cart but it took her a moment to recognize it. She realized that the man who pushed it was the one who had given her work when she had posed as a peddler.

"Hello there!" he called, raised a hand, and waved at the two of them. "I'm not sure if you remember me, Jessie, but I was one of the folks you helped when you first came along."

She nodded and Windchime merely watched the man curiously.

"Caysom," she said when his name slid easily into her mind. It was odd that she hadn't been able to recall it the last time she'd seen him, but maybe that had simply been lack of sleep and too much adrenaline. "I remember you needed a solar charger repaired."

"Damn right I did, and I'm still using it too," he replied with a laugh and patted the device on the roof of his stall. "It works like a dream, for the most part."

"Well, I'm glad I could help," she replied.

"I wish you could have told me you weren't really a

peddler," he said. "I have folk saying I'm blind as a damn cave bat now since I didn't see you weren't the kind to peddle. Although in fairness, you did have the skill set to match what you claimed to be."

"I didn't mean to ruin your rep with the folk of Auburn," Jessica13 said. "But like you said, I wasn't actually a peddler and didn't know the folks to trust when I came in. As far as I knew, you were all happy to be under Lady Hoot's boot and would have turned me in if you found out I wasn't who I said I was."

"Oh, I understand your predicament, and I certainly don't hold that kind of thing against you," Caysom replied and watched her hands as she continued to work while she spoke. "And I don't mean to say I blame you for fooling me. Hell, you and the Knights pulled us out from the clutches of Lady Hoot and for that, I am willing to open my special stores to you and your friend here."

"What kind of special stores?" Windchime asked. "You sell parts, usually ones that need some kind of repair before they're useful. We have piles of those on the Beast."

"Well, see, I'm not only a seller of bits and pieces, mind," the man snapped. "It turns out that's what folks want the most, so I always have those on hand, but the real treasure I carry is from my time as a trapper and a hunter in the woods around here. I'm a great provider of nice fresh meat if you like the taste and haven't the time to raise chickens or pigs."

"Why would they eat the chickens?" Jessica13 asked as her personal dilemma once more raised its head, albeit with a slightly different perspective this time. "A chicken will provide more eggs in its lifetime than the little meat you get if you kill it."

"A chicken doesn't lay eggs forever," Caysom replied. "Anyway, meat isn't the only thing I get to pull off the beasties that I trap and hunt."

"We have animal grease too," her teammate said. "Tinker was actually hoping to trade some of it for what you folks have in terms of food and the like."

"Well, there's more to be taken from the fallen beasties," the other man explained, pulled what looked like a handful of furs from under his cart, and spread them on top for them to look at.

She recalled that a couple of the townsfolk liked to wear them over more tattered clothes, probably to make them a little warmer when the cold months rolled around. They were less thermally efficient than something made from nylon, though, and certainly bulkier. She couldn't wear something like that in the Minato either for fear of chunks being lost in the recyclers and starting a fire.

It still looked nice, though. The way the fur caught the light and shone like something made from metal was certainly appealing in a way. It wasn't the kind of thing she would wear herself, but maybe she could put it on Mini's pauldrons to help the mech fade into the background and be more difficult to see in some circumstances.

It might be especially helpful if she needed to take more shots from a distance. She still had the rifle, although she would have to find or fashion a better holster than the mag clamp on her back. Engaging and disengaging the damn thing was a nightmare in the middle of combat and impossible if she was supposed to carry something into the heat of battle.

Jessica13 made a mental note that she needed to find a solution.

"I'm fairly sure that's the kind of thing that would be worn by someone who doesn't spend most of their time in a mech,"

Windchime pointed out and raised her own concerns on the matter.

"You don't have to be inside those mechs all the time, do you?" Caysom asked, obviously keen to make some kind of sale.

"Basically all the damn time," the other man said. "It might be nice to have them on the outside of the mech, though, to make them a little swankier. It's a problem when your mech has six limbs, or so I've heard. Folks say I look like a giant insect walking on two legs."

"I'm sure you take that as a compliment," she interjected and chuckled at the thought.

"Yes, because every little boy dreams of being thought of as a massive mechanical insect."

"Well, if you aren't interested in any of my special furs, I think I might have another something you might want," Caysom said. "And I'll provide this one to you for free if you're willing to hear it."

"I'm always interested in something offered for free," Windchime assured him.

"Well, the word has spread that you and your Knights want to know any information that might be collected on a place called Citta del Mar."

Jessica13 could see the almost instant reaction from her teammate as he turned fully to stare at the man. The response was a little exaggerated by the mech itself.

"What…what do you know about that?" he asked and tried to keep his voice from betraying his true feelings.

"Ah, well, it's not really much that I know," the townsman admitted, a little surprised by the reaction he'd received. "We get peddlers in and out of here every couple of months, and they always have chat and gossip about what's happening in the world at large. Anyway, the talk is there's a man out in the Wastes who has received a fair amount of attention over the past few years. He calls himself The Prophet."

She narrowed her eyes, a little suspicious. If there was talk about the man out in the Wilderness, the Knights hadn't heard it. He seemed the type Hammerhand would react to. Not many folks in the world at large had the balls to call themselves a prophet, much less The Prophet.

"Anyway, this Prophet has apparently gathered himself one hell of a following," Caysom continued. "The kind who would kill a man who so much as looked at their leader wrong. They are religious zealots and very fervent in their beliefs, and if the talk is to be believed, quite violent about it as well."

"I haven't heard of the like before," Windchime said. "He has to be stupid or something special to call himself something like The Prophet."

"That's what I thought," the other man said. "He has all kinds of talk about the Above, and how Skyfall is his god sending judgment on the earth, that kind of crock, but you hear a few things here or there that stick. One of those things I heard talked about was Citta del Mar. He talked about it like was some kind of land that is promised and where he'll lead his true believers to when the time is right."

"He sounds like a nut," her teammate said bluntly. "Worse still, the dangerous kind of nut—one with power. I have the feeling that if Hammerhand were to run across this character, he would make The Prophet prove his connection to whatever god by entreating them to keep him from being crushed by his hammer."

"No doubt," Caysom said. "But I thought it was interesting that they looked for this place that you are looking for too.

Maybe they might know a thing or two about it, come time to go looking."

Windchime nodded. They could mention it to Hammerhand later.

He turned suddenly to Jessica13. "Get in your mech."

"What's the issue?" she asked, already on her feet and headed toward Mini.

"Hammerhand has word he wants to share over the comms."

She nodded, scrambled into the Minato, and closed the hatch before she inserted the open comm line onto her HUD and listened carefully.

"All Knights Mechanica, hear me," their leader said and his voice boomed into the confines of her cockpit. "Athena and her entourage have been seen approaching a small town about half a day's march from our position. While she is likely supported by highly competent fighters, this is about as exposed as she'll ever be and therefore, this is our chance to strike at her while she does not expect us to attack."

Her heart pounded violently. To attack an unsuspecting supply train was one thing, but a group of attack mechs that were ready for a fight, including a damn Excalibur, was something altogether different. She wouldn't have the luxury of ignoring orders like she had with Windchime or the relative safety of smaller numbers.

"Rally to the Beast. Marching orders will be handed out," Hammerhand continued. "We move at noon."

Jessica13 looked at Windchime, who was already moving toward the Beast to the surprise of Caysom, who hadn't heard any of the conversation. She gestured a hasty apology to the man, who simply shrugged and nodded. "Do you think Hammerhand will make me give up my rifle?"

He looked at her and shook his head. "I doubt it. You have some skill with it, although I can't tell how much is you and how much is your AI. Either way, skills like that can't be wasted. Even if you take a support role, there's always an opening for folks who can hit from a long way off. So keep that damn rifle handy. You might need it."

That was good advice. She took a deep breath as they picked up the pace and hurried to where the Beast had been stopped. Already, all the Knight mechs had begun to leave the city and gravitate to the bunker. When Hammerhand wanted them to rally, they rallied, and they did it as quickly as possible.

Besides, if there was a chance to defeat Athena before she returned to the safety of her bunker, their whole situation would take far less time to resolve.

Hammerhand moved out, already in his mech. He looked over the town and his Knights, hefted his hammer, and positioned it over his shoulder.

He was excited too, she realized.

CHAPTER EIGHT

It was decided that the Beast would follow with a small guard, even though they trusted the good folks of Auburn not to steal from them. Hammerhand wanted to move quickly, and while his Excalibur was only fast over short distances, it still moved faster than the Beast.

The Knights formed up quickly and those who had been selected to follow more slowly weren't happy about the arrangement.

Or maybe they were and simply feigned anger so they wouldn't appear weak in front of their fearless leader. Jessica13 wasn't sure why they would be happier about heading into the thick of the fighting. Maybe they enjoyed the battles or maybe they simply didn't want to be left out of it.

To watch their brothers and fellow Knights move into danger while they trundled behind to tend to their home on tracks and wheels had to be a little disappointing, she finally had to admit. It was only when she felt a tingle of excitement at the fact that she was among those selected to head into the thick of it that she understood.

They set off at a brisk pace and pushed deeper into the land that was controlled by Athena. As they moved beyond the now reasonably familiar territory around Auburn, the landscape changed. Instead of the dry grasslands that struggled to survive, everything became greener and lusher the farther they moved.

The trees were still twisted and fairly small, but they were covered in green leaves and the grass itself now grew thicker and taller. The soil also transformed, now darker and with more nutrients.

"It's still shit soil," Windchime said as they walked in formation. "It looks like this area has far more rain and water than the rest, but all it can grow is tall grass and a couple of dry trees."

"It wouldn't take much to make it good soil again, though," Tinker said and studied their surroundings with genuine interest. "It only needs a little effort, is all. Turn the soil again and direct the water to flow with a purpose. It only gets occasional rain and it's already much richer for it."

His teammate shook his head. "It's still shit soil. You only think about how to improve this land, and you're right. I'm talking about it as it is now."

"Fair enough." The other man shrugged in the comically exaggerated way the mech's tended to mimic the motions of their pilots.

"Have you ever heard of someone called The Prophet?" Windchime asked to break the silence.

Tinker looked at him and his eyes narrowed. He walked with his head out of the open hatch of the top of his mech. "The Prophet? Capital P?"

"That's right. I heard about him from one of the townsfolk in Auburn. The man specifically mentioned that The Prophet had gathered a group of zealots and believers through talk about finding a land that was promised."

"Citta del Mar?" Tinker asked, sensing where the conversation was going.

"That was how we approached the conversation in the first place," Windchime said. "I asked around like Hammerhand told me to, and the man started talking about this Prophet character and mentioned how they ruled out in the Wild and spread word about whatever god they have chosen to follow."

"What is your concern?" the other man asked. "Aside from their knowledge about Citta del Mar, of course."

"I'm worried, is all," he said with a deep sigh. "We're dealing with Athena here, but who knows what might spawn elsewhere in this land? What if this Prophet is much, much worse than Athena and is already raising an army without people like the Knights to keep them in check?"

Tinker nodded. "It is a valid concern, I'll grant ya. We do need to keep our focus on Athena for the moment, though, and can't afford distractions. When we're done, I'll make sure Hammerhand hears about this Prophet and we'll see if we can spare the resources to head in and find out more."

"That's all I could ask for, then," Windchime said.

She had a feeling he would have far more to say, but perhaps he'd decided to save it for when they had the time and weren't being rushed quite so much by Hammerhand.

Their leader was single-minded in his hunt for Athena, and he pushed them at a rapid pace in the direction in which he was most likely to find her given the information they had on her latest actions. She had seen determination in the man previously, but he now seemed driven by something far more powerful than merely resolution or tenacity.

It was both determination and a need to rid the world of a

problem, she realized. Perhaps Hammerhand thought Athena was a problem of his making, a mistake he needed to correct personally before she caused suffering and hardship to anyone else in the world.

He was wrong if he thought that since he was in no way responsible for the actions of someone else, especially as he had attempted to curb her before and it had only made things worse. At the same time, she could understand why he would feel personally responsible for her behavior and want to address it before it became even worse.

"Do you think we should go on ahead to see if there's something that might be a problem for us?" Jessica13 asked. "You know, scout and make sure there's nothing ahead that might be able to ambush us?"

"Not if you plan to rush in there and kill anyone you run into," Windchime said and laughed. "I won't race in after you to save your ass a second time."

"Once was enough," she agreed. "I think I would be able to keep myself far enough away from the fighting, though, even if I do engage in it. I know to keep my distance."

"Don't think you're dealing with silly pirates here, lassie," Tinker warned. "And it's unlikely that the rearguards will snooze through a long march or those on watch will simply assume that no one would attack them and so not pay attention. Athena likes to surround herself with the best of the best, men and women of skill and ability who will not be easy to face. Remember, these are hardened fighters. They were Knights once and know how to handle combat. And there will be Athena herself, of course. You've seen how Hammerhand fights. Don't think his counterpart is any less protected, skilled, or effective, and believe me when I say she will not hesitate to cut you down."

She scowled and felt she was being lectured like she had been in the learning hall at Sanctuary. He hadn't said anything she didn't already know and hadn't considered and maybe even overthought during their entire march. It wasn't like she didn't know they would likely face Athena and her elite fighters along with her.

Of course she knew it. It was merely that it seemed necessary to keep her spirits up through a little banter with Windchime, especially since she would soon face an unfamiliar threat. Worse, it would be in a small and admittedly fast and agile but still vulnerable support mech and she'd be expected to do precisely that—support.

In the light of that, an attempt to buoy her mood didn't seem too bad, yet Tinker thought she needed a lecture about what they might face. She wanted to tell him he was wrong and should rather encourage her good mood but realized that his lecture was probably prompted by his concern for her. The point of it was that she wouldn't head into the battle with unrealistic expectations that might prove dangerous.

While she could respect that and appreciated that he was looking out for her, she still didn't like it. She wouldn't voice her complaint, though, and chose instead to keep her head down, power forward, and make the most of the knowledge he had tried to impart. Despite her good intentions, she did wonder when—or even if—he would stop regarding her like the baby of the family.

"What made you talk about scouting ahead ?" Windchime asked as if he sensed the tension between the two and tried to defuse it somewhat.

"Huh?" Jessica13 asked and snapped out of her reverie. "Oh, I only thought we might want to move closer to investigate that column of smoke rising up in the direction we're heading in."

Both men turned to look at the horizon ahead of them and the very obvious smoke that billowed like a beacon or a warning.

"Fuck me." Tinker grunted annoyance. "How did I miss that?"

"We were bantering, that's how," the other man countered.

Hammerhand hadn't missed it, however, and he had already circled and ordered the Knights into a battle formation. He issued orders while he swung his hammer above his head to draw the attention of the group so they focused on him.

It was how he tended to fight. He used his Hammer, the shield, and his armor to soak up as much damage as possible and hold the attention of the enemy, which left the other Knights free to act with little resistance.

Windchime and a Balthazar took their positions immediately behind their leader and slightly to the side to create the V-formation they used so effectively. Two Lancers formed the rear of the battle line. Taylor, in his Sherlock, had already moved toward the flank, likely in anticipation of a hard, centralized fight that would allow him to cut in if things became too focused. His faithful Watson followed, ready to support him.

The main line, however, was centered around Hammerhand and the others. It was impressive, especially when taking into account the fact that there were so few of them. She had been with them for a while now but was still impressed by how powerful they looked when they advanced in formation like this. Not only that, she'd never seen them practice it and assumed the AIs simply stepped in and directed them into the positions where they would be the most effective or they were so accustomed to fighting together that they needed no orders.

"Jessica13, report in," Hammerhand called over a private comm line.

"Reporting in," she replied. "Where do you need me?"

"It's time to use the mobility your mech is getting known for," he said in the kind of voice she couldn't help but be inspired by. "Head out and ahead. I need you to travel along our left flank. Stay out of the fight as much as you can and alert Tinker if you see any attempts to circle us. Use that rifle of yours when you can but keep moving if you do. Don't let them get a bead on you."

Jessica13 nodded. "Understood. I'll head out now."

It was logical that she would report anything she learned to Tinker since he fulfilled the support role. He didn't like to be in the middle of the fight and would stay as far away as possible, but that didn't mean he wasn't involved and wouldn't help from that position.

In many ways, his role in the battle was much like a field general.

She did as she was ordered, settled onto all fours, and let Mini take over to drive them into the position Hammerhand wanted her to cover. A small hill ran along the left side of the line almost a half klick away from the main force, which pushed forward consistently.

The sun had begun its descent and the source of the smoke was now visible. A large building was ablaze and hungry tongues of flame climbed into the smoke it generated. The sky had darkened around it, both from the sun's slow journey toward the west but also because the smoke created a thick cloud. Despite the fact that it was infused with a dull red light, it seemed to drape itself over the landscape as if to shield it in shadow.

Jessica13 recalled the views she had seen from the top of Sanctuary and how they had filled her with a sense of wonder and excitement about what the world around her held.

All she could feel from what she could see now was dread, however, even before Athena's men came into clear view.

These definitely weren't indolent or tired troops and no one seemed careless or unfocused. While the mechs had obviously been repaired using various spares and parts they had collected from others, the work wasn't incompetent or roughshod to the point where she couldn't even tell what kind they were. They were a group of well-maintained mechs that now assumed a defensive formation ahead of the Knights that advanced toward them.

"What kind of numbers are we looking at?" she asked.

"It's difficult to tell," Mini said, highlighting the group she was looking at. "As far as I can tell, almost forty of Athena's knights now stand ready to face the Knights Mechanica, but a few more groups have begun to march out from the town behind them. The heat signatures are distorted by the fire and the smoke so I can't make out how many of them there are."

"I guess there are many who would rally behind someone who rules with a literal iron fist." She scowled, pulled out of Bulletfoot mode, and settled them into the position Hammerhand had directed them to before she took her rifle from her back. "Especially if they're offered effective mechs and a large group for protection to perpetuate Athena's rule. Is that the town on fire behind them?"

"I suppose that's true, and I'm afraid so," he confirmed and activated the aiming software as she looked through the scope of the rifle.

"Tinker, do you read me?" Jessica13 called over the comm line.

"I read you, lassie. What are you looking at?" Tinker replied.

"There is a large group ready to engage us before we reach the burning town," she said. "I estimate about three dozen of them in a defensive formation, with a couple more groups heading in from behind them."

"Noted," he said. "Keep an eye out for any changes in their position. And try to take any shots you can without being detected."

"Roger that." She eased forward to a better position at the top of the hill and kept her eye on the scope.

Athena's knights were stationed about three or four klicks away from the burning town, and their positions and combat readiness appeared to indicate that they knew the Knights Mechanica were coming. She wasn't sure how Athena had found out but given that she had lost control of a town and one of her supply trains had gone missing, it was really only a matter of time before their presence was at least suspected. She most likely had her own ways to spy on her enemies and wouldn't be as powerful as she was if she didn't make use of them.

Jessica13 leaned in a little closer and tried to identify the individual mechs. They were still too far away to take a shot, and as the Knights continued to move forward, they held their position and their weapons appeared to be already primed and ready for action as best she could tell from that distance.

"It definitely looks like they're expecting our attack," she said over the comms.

"I thought as much," Tinker responded. "I'd say Athena

deliberately burned the town to draw us into a fight she could control. We can only hope they're still getting settled into their defenses and aren't too entrenched."

She continued to move forward alongside the Knights, who had increased their pace. Hammerhand now double-timed them and prepared his force to fight.

Suddenly, Athena's army swung into action. A group settled into an attack formation and raced forward, possibly in an attempt to unsettle their enemy and slow the momentum of their attack.

The Knights merely held formation in response and marched resolutely forward. Their leader seemed undaunted and still held the center of the line to maintain a determined but swift pace. His team maintained their disciplined formation with quiet resolution as if they weren't merely a handful against at least three times their number.

Jessica13 raised her rifle, took a deep breath, and shifted into a more comfortable position. Her task was to keep an eye on the remainder of Athena's mechs, and she refocused as a handful of them broke away from the main force. It soon became apparent that their intention was to circle behind Hammerhand's line, something she could not allow to happen.

Her keen eye identified what appeared to be the leader of the group and she zoomed in before she calmly pulled the trigger.

The rifle's hellebore rounds cut smoothly through the Lancer's armor and into the cockpit. Although the mech shuddered visibly, it continued to move when the AI took control and directed its functions so it could proceed.

"Shit, these fuckers will be a little tougher to destroy than the others," Jessica13 muttered. She waited a little impatiently as the rifle pushed another round into the chamber before she turned to see where the rest of the mechs were going. "You have a small group trying to take you on the left flank, Tinker."

"Roger that," he said, and the Sherlock and Watson team immediately turned to engage them. The Lancers in the enemy reacted almost immediately and assault rifles released concerted volleys while she took a handful of shots and tried to place them accurately to kill the pilots. Even with AIs in control, she reminded herself, there were only a handful of functions they could actually perform. Those that didn't have pilots soon stopped fighting and turned to retreat before they were cut down by the Sherlocks with chainswords.

Literally cut down, she thought with a grim smile and returned her focus to the main battle line. A Guardian had raised its shredder plasma cannon and delivered a series of super-heated rounds at Hammerhand.

The man brought his shield up, and the pale blue film cut into the darkness around it like a knife. The impacts were hard and crisply audible, and she almost had to cover her eyes as the plasma rounds flashed a bright white light each time.

"I'm calling up a light filter," Mini said when he noted the sudden change in illumination around them,

The Knights moved forward. Those behind Hammerhand and the shadow of the shield circled and opened fire on the Guardian in a rapid and coordinated attack. The larger and more powerful mech's armor appeared untouched and it immediately retaliated. One of the Lancers fell back and steam hissed as the plasma round cut through the armor. The pilot had, thankfully, managed to twist aside and it appeared he would make it alive, although he hastily retreated to where Tinker waited to make an emergency repair.

The remaining Lancer moved into the gap where the damaged mech had been and left the Sherlock-Watson duo to fill the other position.

Hammerhand's shield dropped and his Knights released a furious barrage. The coordination between the group was impressive and it was difficult to say whether that was training, experience, or merely the AIs still working their magic.

Jessica13 turned her attention away from the impending clash of the two lines and located one of Athena's knights as it broke away to the side. The Predator V2 was easy to identify due to the point-defense lasers on its shoulder and the sword it carried, which was similar to the two her teammate used.

"I'm breaking away," Windchime said as if the thought had conjured him and immediately drew away from the group and moved to where the Predator attempted to flank them. She could have eliminated the mech from her location but the man already seemed focused on what he had to do and his swords would save them ammo.

Besides, having him come in with his hybrid monster of a mech would certainly play to their advantage.

Although she'd seen him in action a few times already, she hadn't lost the sense of awe he always stirred in her. The Predator saw him approach, drew his sword, and started it. It was a chainsword, an older model than the vibroblades the Knight had, and when their blades clashed, a shower of sparks was unleashed to bathe them in a powerful green-and-yellow glow as they fought.

The Predator pilot was certainly not lacking when it came to fighting skills. He twisted and glided his mech through the fight and maintained the distance that would allow him to fight his adversary's two swords effectively. Its movements were smooth and had most likely been perfected through experience as he slashed and cut, surged forward when his mech allowed it, and drew back quickly before Windchime could take advantage.

To Jessica13's mind, however, there was really only one winner. Windchime had the superior model mech, to begin with. Balthazars were infinitely more mobile and effective than the Predators, and the added swords were merely a bonus. The combination enabled him to constantly drive the Predator back toward Athena's knights' line without endangering himself too much. He wore the other pilot down step by step.

"Windchime, I can take him from here if you want," she offered through the commlink.

He drew away from the fight for a second. "There is no need. I can take care of him and it'll let me inch in closer to their formation while I'm at it."

The rockets on his back flared. The added weight of the hybridization meant it couldn't actually fly like Balthazars were supposed to, but it could still gain some elevation.

Which was obviously what he wanted to do and he had waited for the right opportunity.

The rockets activated suddenly and launched him vertically as he hurdled a swipe at his legs. Windchime lashed his boot out in midair, drove it into the cockpit of the Predator, and shoved hard. The mech stumbled as its gyros struggled to compensate for the sudden change in weight distribution.

The Knight was quick to take advantage and landed smoothly again, only to leap forward over the ground that had been scorched by his rocket to thrust his right vibrosword into the Predator's chest. The blow was blocked, but the strike with his left hand wasn't and another flurry of sparks spiraled when the blade slashed the legs and seared into the hydraulics.

Jessica13 frowned when the power in its legs suddenly cut off. Some of them would have compartmentalized hydraulics, and it seemed to be the case in this one. It was still able to move its sword even though fluid gushed from the damaged area.

The pilot within still attempted to fight, and she could respect him for that, but the fight was well and truly over.

Windchime darted back another step to avoid the chainsword. It was a sensible precaution as he wouldn't want to be hurt or risk any damage to his mech in a fight that he had already won.

The Predator balance was totally compromised and it barely managed a few swings before it fell. Her teammate stepped in to finish it and drove his vibrosword into the back. It took a few seconds for the rapidly vibrating blade to slice through the weak places in the armor until it finally reached the pilot. The mech suddenly stopped moving and sprawled silently. Windchime used one of his free hands to grasp the pilot and haul him out.

The man appeared to already be seriously injured but still alive as he was flung aside without so much as a thought before the Balthazar kicked the downed mech and strode around it to rejoin the fight.

"Jessie, report in," Tinker called.

"Reporting," she replied.

"Hammerhand needs help with that fucking Guardian," he grumbled. "Is there anything you can do to cover for him?"

"I think so," she responded and silenced her comm for the moment while she zoomed her rifle into the Guardian that centered Athena's line.

The cockpit was fairly easy to find, despite the size and the bulk of the mech. She had worked on them enough in the past that she could probably find her way into the cockpit blindfolded. While she'd never piloted one, she knew she would be able to do it if she were given the chance.

Not that she would ever trade in her Minato for one of the hulking bastards.

She fired a couple of the hellebore rounds and attempted to hit the pilot. The Guardian was bound to have its own AI operating it, but it would still be less functional without a pilot.

Both rounds had no effect and it continued to fire its plasma cannon at the Knights.

"The armor is too thick," Mini pointed out. "Those plates were made to protect against hellebore rounds. You won't be able to kill the pilot inside."

"Is there anything I can do?" she asked. "Can you scan for any weaknesses in the armor? Someplace where I can do some damage?"

"Scanning now," he said and data scrolled as he ran through a variety of subroutine scans on the moving Guardian. "Vulnerabilities detected and highlighted on your HUD."

Jessica13 scowled skeptically as she studied the positions he had highlighted. It was difficult to understand what the AI had seen in the places he'd identified. While she could do some damage to the armor, it wasn't like hitting the cooling system in the knee and ankle joints would really achieve anything in the long run.

Then again, neither would wasting bullets on the hardened armor anywhere else.

"Fine." She hissed through her teeth in irritation, decided

to trust him, and took aim. All she was asked to do was slow it anyway, and she could at least do that if not anything more important.

The rounds punched through the weaker armor around the joints and stirred a moment of satisfaction in her. A flurry of sparks drew the gazes of the men flanking the Guardian and they attempted to determine what was shooting at them while they continued to push to find a weakness in the Knights' advance.

As Jessica13 studied the battle, it became clear that Athena's advance troops were only in place to slow their enemy. A handful of them had already pulled back and they worked in a layered defense. They made no effort to win the battle and were there to delay the Knights, which meant she had most definitely sent them in anticipation of an impending attack.

Which meant, in turn, that they would encounter far more resistance down the line. And, as Tinker had said, it was possible that Athena had set the town on fire deliberately to draw her adversaries out.

She didn't like the fact that they were pulled and drawn out into the open like this and wondered if Mini had noticed it as well. Not only that, but she also didn't want to think about what the woman might have in mind for them when her trap snapped shut.

The Guardian continued to move but it was clear that the pilot struggled to compensate for the compromised balance. It lagged somewhat on the left and almost bumped into the mechs on its flank. The change might be small but it was a distraction, and most of the shots from its cannon went wide.

It provided the opening the Knights had looked for.

Hammerhand kept his shield up and moved forward as his team readied themselves behind him and used the cover to surge toward the defenders in a sudden attack that was coordinated and precise. The moment the shield dropped, they pushed forward and battered the group with consistent fire while Windchime surged in from the side and used his rifles and swords to deal with those who tried to escape the onslaught.

The Guardian attempted to contain the assault and drew as much of the fire as possible. A couple of its plasma rounds hammered home in an attempt to disable Hammerhand, even with its balance awry. The rounds made little impression on the Excalibur, fortunately, and with the damaged but determined mech focused on what they perceived as the greatest threat, the Knights were able to focus on its team with brutal efficiency.

To protect the rest of his comrades, the Guardian's pilot fought hard to keep it on its feet when Hammerhand stepped in.

Jessica13 almost didn't want to watch but it was hard not to. Like watching Skyfall for too long, she didn't want the blaring headache that came from blinding light that accompanied it.

But Skyfall was something external and these were her teammates. She simply had to watch.

Hammerhand stepped in and swung the weapon he was known for up and over his head. The Guardian took a step forward and into the swing of the hammer.

The leader of the Knights Mechanica anticipated it and the film of blue emerged once more, illuminated the world around it, and pushed the enemy back a step. Its legs were already less than fully functional when the shield descended, immediately followed by the hammer powered into a crushing blow by a rocket blast from the back.

The mech was too sturdy to be flattened like most others would be, but the force of the weapon was still enough to pulverize the top half and leave it a sparking and shuddering mess. The pilot had no doubt been killed instantly and the AI struggled to bring the ruined mech back from the dead.

It was an effort in futility, and it wasn't long before the critical functions gave out and shut it down as a defense mechanism.

The AI core would have been undamaged, and if they opened it and plugged it into another mech, it would likely be perfectly capable of taking control and operating at the same capacity as before.

Which was why Hammerhand now called the Knights to a halt as the remainder of Athena's men beat a hasty retreat.

"This isn't the end of it," he said, his voice loud across the plains. "Those who fight for our enemies are not so easily stamped out, but enjoy the victory, my friends. Let it lift your spirits, for there are those who would drag them down and curse you for the effort."

The Knights raised their weapons in response, but there was no cheer. They understood that the battle was far from over and they did what Jessica13 had come to expect from them in these situations. Without a need for orders or discussion, they worked quickly to scavenge what they could, treat those who had been injured, and eat or drink a little as needed.

It was a practiced and efficient routine and although it seemed a little odd in what was essentially a lull in the battle, it was a necessity for them. They needed to renew their strength to keep on fighting and surviving in the Wild but also had to be sure to leave nothing their enemy could use against them.

Those whose mechs had been damaged quickly moved to Tinker to have them attended to. A healthy pilot needed a working mech. Those that could be scavenged from the fallen needed attention since they had been disabled in one way or another, but they would provide valuable resources for future repairs or possibly even become replacements if needed.

Jessica13 helped them quietly. Hammerhand consulted with Tinker before he decided to take those who were still functional and eager for action.

Tinker worked double-time to check that each of the mechs was functional and cleared them for duty while those who waited gathered whatever they could as quickly as possible. The priority was on the former and the latter was a way to fill the time constructively and appease the mechanic's insistence that nothing be wasted.

She hurried to join the support effort but he stepped in front of her.

"Hammerhand needs a support mech with him," he said.

"I'd be more useful making sure the mechs are up and running," she pointed out, unsure of why she said that. Despite her every instinct telling her to stay, she wanted to keep moving forward and fight with Hammerhand.

"I know, but you're most useful at the front, lassie," Tinker said. "You have skills that will be used best there. Hammerhand said so himself. Get going now. There's no point in being left behind."

Jessica13 nodded and shifted Mini into Bulletfoot mode. They would hopefully be able to spare some of the resources and parts for the folks in Auburn to use for their own defense. Those who manned the Beast would arrive soon and help with the advance, which was doubtless why their leader had insisted it be brought and not left in Auburn. Hammerhand had experience with an operation like this and obviously knew he now needed every available member of his team as well as their stores.

What worried him—and, of course, the other Knights—was that Athena knew him and would be very familiar with his strategies and tactics. None of them mentioned it, but it was something all of them no doubt thought about.

The smoke had grown thicker and hung closer to the landscape as more and more was pushed out by the growing fire. She could almost see the awe and disgust in the posture and attitude of the mechs the Knights Mechanica piloted. Part of it was in the way they slowed to look at the flames that had now grown to the point where they were all that could be seen ahead.

It was almost like she could feel the heat, even from this distance.

"We have no time to ponder the power of evil deeds," Hammerhand said when he noticed the dispirited silence of those around him. "Consider instead how to make them right."

CHAPTER NINE

Jessica13 couldn't begin to imagine the condition of the town. The smoke had built to the point where they couldn't see anything beyond ten yards and it grew denser by the minute.

A conflagration this size would be difficult to contain. It would begin to spread into the wilderness around the town and from there, it could sweep through the whole area.

She sighed and coughed when some of the smoke came through the filters.

"My apologies, Jessica13. I will update the filtering software and elevate the protocols," Mini said and immediately did precisely that while she watched through the HUD.

"Why would someone do something like this?" she asked and shook her head. "What's the point of this kind of wanton destruction?"

There was a pause from his processors and a series of protocols activated. They were from deep inside the AI core where Mini's "personality" was stored. She had seen it activated like that in situations where he contemplated updating his personality software.

He had explained that it was what humans called introspection.

"I cannot say," he said finally and displayed a sad face on the HUD. "My knowledge of human personalities is based almost entirely on my personal interaction with other humans. The people who developed me were the basis and you, of course, have played a substantial part in it, as have the other members of the Knights Mechanica as well as the inhabitants of the Sanctuary Bunker."

A slight pause followed, accompanied by the hum she now knew meant he was searching through his stored records. Not sure where his reasoning would take him, she simply waited for him to continue. "I have found nothing in people's overt personalities that is any indication why they are capable of such violence. Of course, it could be something subconscious. But according to my files, I would say humans should be incapable of such actions. These are open to update, of course. Based on my records of human history, such things have been perpetrated by humans in the past, which means humans are capable of such acts, but I cannot find any reasons as to why."

Jessica13 shook her head. "I wouldn't have thought humans were capable of that, but yes, I suppose I can't really ignore the fact that we have been guilty of such a thing in the past. I merely don't understand how."

"Do you think there would be anything that could cause you to set fire to an entire town?" Mini asked, still running his updating subroutines on the AI core.

"I...don't think so," she responded. "It would take some kind of trigger to elicit this kind of reaction from me, I think, but even then, something that draws out an extremely violent response would be limited to the person or persons responsible for that. Not an entire town."

"I do not think you are capable of this kind of mass destruction," he replied. "Which is interesting as it would suggest there is a psychological discrepancy between those who can and those who can't, which cannot be identified until the action is perpetuated. In every case in history I have been able to find, the perpetrator always felt his or her actions were warranted in some way. Forms of zealotry, religious or otherwise, appear to manifest in actions that are believed to save more lives in what is ambiguously termed 'for the greater good.' In the end, however, the assumption is that such actions would never be considered by those who are incapable of them, while those who are regard themselves as willing to make the 'difficult choices.'"

It was an interesting thought and one Jessica13 both loathed and yet felt drawn to somehow. It was because of those types of people that the world had ended all those years before. Humans and invaders alike saw mass killing as a viable option for some reason, and that reasoning had been perpetuated in the world that survived.

Hammerhand appeared to think Athena was a threat to humanity as a whole and she could now see why he thought that. If she was willing to burn an entire town for no reason other than to lure her enemies into a trap, what would stop her from destroying something larger and killing even more people? How much of a reason would she need for that?

As they approached the source of the flames, things oddly became a little clearer around them as the heat from the fire forced the smoke upward so everything at ground level was more visible. The heat could be felt in her mech already and beads of sweat trickled down the ridge of her spine.

Her growing discomfort, however, lost relevance like a

nagging noise she pushed to the back of her mind. It all felt so unimportant compared to the sight in front of her.

The town they looked at was almost as large as Auburn. It might have been a little smaller but the fire made it seem much larger, especially as the trees and the underbrush on the outskirts burned as well and contributed to the blaze.

Almost all the buildings were alight and the wind pushed the flames rapidly beyond to the outer reaches. It would soon reach the hills behind it, driven to consume anything in its path if the wind picked up or the blaze wasn't extinguished.

"Fucking hellion bitch," Windchime muttered under his breath and sounded cold and angry at what he saw.

Jessica13 realized that she shared his rage. It was hard not to as they stared at the kind of destruction they confronted.

There were a few indicators in Mini's AI core that suggested he might be dealing with something similar. For a brief moment, she was impressed as she hadn't thought he was capable of that kind of emotion.

It was short-lived, however, as her mind was otherwise occupied. She would bring it up with the AI another time.

"It is a message," Hammerhand said through their comms. "Athena has found out what we've done for Auburn and she doesn't like it. More importantly, she cannot bear that kind of challenge to her authority. She wants to make sure the other people in her little domain know that any rebellion against her power will be thoroughly punished. The flames will be seen for hundreds of klicks, a clear warning sign to all who would dare to challenge her authority."

"And an effective one as well," Windchime pointed out. "It is also one she has used before. It would seem she enjoys the act of killing these people and destroying them but manages to contain herself until she finds a reason to unleash the beast she keeps so poorly hidden inside."

"We could contemplate the darkness Athena has inside her from now until the heavens collapse and the Invaders return, but I feel our efforts would be better focused on scouring the town below and finding any who might need our help," their leader said. It was disguised as a suggestion, but she knew better than to assume it was anything but an order. The group seemed to share her opinion and headed into the settlement.

The priority had been made very clear—find any survivors and get them clear of the burning buildings. The unspoken idea was to find any useful salvage to take back to the Beast, but that held a very distant second priority in her mind. It seemed that for the present, the enemy forces had retreated beyond the burning town. There was certainly no indication of their presence and no resistance was offered, but the Knights moved warily with an inherent caution based on the fact that they knew they could be walking into a trap.

She moved between the houses first and tried to find anyone who had escaped the inferno that ravaged the town. It seemed unlikely that anyone would be able to survive unless they were in mechs themselves—or maybe had some kind of breathing apparatus since the smoke would be what killed most of those caught in the buildings.

The flames licked at the Minato's armor, and scorch marks were visible where they burned into the green paint she had coated her mech with in traditional Knight Mechanica fashion. It would take a little more than fire to get through the mechs' defenses, however. She could feel the heat transferred into the mech, but Mini had increased the insulators in the armor so she would be safe from being burned. The worst damage the mech would see was if a few copper wires lost their rubber insulators.

It could cause a short here or there, but the rest of it was insulated against that kind of thing. For the moment, at least, she was safe. If there were any problems, they would appear on the HUD and alarms would blare long before they became the kind of issue that would end with her dead or injured.

Jessica13 couldn't move through the town without shock at the extent of the destruction around her. It appeared as though Mini was in a similar situation and they simply proceeded in silence and stared at the carnage. Charred corpses were huddled in sections of the houses where the doors had been jammed shut with metal bars that were now all that remained to indicate the occupants' imprisonment. A couple of bodies hung out the windows, a sign that those who had attempted to escape had been gunned down.

More bodies littered the streets and she assumed those had tried to run. A couple of mechs had been stripped for parts so she couldn't tell if they had been for defense or merely used in the fields, but they had been stripped before the town was set ablaze.

"Great Prophet," she said softly and shook her head. "How many people died here? How many lived here?"

"Census data is not available," Mini said. "But extrapolating from the size and density of the buildings all around us as well as the population numbers of a city like Auburn, an estimate can be made of at least three thousand people living in this town."

"Three thousand people?" she asked and tried to put it in understandable terms. "That's more than they had at Sanctuary."

"My estimates similarly conclude a minimum of ninety-five percent casualties," he continued. "The fire and the smoke, as well as the systematic execution of those who attempted to flee, leads me to conclude that while the possibility of those escaping the massacre exists, it is rather unlikely. Not many people would be able to survive Athena's cruel but effective message, and not without any mechs or defensive armor."

Jessica13 shook her head. "Athena wouldn't have allowed the people under her domain to have any defense. From what I was able to learn from the people I talked to in Auburn, she tried to push her role as a protector against the pirates and the dangers of Outside. She would have seen anyone who might have attempted to leave her protection as much the same kind of threat as the pirates and could have twisted it to explain her actions against them. In doing this, though, she's revealed herself as more of a threat and an abomination than any pirate could ever be. This isn't a message for the people under her dominion. This is a message for us—or, more specifically, a message for Hammerhand."

"The message appears to be that any further attempt to resist her presence will lead to more deaths," Mini said.

"Yes," she agreed. "Although she has to know that these kinds of extremes will only incite him to work harder to depose her, not stop him."

"Do you think she wants a final showdown with him?" he asked.

"It was something she was deprived of in their first confrontation," Jessica13 said. "If she has the same combative instincts as Hammerhand does, I'll bet she is aching for another attempt."

"I suppose that is a fairly sound assumption, all things considered," Mini agreed as they continued to search the town, although it looked less and less like they might find anyone who might need their assistance. "It would be interesting to know if Hammerhand and Athena are related by blood or if it is a relationship based solely on interpersonal interactions."

"What's the difference?" she asked.

"While looking for data that might assist us, I stumbled across other information that might not be relevant but is interesting. From what I have found, the difference would be that those who feel a necessity to conform to siblings' expectations are more likely to lash out when the siblings aren't present as well as more likely to hide it when the sibling is present," he said. "It might be a possibility to explore should the two run into each other."

"I have the feeling that them meeting again is almost a foregone conclusion at this point," she said but something distracted her and she narrowed her eyes. "Wait a moment—what is that?"

Mini quickly scanned what appeared to be a structure in front of them, although it wasn't shaped like any kind she had ever seen. It appeared to be a manufacturing building of some kind but something about it rubbed her the wrong way although it was difficult to say what.

"Scans indicate a high level of reinforced steel and titanium," he said. "There are also indications that it might not be a structure at all."

"Then what is it?" Jessica13 asked but her question was answered when the scan results were shown on her HUD. Without the smoke and darkness, it was easy to identify arms, legs, and even a cockpit. "It's a mech."

"Larger than any of those we've seen in this town thus far," he pointed out. "And not stripped for parts."

"Oh, shit." She pressed her comms hastily. "Alert to all Knights Mechanica. We're about to have company."

"What are you talking about?" Windchime asked. Thankfully, their small numbers meant that her teammates were close by, so she knew she'd have help in moments.

"There's a mech here and it's still intact," she said and retreated slowly. It appeared that the larger mech had realized it was being scanned and now began to move. "And it looks like it's getting ready to fight."

"It would be good to note that I pick up more movements across the town," Mini said.

"And I guess those aren't Knights?" she asked and looked around when the activity became visible even without the HUD.

"No," Mini replied simply.

Combat mechs emerged from the hidden corners and crevasses of the town. Most were Lancers, but a couple of Cinders appeared as well. They had been positioned at strategic points along the paths and roads leading in and out and had managed to remain utterly motionless and completely hidden among the smoke and wreckage.

It was, like many had suspected, an ambush but given that they made no effort to attack directly, it seemed it might be designed to trap the Knights inside the town and prevent them from leaving. Which meant that whatever it was they had been caught inside with was the real trap, and Athena didn't want them to escape it.

Jessica13 turned her attention to the mech she'd first seen that activated slowly and straightened to its full size, which resembled that of an Excalibur. It was perhaps a few meters shorter than the one Hammerhand piloted but made up for it with a large ballast around the midsection. It looked rounded and even the limbs had been given extra padding that was almost like armor, which would make it much slower but almost impossible to break through.

"What the fuck is that?" she asked. "There are pieces on it from about seven or eight other mech designs, but it's not based on a central design. It looks like…all those pieces have been put together with tons and tons of armor."

Windchime rushed to her side and gaped as the massive mech activated itself fully and exposed a variety of steam vents across its body, obviously for cooling purposes.

"Holy shit," the man said. "That's a Golem."

"A what?" she asked but he made no reply and instead, quickly called to the other Knights to form up. Hammerhand had engaged a group of Lancers and kept them busy for the moment. He would keep them at bay on his own and let them deal with the other threat, whatever it was.

Mini was quick to answer the question. "Golems are created from whatever scrap can be found. They are dangerous to pilot by a human, which is why they are generally operated by an AI with basic combat programming. They're difficult to destroy but generally not that much of a threat."

"Unless they're about twenty meters tall and carry more armor than your average bunker," she pointed out.

He paused. "Yes, that is correct."

"How the hell will we be able to get through the armor?" Jessica13 asked as Windchime turned to the Knights who had responded immediately to his call. The Golem appeared to be fully activated and moved ponderously out of its hiding place. It crushed the remains of a couple of nearby buildings and released showers of bright yellow sparks that almost suggested a pair of flaming wings.

She gulped instinctively, took a step back, and glanced at her teammates. Windchime positioned them quickly and snapped orders to arrange them in fighting formation. None would engage the massive mech alone or even attack it all out.

"Keep it busy," he said. "Hit it when you can but jump back quickly too. Don't let it get a lock on you."

The others appeared to agree with the tactic. While they were all the bravest fighters she had ever met, none of them would risk their lives unnecessarily. She knew they would follow the orders of Hammerhand, Tinker, and Windchime mostly because they knew there would be no lives risked without reason.

"Jessie, try to keep it distracted but do so from a distance," Windchime said once he'd connected with her over a private line. "And keep any of the other mechs off our backs."

"Understood." She removed her rifle from its place on her back and focused on three Lancers that approached, obviously intending to distract the group from their attack on the Golem.

"It's time to get to work," Mini said and called up the aiming software.

Jessica13 looked down the scope and used some of the upgrades on the motion sensors to give her a better view of the mechs that moved steadily closer.

"Mini, keep us moving away from them," she said, handing the controls to the AI. "Draw them away from the fight and away from the Knights."

"Understood," he replied and guided the Minato back slowly as she lined up her shot. The Lancers didn't appear to pay her much attention and focused instead on the Knights who had begun to engage the Golem. They quite probably hoped to find easy targets among them and so moved steadily closer while they believed their quarry was distracted.

She took a deep breath, exhaled quietly, and pulled the trigger. Her target was the cockpit area to eliminate the human control of the mech, which would in turn remove most of its combat capabilities.

The Lancer slumped forward since the AI still needed to gain control when the human input ceased, and it was immediately apparent that it was out of sync with the other two. They had already turned to try to identify the origin of the shot fired at them.

"Keep us moving," she reminded Mini.

"I will, but there are some…complications," the AI said and sounded almost uncertain. She had never heard him like that before and looked quickly to where the Golem advanced on her teammates. She noticed that they seemed to use evasive tactics but wasn't sure what they tried to avoid until she registered the weapon the AI-controlled mech used.

It took her a few moments to realize that the mist that issued from the exhaust vents wasn't the usual steam but carried something a little heavier that made it swirl and hang only a short distance above the ground until it came into contact with its adversaries. A pale-white and noxious smoke rose when it connected with the metal of the Knights' mechs.

Jessica13 wasn't sure, but it seemed like the vapor was incredibly caustic or acidic and it had begun to eat into the armor. It would take a long time to destroy it sufficiently to reach the pilot, but it was certainly cause for concern, at least in her eyes.

"Windchime, stay away from the steam the Golem is emitting," she said. "It's acidic and it could eat into something important in your mech."

"I…are you sure?" He sounded a little stressed.

"Your mechs erupt in white smoke whenever you step into it," she told him firmly. "It's safe to say there's some kind of chemical reaction."

"That complicates things," he complained.

He was unfortunately correct. They needed to get in close to the Golem to inflict any real damage and he accomplished most of it with his vibroswords. They sliced deeply, but the laser-point defense grid that was mounted on its shoulders protected the vital functions from any shots, which meant shooting it from a distance wouldn't work. His close-quarters assault was the only option, and with its large, thick arms swung around like clubs, it had appeared this was the only defense it had and which Windchime's speed and dexterity could easily avoid.

The acidic mist, however, created a dangerous complication that had bigger repercussions than simply the potential damage to their armor.

"Shit!" Windchime shouted over the comms. "Keep attacking but run systems checks every time. If there's any kind of breach in your armor, don't go in again. Leave us and help Hammerhand engage the escort."

The team highlighted their understanding of the situation and continued their efforts. Jessica13 turned her attention to the Lancers that had now resumed their approach. The one with a dead pilot began to walk around in a circle when the AI started to malfunction, and the other two seemed to realize that she was the shooter.

She selected her second target and pulled the trigger before they could attack. The mech immediately displayed the same kind of devolving function and she trained her weapon on the third one.

"Jessie, get down!" Windchime called.

Jessica13 looked up gaped at a new weapon that had appeared on the Golem's shoulder.

"Radar targeting systems detect that we have been acquired," Mini said and displayed the system in question.

"Shit." She turned to the building above her and aimed her grappler at the top of the building.

"Oh, I will regret this," Jessica13 mumbled and wracked her brain for any other possible solution.

"What is the alternative?" Mini asked as two missiles flared from the massive mech's launcher.

She made no reply and simply fired the grappler at the still-burning building. The dart struck top the corner and embedded itself as she hastily engaged the retractor and hauled them up abruptly enough to make her head snap back. They climbed quickly while the missiles spun toward her and attempted to arc and adjust for her sudden change of location.

They weren't quick enough but their impacts with the building she was climbing were immense. The explosion caught her in the back, shoved her upward, and thrust the breath out of her lungs.

More importantly, her grasp on the building shuddered and suddenly pulled free as the entire side of the structure began to fall.

"Oh shit!" Jessica13 shouted and her stomach lurched into her throat as her upward motion ceased and she hung in a moment of vertigo before gravity pulled her down again.

Unfortunately, the structure toppled with her.

"Brace your neck!" Mini warned and she did as she was told, clasped her hands around her neck, and hunched herself in the cockpit when he took control of the mech again.

She grunted as they landed harder than she had anticipated with a jarring thunk, but Mini had already fired the grappler as another two missiles streaked toward her. She curled as best she could to protect herself as the grappler dragged her across the ground, away from both the projectiles and the falling building.

It wasn't a clean escape as chunks of construction material showered over them as they moved. Unfortunately, the missiles also struck home and hurled them forward. This caused a loss of traction on the retractor, which displayed a couple of malfunctions.

She was hurled around inside the cockpit and felt every shake and shudder. Something was wrong with the inertia dampeners and some of the jarring and pounding affected her more than they should have.

"Crap," she exclaimed when they finally came to a halt. "Why did it target us?"

"Core programming," Mini explained. "It's meant to contain us and you threatened to break that containment."

"Very helpful." She hissed in pain and rubbed her sore shoulder. "Run a systems check and make sure nothing's broken."

"Affirmative," he said. "Although it should be noted that the targeting system on the Golem is still locked onto us. You should eject."

"I wouldn't survive out in the smoke without help and you know it," Jessica13 said. "I'm not going anywhere."

"Our funeral," Mini said.

"Was that a joke?" she asked as she struggled to get the mech upright. "Are you making jokes now?"

"I have attempted to upgrade my human-friendly functions," he said. "I am glad you appreciate it."

The missiles flared again as the Knights continued to

attack. There were many ways to kill something like that but the most basic was, of course, to tear it apart, piece by piece. It wouldn't come close enough to achieve that, however.

She gaped as the missiles fired upward instead of at her to twirl and twist before they detonated hundreds of meters in the air.

The reason why was suddenly made apparent. The shield's blue film was distinctive but she had somehow missed it despite that. She realized she had Hammerhand to thank for redirecting the missiles and was about to warn him about the vapor when he charged the Golem and shoved it forward again.

It turned and tried to see what had attacked as the shield dropped.

Jessica13 knew what would come next, and she really wanted to watch. The hammer arced above Hammerhand's head and swung to catch the monstrosity across the shoulder. It wasn't a clean blow but still powerful enough to make it stumble.

The blue film of the shield appeared again and seemed oddly clear against the smoke and fire in the background as the man surged forward again. The massive Excalibur moved faster than the Golem could, and the impact was enough to destabilize the monster's gyros and it lurched into a smaller building that toppled with it.

The shield fell again and the hammer raised and activated the rockets on the back.

She flinched as it descended. Cutting into the mech was effective but crushing it was equally so, and after four strikes of the hammer, scrap metal was all that was left.

Windchime came over to where she still struggled to right herself and helped to pull the Minato to its feet.

"Are you all right?" he asked. "Are there any breaches in your armor?"

Jessica13 ran a spot check. "None that I can see, anyway. I'll need to run a quick systems check to be sure."

"Until you do, stay away from that mist," he said and removed a few pieces of rubble from her joints, which had probably been what prevented her from standing in the first place. "Go out there and help them take care of the rest of Athena's assholes. We'll clean up around here."

She nodded and turned carefully. The Minato's movements were still a little sluggish although she didn't detect anything she couldn't bang out herself once they were clear of the smoke and caustic steam. She moved over to the rubble, retrieved the rifle she had dropped there, and brushed some of the debris from that too.

"Will it still work?" she asked.

"Scans indicate that it should be as functional as it was when you held it before," Mini said after a moment. "Rifles like this were built to take a great deal of punishment."

"Well, there's only one way to find out." She raised the rifle and peered through the scope at the Lancers and Cinders the other Knights had begun to engage now that the Golem had been dealt with.

She pulled the trigger and was a little startled by the kick as the hellebore round exited and flew true. It bored into a Lancer and its AI took the functions over when the human was killed.

"There's something wrong with the inertia dampeners," she grumbled and rubbed her shoulder again. "I'll need to check on it when we have the time."

"Of course," Mini said. "I am already running diagnostics."

"Show me," Jessica13 said and checked the rifle again. She'd had no idea that it had that kind of kick since it was usually absorbed.

The diagnostics were running slow due to the external heat acting on the mech.

"The Minato should be functional for the moment, but there will be some malfunctions," Mini said. "My apologies."

"There's no need for apologies," she said and peered down the scope again. "Let's get this finished."

CHAPTER TEN

The confrontation dragged on. Athena's knights were well trained, and once they realized they were no longer merely in a containment role, they quickly reorganized, pulled together, and mounted a strong defense. If it had been only the Knights, they would have put up one hell of a fight and might have won.

But the group wasn't built to face the might that came with an Excalibur in the attackers' ranks. Hammerhand worked quickly once he'd eliminated the Golem and focused on the mechs. Jessica13 continued to keep herself away from the fight as Mini conducted the work on the suit to keep them functional. The acid mist was rapidly burned away in the fires that still consumed the town around them, which made it safe again for her and the others who might have compromised their mechs had it remained.

It was slow, steady work, but it wasn't long before Athena's knights were defeated deftly and without quarter given. Hammerhand was in a state of fury, cut down those who attempted to retreat, and demanded that his team do the same. He intended to send a message of his own, not that there would really be anyone left to deliver it to Athena.

"Killing the messenger sends a message in its own right," Windchime explained to her once all the other mechs were destroyed and they went about the work of scavenging and recycling them. "Even if they don't return to Athena, she'll know none of them returned and that is a message in and of itself."

"I don't think it was an intentional reaction from Hammerhand," she said and shook her head. "In fact, I would go so far as to say that he is in the kind of mood where he would kill anyone who so much as looked at him the wrong way. He's not thinking right now. He's angry."

"It doesn't mean both can't be true," he pointed out and cleaned his mech while other Knights worked to extinguish the fires. They were already starting to burn out, and it was only a matter of containing the blaze and preventing it from spreading into the nearby grasslands.

It would have been providential to have a rainstorm to put the flames out, but unlike Auburn, this town didn't appear to have its own connection to the weather control system.

They did what was required in the conventional way with what water could be found and by clearing the land and letting it die naturally.

Hammerhand appeared to take part in their efforts with a little too much enthusiasm. A single strike of his Hammer collapsed one of the buildings they had made sure was clear of live occupants, and with ground-shaking thuds, he attacked the fire with his hammer and used it to quell any flames.

She wondered if he didn't also take a little of his frustration out as well, as he had no other enemies to focus on.

It was long, arduous work, and while the smoke would

linger around the area for days and possibly weeks, the fires were out. They could all focus on scavenging and finding anything they could use, not only from the fallen mechs but also from the town around them. It felt almost disrespectful to the people who had died in their homes, but they lived a life that didn't allow for respect of the dead to take precedence over the survival of the living.

Jessica13 sensed the despondency among the Knights as they went about their work with their usual efficiency. A few hours later, the Beast rolled in together with those who had been tasked to bring it safely. It was impossible to miss the shocked and awed looks in their eyes as they moved forward almost seamlessly to do their share of the work.

"Fucking savages," Tinker said as he came over to her. "She needs to be all kinds of insane to do something like this. I'll never be able to understand what drives that woman to go to these lengths. A part of me wants to say it's not human, but I've seen too many humans acting like her to truly believe that. But never quite on this fucking scale, though."

She looked around, unsure of what she was supposed to say to him. Did he expect her to have something to say on the topic?

He didn't seem to notice that she hadn't replied. Maybe he had talked mostly to himself. After a second of reflection, he turned to face her fully. "How are you doing, lassie? I see you're not much the worse for wear, aside from a couple of bumps and scrapes and…what looks like acid eating into the nethers of your mech. Did you step into a vat of it?"

"Nothing quite that concentrated," she said and shook her head. He had not been present for the fight as he had doubtless been in contact with the three Knights in the Beast and had waited for their arrival. "We encountered a Golem that spouted an acid steam from its vents that settled on the ground around us. I almost didn't realize it until Mini picked up on it."

"Wait, hold yer horses," he said. "You battled a Golem? What kind?"

Jessica13 wanted to show the man but remembered that the monstrosity in question had been crushed by Hammerhand. "Well, it was big—almost as big as the Excalibur—but rounder and it didn't have any assault rifles. Instead, it had a laser-point defense grid, big clubs for hands, and shoulder-mounted rocket launchers that it turned on me once I tried to destabilize their containment technique. And there was the acid steam release that I thought was very interesting from a mechanical standpoint at least."

"The acid steam came from its cooling vents?" he asked and moved closer to her where she took one of the Lancers apart. "That's incredibly dangerous. It would corrode the vents themselves and it would kill the pilot when he was exposed. When, not if. I know the kind who work for Athena, and while they enjoy danger, the suicidal type they are not. Usually, they're quite greedy and like to take what they want, but they would never put themselves inside a mech that would kill them."

"I don't think there was a pilot inside the Golem," she said. "There were dozens of bits and pieces put together and a huge amount of armor. It was meant to take as long as possible to eliminate it, but Hammerhand was a little more motivated than usual."

"What do you mean?" Tinker asked.

"I think this whole thing affected him," Jessica13 said. "Seeing this many people killed and that Athena wanted to lay a trap for him and his people—and the fact that he walked right into it—well, he destroyed it on his own, then attacked any of the mechs that stepped in front of him. And one of the buildings that were on fire. Well, it was effective and did put the fire out, I suppose, but in the end, it seemed like he needed to vent heat of his own that had nothing to do with his Excalibur."

Her companion nodded and looked pensive for a moment. "I've known the man for years and I can say that sounds exactly like him. Seeing folks killed like this would tick him off something special as he's an empathetic man. He feels their pain rather acutely and will go to great lengths to make sure it's reduced, at least somewhat if he can."

She sighed, looked at the man who stood over her, and shrugged enough that her mech would exaggerate the motion with a hint of annoyance. "Be that as it may, I can sense his despair. More importantly, so can the Knights, and I fear it is starting to spread. I wouldn't want to overstep or comment on something that is not my place, but if he needs something to lash out at, it should be Athena and not random buildings."

"It's not overstepping to speak your mind, lass," Tinker said. "And what you have to say makes a good deal of sense, I won't deny that. Hammerhand is a leader, and with his position comes the expectation from those he leads that forces him to be better—and sometimes better than human. I am concerned for the man, make no mistake, but you are right. He does need to collect himself."

Jessica13 scowled. She hadn't meant that he wasn't allowed to grieve for the people who had been killed by Athena, especially since the most admirable trait about the man was how he was able to feel the pain of others and allowed it to fuel his own actions of heroism. She didn't want to change that about him.

But at the same time, the Knights needed Hammerhand to take that grief and pain and make it into something that would drive them forward to confront Athena to make her answer for her crimes against the people she had hurt and killed. It would protect the other people in the area and it would help them to see there was a better way.

The scavenging efforts began to wind down. Most of what could be recovered had been gathered and the rest had been thoroughly ruined by the fire. It simply wasn't worth the effort it would take to make them functional once more.

The group gathered at the edge of town where the Beast waited, and it was immediately apparent that Hammerhand's mood had not improved. He still looked like he was ready to crush anything and anyone that crossed his path. The mood was reflected in many of the group who paced impatiently ran weapons' checks far more than was necessary. It wasn't hard to imagine that their despair had turned to hatred, anger, and the desire to avenge the fallen.

Windchime was one of the few who appeared to not share the same state of mind as the rest. He had withdrawn himself from the others and now moved to where Hammerhand stood and communicated with other members of the Knights to coordinate everything so they could head on out into combat again. They obviously wouldn't have much rest, even though night was falling.

Jessica13 doubted that any of them would want to sleep anyway. The day was the kind that would lead to nightmares.

"Hammerhand, if I might have a word?" Windchime asked, stepped forward in front of the leader, and spoke clearly enough to be heard.

"Of course." Hammerhand sounded a little hoarse.

"I feel like I am responsible for what happened here," the

other man said. "There were a great many factors involved, of course, but I feel as though it was my responsibility since we acted on what happened in Auburn, which in turn caused Athena to exact her revenge on the innocents of this town. If you would allow it, I would like to regain my honor."

A shocked silence settled over the group of Knights around her, but Jessica13 wasn't sure what he was talking about. She knew honor was something that was considered rather important to the people she had been with, but there had never been a mention of regaining that honor if it had been lost. It seemed to her that the best way to do that was to simply keep fighting.

But whatever it was Windchime had referenced was something far more important to those around her. She sensed that they felt it needed to be addressed out in the open and in the presence of the rest of the Knights like some kind of group action would allow him to regain his honor. None of it made sense to her at all.

"Mini, do you know what he's talking about?" she asked.

"Nothing in my files provides any indication of what this might mean," he said. "There are a handful of elements in past human civilizations that would allow honor-based soldiers to regain honor if lost, but there are too many for anything other than broad speculation."

She turned to Tinker, who was already beside her. He appeared to know what her question was before she even asked it.

"Windchime feels responsible for what happened to the people in this town," he explained. "He feels that he lost his honor through the choices he made and their consequences and would therefore like the chance to regain that honor by..." He trailed off, his expression grim.

She scowled. "How?" she demanded.

"He wants to donate his parts to his brothers," he explained. "And once his mech is gone, he will take himself into exile with nothing left to his name to die either from the elements or the dangers of the Wild."

"What?" She stared at him in shock for a moment. "Why would he do that? Why wouldn't he simply earn that honor back by fighting harder than ever? Why kill himself like that?"

"To his mind, his failure is so great that he would never be able to overcome it," Tinker continued. "He would rather give the parts to those who need it as a final gift to his brothers and leave the Knights to avoid ever making a mistake like that again."

"No, he can't do that," she protested. "It wasn't his fault. He followed his orders. If anything, I was responsible for heading into the town and putting myself at risk. He wouldn't have bothered to try to retake Auburn if I hadn't insisted on it. If anyone needs to be punished or dishonored for what happened here, it should be me."

Her companion shook his head. "Wrong again."

"What?"

He didn't reply and instead, he pushed forward through the other knights and stepped in front of the group, his thick brows furrowed.

"Windchime misplaces the blame," Tinker said loudly and made sure that all present, including Windchime himself, could hear it. "If there is responsibility over what happened here today and if it belongs to any of us, I feel it lies squarely on my shoulders."

"What are you doing?" Windchime asked and placed one of his mech's hands on the other man's shoulder. "You don't have to do this for me. I know what I've done."

"I was the superior officer on the scouting mission and I certainly outranked you," Tinker said firmly. "If there was danger in our actions to be considered, I should have done so. As I have said, if there is any responsibility, it lies squarely on my shoulders. It was my decision and I made it."

Jessica13's eyes narrowed. Was Tinker suggesting that he would be the one to head out in what felt like a ritualistic suicide?

"Besides," the man continued," if I had stood my ground when we were still on the road and insisted that we continued to move without pausing to help anyone, Athena would have made her collections and moved through the land without so much as a blink. There would still be the dead from the burning of the church and they would have been a little the worse for wear after having dealt with the collections, but they would have been alive here."

Hammerhand turned to face Tinker. He looked like he wasn't sure where the man was going with what he was saying and wasn't sure if he liked it either.

The group of Knights assembled around them appeared to choose one side or the other and began to argue over the valid points each of the men had raised. Jessica13 lowered her head and moved back a few steps, not wanting to be caught in this argument as she felt both the outsider and way out of her depth.

"Enough!" Hammerhand commanded sharply, his speakers very easily heard in their small area. "We are clearly in a position that requires you all to listen to reason, and here is the reason I give you. No one will restore honor through killing themselves. If any want to earn their honor back for whatever reason you feel it's needed, you will fare better in the effort by staying alive, do you understand?"

Tinker and Windchime still looked less than convinced.

"Do you understand?" their leader snapped and took a step toward them.

There were few things in the world more intimidating than the sight of an Excalibur staring at you and expecting some kind of answer. The two men weren't affected the same way Jessica13 would have been, however. They didn't take a step back from the man, but their heads lowered and what looked like dejection settled over them as far as she could see.

They felt ashamed. Hammerhand had a point, and they knew it. Windchime had looked for an easy way out, wracked by guilt as he was, and felt he couldn't look any of his brothers in the eye after what he perceived as a lapse in judgment. Tinker felt similarly disappointed with himself.

But this was not the moment for guilt or self-recrimination. They had a job to see through and trying to get themselves killed any other way wouldn't do anyone any good. The only way they could make up for whatever foul deeds they believed they were to blame for was if they powered through the battles ahead and emerged at the end having rid the world of the likes of Athena.

"We can't afford the waste of losing either of our finest members," Hammerhand continued in a softer tone. "We are all to blame to some extent or another for this. That is what being in the Knights Mechanica means. We are all brothers, and our problems belong to the group, not only to one or the other. None of us could have anticipated that Athena would do what she did, and in that, I am to blame. No matter how unhinged she was before, I would never have thought she had fallen this far. The three of you did the correct thing in liberating the town of Auburn from Athena's grasp. You could not have weighed the lives of the one against those of the other."

Jessica13 lowered her head, drew deep breaths, and tried to pull away from the memories of the bodies she'd seen burned in the buildings around them.

"I need every last one of you to steel yourselves and clear your minds," Hammerhand said and addressed the Knights as a group. "The responsibility for what happened here belongs on the shoulders of Athena and no one else. It was her choice, and all we can do is make her pay for her wanton destruction and her cruel decisions."

The Knights raised their hands and a cheer came from them. Windchime and Tinker did as well, even if they did appear to still be despondent over what they'd seen.

"Now, we still need to find a way to engage Athena that won't allow her to destroy another city like this," Hammerhand said. "She would be insane to repeat the carnage, given that they are the ones supporting her and her people. But if there is anything we've learned from this town, it's that we know we can't expect her to do the right thing or even the logical thing. Her actions prove only that she needs to be stopped."

Another cheer erupted from the group, who already felt a little more lighthearted when they saw their leader with a better attitude than before. Jessica13 couldn't help a small smile. She knew she wouldn't be able to help them much with planning their attack on Athena, but there was still collecting and packing the parts and pieces they had scavenged. That did appear to be the one thing she could do while the others began to formulate a battle plan.

Something crackled and sparked in the sky above her and she looked up as she made her way to the Beast. Curious, she tilted her head and squinted in an effort to make out what hung above them in the growing darkness. Not only had the sun already begun to set as the smoke cleared slowly, but heavy, dark clouds gathered and flashes of lightning arced through them to illuminate something that wasn't a cloud.

"What the hell?" Despite her best efforts, she simply couldn't make it out. "Mini, can you see what is up there?"

A couple of scans ran across the HUD. "All scans are inconclusive. You could look through the scope of your rifle for a better view."

She did as the AI suggested, took her rifle from her back, and peered through the scope. It provided a breath-taking sight of the massive clouds above her head as they darkened and surged with streaks of lightning quickly followed by a crack of thunder. As she'd suspected, there was definitely something else there. It was hard to tell what it was, exactly, until she zoomed in closer and realized that the lightning reflected off something made of steel.

Finally, she discerned the outline and realized they were balloons. They seemed identical to those she had seen tethered at the top of Auburn's bunker, but these moved in and ahead of the clouds. Fascinated, she fiddled with the zoom for a clearer image and noticed small, metal nets extending from the front. The lightning either moved from the nets into the clouds or they collected the lightning from the clouds. Unfortunately, they moved too quickly for her to confirm which it was.

"Tinker!" she shouted and turned to locate him. The older man was still with Hammerhand and in discussion about their plans for an attack. "Tinker, you might want to see this."

He turned to her and looked a little annoyed that she had interrupted him but also heard the alarm in her voice. She wasn't sure what those balloons were supposed to do, why they weren't tethered to a bunker, or how they were able to move freely like they were propelled by something.

"What's the matter, Jessie?" Windchime asked and she handed him the rifle and pointed to the place ahead of the clouds where the balloons were.

"What the fuck?" he asked and handed the rifle to Tinker who immediately trained it on the area in question.

"Those are the same as the weather balloons tethered on top of the Auburn bunker, aren't they?" Jessica13 asked.

"These aren't tethered," he said. "And they are what's causing the weather to turn sour, or I'll eat my mech's nuclear power core."

"Imagine shitting that out," one of the Knights commented.

"Given that it weighs half a ton and is about a half-meter square, I'd say I'd have many more problems before I had to deal with shitting it out," Tinker said without moving his gaze from the vessels. "My question, however, is trying to determine what they're doing up there and why they're moving. Or where they are going."

Hammerhand looked up and Jessica13 assumed he had the software to see that far without needing a scope. "They're moving to Auburn. And if they aren't a vanguard for another of Athena's invasions, I'm a fucking pirate."

"That might be true," Tinker said. "Or they could be a distraction—a way to punish Auburn while she burns more towns to distract us. She wants to draw us out and stretch our resources thin, which would allow her superior numbers to take us on piecemeal."

Their leader nodded. "Shit, I should have thought of that. Athena has always been a crafty bitch. This is her land and she controls a great deal about it. We should keep that in mind while moving forward."

"Would her power over the weather be a threat to us?" Jessica13 asked.

"The only threat would be the lightning, and I don't think she would be able to control that, not with a hundred of those balloons," Tinker said. "Even then, it would take tremendous power to destroy even a Watson, much less a combat mech. They've been designed for that. Still, the weather could slow us. The Beast doesn't move too well in mud but it still moves. We'll merely be slowed a great deal."

"And that's enough for her, I suppose," Windchime said. "What is our plan?"

Hammerhand paused and looked pensive for a moment before he turned to face the younger Knight.

"You asked for a way in which to regain your honor," he said and his voice boomed across the group and immediately captured their attention. "I offer this to you now. Choose two of your brothers in combat mechs. Go to the next town on the map and protect them there. Keep Athena away from them."

Windchime nodded and took a deep breath. Protecting the people of the town would be a good way to make up for whatever it was he believed had cost him his honor, and if there was a good deal of fighting to clear them of Athena's influence, so much the better. Jessica13 still wasn't sure why he felt he owed something for helping the people of Auburn, though.

Still, if this would clear his conscience and keep all those thoughts about killing himself out of his mind, she was all for it.

"As for the rest of us," Hammerhand said and addressed the group as Windchime selected his team, "Auburn appears to be next in our enemy's sights. You saw the destruction she caused here. This I swear—as long as I breathe, I will not allow another town to be murdered in such a manner. I invite you to take the same oath. Fight with me with that oath in mind."

Another roar issued from those gathered and they began to prepare for the march. Every one of them was still exhausted from the previous trek and the battle they had so recently been a part of. Hopefully, like Jessica13, some would be able to rest in their mechs while the AI controlled it during the night's march. Others would try to take turns to rest in the Beast when they could. They didn't, unfortunately, have the luxury of taking adequate time to rest and would have to snatch what they could without slowing the march. Lives were at stake, and they had more important matters to attend to. When the need was great, people somehow found the reserves to do what they must.

Tinker moved to where she stood and handed her rifle to her. "Are you all right, girl? You do understand that none of what happened here was our fault, yes? You don't have any silly ideas of sacrificing yourself?"

She took the weapon and slung it onto her back. "Athena's actions are her own, and we're as responsible for them as much as we are for the weather or the attack of the Invaders. We have already begun to end her oppression of the town of Auburn, and if she chose to retaliate by oppressing even more people to the point of killing them, that is her guilt. Our only problem is not having destroyed her sooner."

Tinker nodded. "Good. I wanted to make sure you weren't having the same thoughts as Windchime."

"I know and I wasn't," she said and tried to force a smile, but there was no happiness in it. "I only want to make sure that Athena pays for the lives she took today. I think Hammerhand will want to exact that price from her, but after what I saw… Well, I wouldn't mind a piece of her myself. I want to send the kind of message that would make anyone of a similar mind think twice."

"Agreed," he said. "Use that anger but don't let it consume you."

"How do I do that?" Jessica13 asked.

He shrugged. "Fuck if I know. But you'll know the anger that consumes when you see it once you've seen it before."

"And where have you seen it before?" she asked, even though she knew the answer.

"A woman we call Athena," he stated coldly. "Or Lady Hoot. Whichever you prefer."

CHAPTER ELEVEN

Night had fallen and shrouded the land in the kind of darkness that was practically palpable. There was no moonlight and the stars were hidden by the cloud cover that draped the entire landscape in what felt like a blanket. The air felt thick, even through the filters of the mech.

The flickers of lightning were all that illuminated the area for the first few hours of their march. Jessica13 wasn't sure if she liked it better than what began to cast light across the horizon they were approaching. She'd had her fill of fire for the day.

But at least that was enough warning for them to know that Athena had sent mechs to slow them. When she looked through the scope of her rifle, she identified a group of Cinders that used their flame throwers to set fire to the dry grasses. The wind had picked up and the flames spread fairly quickly, driven by the gusts.

"It could be they're trying to burn Auburn," Tinker said when she pointed it out to him.

"Or it could be that they're trying to build something of a

wall of fire to keep us away," she suggested. "Either way, she knows where we're going. I think she might not expect us to split our forces, though, so if she has a mind to corral us, we would be able to call Windchime to help us. I…hope it won't come to that, however."

"Hammerhand has a talent for tearing out of holes we manage to get into," he agreed and motioned at the combat mechs that began to take a V-formation in response to their leader's orders.

They expected an attack from the Cinders that hung back but the Knights didn't let the possibility deter them and pushed forward once they chose a path through the places that had already been burned. The speed at which the grass caught spread the fire effectively but it didn't last very long in places, which resulted in open patches of burned grass that posed little risk. There were a few places where it was obvious the fire had grown a little too intense and the sandy earth had been scorched and even crystallized. It crunched underfoot as she moved forward.

"They're using too much fuel," one of the Lancers noted. "The fire burns too hot and turns the sand into glass. What a fucking waste." He shook his head in disgust and the mech responded, but this time, there was nothing amusing about it.

"I don't think Athena hires her folks with saving resources in mind," Taylor replied from the Sherlock that moved on the right flank. "Lavish usage of resources is a way to show the people she rules over that she's better than they are and they would be better with her than without."

"I suppose," the Lancer pilot conceded. "Still, it's the kind of waste that heats the blood, if you know what I mean."

Jessica13 did know what he meant. Waste like that was foreign to her, having lived her whole life recycling every drop of sweat and not letting anything go to waste. Burning grass for the hell of it or even to send a message was plain wasteful. At least this time, her confusion over the waste debate didn't even try to raise its head.

They continued their determined march as more of Athena's mechs began to move closer to the group. Battle lines drew into a formation that would allow the Cinders to take the front of the line. It was an odd tactic, but if they got in close enough to Hammerhand's group, they would be able to do significant damage with their flechette guns and flame throwers.

Then again, Hammerhand could come in and hold the front line against them, use his shield, and knock them back with his hammer. It would be a risky tactic.

When they ignited their throwers, she realized they had no intention to attack and instead, merely held their ground and started fires in front of them. The flames caught a little too quickly. They had soaked the ground with fuel, apparently, and the blaze spread swiftly and covered almost thirty meters to force the Knights to a halt.

The fire wouldn't go so far as to ruin the mechs if they elected to go through it, but it would make them vulnerable. There was also the possibility of shorting something out, which would bring the small group to a sudden and unwanted halt. No one wanted to have to do sudden repairs while they walked through a veritable wall of fire.

Hammerhand didn't appear to be concerned, however, and strode forward to stand in front of the flames. A mech the size of his would have little trouble pushing through and it would take a few hours for something like a gas fire to even begin to heat the heavy armor the Excalibur was known for.

But the Knights' leader made no effort to approach the

flames as yet. Jessica13 tilted her head curiously and remained where she was at the back. The man stepped forward, lowered his weapons, and looked like he intended to speak to their opponents on the other side of the wall of fire.

"My brothers!" Hammerhand called and his speakers carried his voice well over the roaring blaze between them. It was hard not to pay attention when he spoke. "Why do we fight?"

It was an odd question and yet a good one at the same time. She wasn't sure why she hadn't thought of why these men would follow Athena to the point where they risked their lives against opposition who could actually fight back. Bullying folks in towns and villages into giving up their resources was all well and good but usually, when faced with stiffer resistance, pirates and the like tended to turn tail and run. To them, it was always better to live to fight another day, and she couldn't blame them for it.

There was no answer from their adversaries and they appeared to be as surprised by the question as she was. The group of Cinders she'd noticed before were flanked on both sides by almost two dozen Lancers in formation, what looked like their escort out in the Wild.

"Why must we fight?" Hammerhand asked again. "You engage yourselves in acts of depravity and evil that would corrupt any living soul, but know this—there is a way out, a way to disengage yourselves from such horrors that you have witnessed and even committed. You have fought for a side you must know to be in the wrong and a group that must be brought to answer for what they have done, but you need not be among those punished. You need not be among those who fall in the name of justice."

She frowned, not at all sure what his point was. There

were those who had fought for too long at Athena's side to question her methods and morals now. Maybe there were newer arrivals who could be convinced to turn against her. Or better yet, maybe he considered something more long-term. His words of peace and mercy would resonate in the men and women across from them, and maybe after they'd had time to think, they would see the wisdom of it.

Perhaps, in the long run, there would be those who elected to surrender rather than fight, knowing there was a way out now.

Jessica13 hoped for all those things but somehow doubted any would be the case.

"Instead of fighting alongside a tyrant who you must know will turn against you too, eventually, you could fight alongside the Knights Mechanica as our brothers," Hammerhand continued, took a step forward, and extended a hand to the mechs on the other side of the fire. "Make restitution for your sins. Pay penance for them by standing beside those who cannot protect themselves against those who would take advantage. Your lives and souls may yet be saved from the darkness that has consumed you. You have hurt and killed the innocent, and you must know that in time, you will meet justice, one way or the other. Stand with us and you will be spared and be able to face that with the knowledge that you have done something to right your wrongs. Do not, and that justice will meet you a good deal sooner than you would like."

Athena's knights appeared to confer with one another if nothing else, as their body language seemed to indicate that a discussion was in progress. They didn't look like they would take Hammerhand's offer and really, no one expected them to. Each of them had elected to side with Athena for a reason, after all.

But they would have the offer firmly in mind when he powered through their lines like he was some kind of machine of vengeance from above.

A Lancer finally stepped forward. The hatch twisted open and the pilot climbed out to stand on the shoulder of his mech. He stared at the silent Knights Mechanica and she used the opportunity to study one of the enemy.

Given the numbers Athena had committed to the burning town and again in this location, she had begun to feel that they had vastly underestimated the forces their adversary had at her disposal.

The man opposite looked lean and hungry and was most likely completely shaven as most mech pilots tended to be. He wore a patchwork coat of a variety of colors and mismatched pieces and looked much like the coat Athena had worn on her mech, she now recalled. Most of the scraps appeared to be some kind of leather about the size of a hand each, with a few patches of canvas sewed in as well like they were placeholders.

His helmet consisted of the same kind of work that even displayed a few sections of canvas too and covered his skull. The over-sized goggles he wore made it look like his eyes were popping out and created the impression that the head-gear was way too tight.

He started to speak but lacked the powerful external speakers Hammerhand's Excalibur had so it was difficult over the roaring flames between them. She couldn't actually hear a word but it seemed fairly obvious that he attempted to convey the fact that he wasn't open to the idea of being accepted by the Knights Mechanica. He beat his chest and shouted to the other mechs, calling what might have been a challenge and was very obviously an attempt to rally them with far more noise and gestures than Hammerhand ever needed.

Jessica13 pulled her rifle out and looked down the scope to see more clearly. He pulled the helmet and goggles from his head and she realized that his skull was covered in thick black tattoos. They appeared to be rather crude and depicted a wide variety of animals—some of which she had never seen or heard of—but the most distinctive was on his forehead and seemed to look down at him.

It was rough like all the others but the depiction of an owl was unmistakable. It seemed impossible that Athena would have made all her followers mark themselves with her sigil, as forcing them to do something they didn't want to do would be entirely counterproductive to her efforts.

If they had been convinced to do it on their own, however, it painted a very different picture. It seemed unthinkable that they liked the idea of her looking over their every action, seeing everything they did, and showing them that they could never escape her grasp, but the man seemed proud of it. If that was an idea they considered desirable, she wondered if there was anything that could be done to pull them away from what Athena wanted them to do.

She wondered how they had become that way. They had likely been selected from those who were already terrible like pirates and quickly beaten, pounded, and forged into weapons who would follow Athena's orders without question.

"I don't think they'll go for it," Jessica13 said softly.

"Give them a warning shot," Hammerhand said through her commlink. "Target the one who's out of his mech."

"Understood." She already had her rifle trained on the man and took a deep breath. He was still showing off his tattoos and his allegiance to Athena to the cheers of his fellow fighters when the hellebore round punched through his skull. The soft bone offered almost no resistance and the bullet drilled through and into the mech to knock it back a step before the AI inside was able to correct it.

The cheers around him ceased when they realized their apparent leader had collapsed with most of his head splattered across the outside of his mech.

"He should have known better," Tinker said. "You don't climb out of your mech in a combat situation. That's asking to get yourself killed."

"Agreed," Hammerhand said and raised his hammer.

The crack of the rockets on the back no longer caught her by surprise and his weapon quickly increased its speed as it swung into action.

By the time it impacted, she could almost hear the wind whistling around it as it pounded into fire-covered earth. The speed that propelled it generated a shudder and a powerful boom that seemed to drive the fire away from the head of the weapon.

The effect on the fire itself was negligible as it quickly regained the ground it had lost since it was still soaked in fuel. Athena's fighters took an instinctive step back, however, as Hammerhand advanced through the flames, the spectacle rather gratifying.

"Get out from behind the shield and keep on firing," he said and activated the barrier. The heat made the vents around his feet open to cool the mech as he moved through the blaze. He was through in a few strides, and from the look of the men ahead, it didn't appear as though they wanted to actually fight. The stood frozen as if their will had suddenly and painfully been dragged out of them.

Jessica13 pushed out from behind the shield but remained

on their side of the fire while the other knights crossed through and advanced in formation. The enemy suddenly seemed to realize that their dead leader had elected to fight rather than surrender and hastily began to prepare.

She lined up another shot. The Cinders' pilots appeared to more anxious for action than the Lancers, unsurprisingly, and that made them the perfect place to start her attack. They had some armor but it was mostly frontal, and as they turned to face Hammerhand head-on, she had a clear shot at their fuel supplies.

It was tempting to simply act quickly but she forced herself to wait as they started the throwers. Only when she was sure they were drawing from the supplies on their back did she choose the one at the front who attempted to push his flames against her leader's shield. She pulled the trigger.

The result was a little less immediate than she thought it would be. The pressure was suddenly lost in the fuel supply and the flame was quickly drawn back into the thrower itself to travel up the pipes and into the fuel. It took almost five seconds for the full effect to come to fruition, but by the time the flame reached the tank, she had turned away. The blast was bright enough to light up the entire area around them.

She grasped the rifle and let the mechanism load another round before she selected her next target. The Lancers needed to retreat slightly as the blaze from the destroyed Cinder was too intense for them to approach. A couple of the others had been eliminated in the same blast.

The Knights moved around the flames, but Hammerhand simply kicked the ruined mechs out of his way and marched between them with his shield up. The enemy finally opened fire.

And not only on the knights, she realized, when the earth was kicked up by a few rounds aimed in her direction.

"It's time to move," Mini announced and she already understood what the AI had in mind before he even had to say it. She tucked the rifle away on the back of her mech and let him take them onto all fours and bound to the side as the volley directed at them grew more and more intense. She braced herself in anticipation of his next action and he pushed the Minato into a sprint toward the tall wall of flame between them and the Knights who began to engage Athena's men.

Mini bunched the mech and used their momentum while he drove forward with the more powerful back legs to launch them high above the fire and over the tongues of flame that licked at them. She could still feel the heat, even through the insulators, but in seconds, they landed heavily on the other side.

The impact was more intense than it should have been and her whole body jolted with pain.

"Shit!" she shouted and braced herself a little harder. "I really need to fix those fucking dampeners."

"Agreed," Mini said simply and raced into an evasive pattern that allowed them to approach while taking as little fire as possible. The few rounds that actually found them ricocheted off of the angled armor and they were able to keep moving.

"Am I to guess that you have a plan of some kind?" Jessica13 asked, still holding on for dear life.

"My thought was simply to surprise them with our presence, distract them, and give the other Knights a chance to breach their line with a minimal loss of life," he replied.

"That doesn't sound like a plan," she retorted waspishly. "That's barely even a concept."

"I am open to additions to the plan," he replied and she could almost hear a hint of hurt in his voice. Unfortunately, this wasn't the time to explore it or attempt apologies.

"Can you keep us moving?" she asked. "I think I have an idea but I need to use the grappler."

"Understood," Mini said, quickly disengaged them from Bulletfoot mode, and kept their movements sporadic and unpredictable as the gunfire around them grew more intense.

"I will definitely regret this," Jessica13 said. The bumps and bruises from their last fight still made her body ache, and their erratic course at breakneck speed only made it worse.

Mini guided them toward the line the enemy attempted to hold against the Knights. The Cinders were at the front and coordinated their defense to halt the Knights' advance and more importantly, try to keep Hammerhand at bay. That was the weakness she intended to exploit. Hopefully, she thought grimly, but pushed the doubt aside and readied herself for what she needed to do.

It was difficult to aim the grappler while they were in motion, and Mini called up the same software they used to aim the rifle on her back. It wasn't quite as accurate but at this range, it didn't really matter. She found her target and launched the dart to streak forward and drive home in the arm of one of the Cinders.

She wasn't sure what she had expected to do other than distract it, but the mech didn't budge from its attempt to keep Hammerhand pinned in place with its thrower. The flechette gun turned toward her and while it was angled a little awkwardly, the effect would be the same. The type of rounds that were fired from that kind of gun would cut through her armor and find her rather vulnerable inside with ease.

Jessica13 twisted away from the Cinder's line of fire and

yanked at the chord that was still attached to its arm. The motion hauled the mech around without her realizing what she had accomplished at first. As soon as reality clicked in, she continued to drag the mech's thrower away from Hammerhand's shield and toward the Lancers that tried to protect it.

Flames coated the enemy mechs and the screams were audible. The heat wouldn't damage the steel or even the mech itself overmuch, but they would cook the inside, which happened to be the pilot. The temperature would rocket in their cockpits to the point of being unbearable.

A few tried to climb out, but that only let more of the heat in along with the flames. The shrieks sounded almost inhuman as the men tried to beat the fire away, but the fuel stuck to their bodies and it wasn't long before a few hung half-outside their mechs, wreathed in smoke and filling the air with the acrid smell of burning meat.

Those that had actually encountered this problem before were easy to find as they acted quickly to scoop up dirt from the ground around them and shoved it onto the places where the flames burned to stifle them quickly before things grew too hot.

Even with only five of the Lancers dead and a few more distracted, it was the only opening Hammerhand needed. He dropped the shield and advanced quickly on the Cinder that still had her dart attached, which she retracted hastily when she saw the hammer swing in from the side.

The enemy mech was busy trying to acquire her and Mini for another shot and didn't realize that the Excalibur was behind him until it was too late. The blow from the rocket-powered hammer resulted in an audible crunch that lifted it off its feet and catapulted it into the wall of fire that still burned brightly.

The sight of Hammerhand bathed by the red glow of the flames and the occasional flicker of lightning was truly awesome to behold, especially when he was surrounded and flanked by his fellow Knights. Power seemed to radiate from his mech as the vents opened quickly and appeared to cool the fire around it as well.

Jessica13 stowed her grappler, moved herself to the safety provided by the Knights' position, and once again assumed the regular role of a support mech. She reloaded her rifle's mag before she took a handful of crates to where her teammates fought their way through Athena's forces.

It had seemed like the mechs had only been there to slow them, but they fought with every intention of trying to win. They had to know they had no chance, especially when Hammerhand gave legend to his name and simply crushed them, sometimes two or three at a time, with his hammer. The Knights dealt with those that hadn't been removed from contention already with their own unique sets of skills.

Taylor moved quickly in his Sherlock, supported by his Watson, and protected Hammerhand's flanks to ensure that none could get around his shield and hammer. At the same time, the Predator broke away, circled its leader, and surged into the enemy ranks.

It moved swiftly and deliberately and used the close quarters to its advantage. The chainsword dealt severe damage to the limbs of the mechs and rendered them immobile before it cut carefully into the cockpits so as to leave the mech itself intact while it could still drag the pilots out.

None of them retreated, asked for mercy, or even thought to take Hammerhand up on his offer.

Jessica13 shook her head at their foolishness as the chainsword executed the pilots methodically and splattered their blood across the grasslands. The bodies were simply left there to rot.

It was harder to watch the men killed outside their mechs than to simply shoot them almost clinically while they were still inside. There was a lack of connection as if the man being killed was simply a part of disabling the mech. No matter how terrible he was supposed to be, it was far more emotionally charged to witness him actually dying.

Hammerhand turned to his team. "Put the fires out so the Beast can come through. Once you're finished with that, we'll strip the parts from these and move on, as is our way."

As was their way, she reminded herself. It helped to focus on the routine. She wasn't sure how they would manage to extinguish the blaze so watched the others as they dug the dirt to spread it over the flames. She moved closer to the Cinder she had shot and realized that while the flames had eventually burned themselves out in certain sections, they had been so intense that the sandy earth around it had been turned to glass. It crunched under her boots as she gathered as much soil as she could and carried it to where the fires were still a problem.

There was too wide a section by now to completely extinguish, but a pathway was quickly created through the flames. Smoke seeped through where they had smothered a section of the fire but it would allow the Beast to travel through.

With that accomplished, they turned their attention to the battlefield and scavenged what they could from the parts that hadn't been crushed or melted. The Beast moved slowly along the route they'd created and carefully avoided the sections that were burning on either side. The parts they collected were gathered and put in the back.

As was their way. The thought came unbidden again, but it

seemed to ground her. Despite the trauma of some of the things she'd witnessed, the idea that she was part of something solid and normal and lasting brought solace.

It was all slow, hard work, but it needed to be done. Jessica13 recognized that her body felt like it was at its limit. She was exhausted after a long, hard day of marching and fighting, and she didn't think she could take much more of it.

And yet there were still a few things that needed to be done before they resumed their journey to Auburn. Once again, those who had sustained injuries were attended to, mechs were examined, and any repairs that could be done were completed. Fortunately, the Knights had sustained little damage and most of it was easily remedied.

Thereafter, as if by some unspoken command, the mechs began to fall into their usual formation, ready to march once again.

Tinker moved over to where Jessica13 tried to make a wide berth around one of the dead bodies.

"How are you feeling, Jessie?" he asked as he fell in beside her.

He only ever called her Jessie when he was concerned about her. That much was familiar, at least.

"I'm fine," she lied. "A little tired, though. I thought I might snatch a little sleep on the way to Auburn. Well, unless Athena has left any more of her minions to give us problems."

"I think it's safe to assume she won't have. Of course, we have no real idea of the number of her forces but I imagine it couldn't have been easy for her to have this many people spread out so quickly," Tinker said. "I wouldn't be surprised if we find our way to Auburn clear and clean, although that might change if those fucking balloons keep moving."

She looked up when he mentioned them, and sure enough,

despite the delay they'd had while they dealt with Athena's men, they were still a good way ahead of the slow-moving balloons.

The fact that they were still moving inexorably toward Auburn played on her nerves and made her heart sink into her stomach a little. Their slow pace, however, meant the Knights at least had time to reach the town and prepare before whatever it was that Athena had in mind for them arrived.

"We'd better keep moving, lassie," Tinker said and patted her shoulder lightly. "There's no point in waiting for them out in the open."

"What about the fires?" she asked. "Isn't there something we can do before they sweep through the whole land?"

He looked at the flames that crept across the landscape around them. "I'm afraid there are a few troubles that are too mighty for even the Knights Mechanica to handle. Let us focus on those we can deal with."

She nodded regretfully and ran a quick check on her rifle before she joined the Knights.

CHAPTER TWELVE

Jessica13 did manage to get a few hours of sleep while the Knights continued to move across the grasslands toward Auburn. She also noted that Windchime had sent an encrypted message across their private lines to tell them that he and his team had arrived at the next town. A handful of Athena's men was in place, but they wouldn't engage them yet.

It was a wise decision. There was really no point in letting the enemy know about their presence in the area before they could make a real difference.

The few hours of sleep she snatched were rife with nightmares filled with mechs that rushed through flames to attack her, while she was always unable to protect herself. The Minato didn't respond to her controls, and Mini remained silent. Every time, she jerked instinctively to avoid being injured or killed, but it simply repeated itself when she closed her eyes again.

By sunrise, she decided to simply give up on the concept of sleep for the moment. She'd had some rest, at least, and that would have to be enough for now.

"If you like, I can study your sleep patterns in order to try to find a method to help you get decent rest," Mini said as she rubbed her eyes, which felt like someone had put a grinder to her eyeballs.

"How did you know I had trouble sleeping?" she asked and growled softly. "Do you spy on me while I try to get some rest?"

"Of course I do," he responded in a matter-of-fact tone. "But I can't study something as intimate as rem cycles and the like while you sleep. At least not without your express permission."

"Wait, is the issue with my express permission?" she asked. "Because I don't remember permitting you to watch me sleep."

"You tasked me with keeping you safe," he pointed out. "In that, there were certain permissions you implied. You can withdraw those permissions, of course, but until you do, I will continue to observe as I have been, as keeping you safe is my highest priority."

"No, no, it's nothing like that," she said and shook her head. The rising sun illuminated the landscape around them despite the fact that the sky was covered with a thick layer of clouds. It would be a dark day, but some light was better than none at all.

"What is it?" Mini asked.

"I'm a little cranky, is all," she admitted. "Getting little to no sleep ever since we started on this mission is really telling on the nerves. I know you've always looked out for my best interests, even if I haven't done the same."

He paused and ran a number of processes, and Jessica13 realized that the AI was trying to determine if she was being sarcastic or not. After carefully determining that she was not, the processes closed.

"Well, again, if you would like me to, I think I could help you get better sleep if I was allowed to monitor your sleep cycles," he said finally.

"I appreciate that, Mini, and I might actually take you up on it," she responded with a small smile and ran her fingers over the inside of the cockpit. She knew she couldn't take a mech like the Minato and especially not an AI like Mini for granted, no matter how much she adjusted to having them around. The mech and AI both had brought her through some tough situations when she had been absolutely sure she would be killed.

"We're approaching Auburn," one of the Knights said. "It appears to still be intact. Thank the Prophet."

"I didn't think they would get here before the balloons did anyway, but it's still good to verify it," Tinker said over the group comm channel. "Let's head in there and make sure all the folk are well and surviving and then we'll figure out what to do about Athena's impending attack."

"Why didn't she simply send her men ahead to take the town?" Jessica13 asked quickly. "Why did they come back to try to deter us if she wasn't already attacking?"

"It could be that she wanted to catch us by surprise," Tinker replied. "Or she simply wanted to slow our progress and leave us little time to mount any defenses. Maybe she wanted us to be in the town while she sets it ablaze."

She turned to look at the hilly grasslands they had left behind in the far distance. It seemed there were some places where sheets of rain fell and would hopefully put the fires out. Others had simply gone out for lack of fuel or wind but a few still burned steadily through the grass and left black, scorched earth behind it. For all she knew, it was simply how Athena wished to be remembered by those who came after her.

Hammerhand indicated for them to keep moving and they left the semi-arid grasslands and entered the denser shrubbery, an indication that they were coming into an area with a more abundant water supply.

The balloons still cruised behind them but were now ahead of the storm they appeared to be forming and the rising sun glinted off their steel or aluminum hulls.

Those still tethered to Auburn's bunker were clearly visible as well where they drifted lazily in the winds that buffeted them. They were almost completely useless both to the people of Auburn as well as Athena now that the connection to the weather-influencing network had been severed.

Maybe that was why Lady Hoot was sending her own balloons. Perhaps she wanted to reconnect those that had been lost—as well as likely burn Auburn to the ground. Networks like the kind the weather-influencing system worked from tended to be less effective if critical pieces were cut out.

Aside from the practical considerations, it was a challenge to her authority and also a direct strike against her influence over her domain.

A handful of townsfolk seemed to have begun to use their own mechs for protection rather than simply to help in the fields, although they were unarmed and would be of little use in an outright attack. Still, at least they had made the attempt to participate in their own defense. The pilots were out of their mechs and seemed to be in discussion about something but the conversation ceased when they noticed the unmistakable sight of Hammerhand's Excalibur striding toward them.

She wondered if maybe they would think it was Athena's mech since it was built in more or less the same style. From a distance, they could be mistaken for one another, but closer inspection revealed the banners hung from his shoulder pauldrons, the lack of the patchwork cloak Athena wore, as well the absence of the owl carved into her helm which inspired her moniker.

As the Knights approached, a group from the town began to move toward the bunker as well. In a few minutes, it grew larger as people abandoned their work in the fields to join the new arrivals.

Any hopes that they might have a friendly greeting from the citizens of Auburn were dashed, however, when she saw their expressions up close. Some looked scared, but the majority appeared to be angry.

"What is their problem?" she muttered, more to herself than to Mini.

"It could be that they saw the fire or at least the smoke from the burning town and want answers about that," he suggested. "Or they can see the storm clouds gathering in the distance and want to know about them."

"But why do they seem angry with us?"

Mini paused. "I have no idea. Maybe they are angry at the situation rather than with us and simply think we can protect them. Or perhaps they think we are to blame."

Either of his situations might have made sense, but she was too tired to consider them fully. All she could think was if these people wanted to know about what happened to the other town or the clouds approaching them, there was a nicer way to go about it than approaching the Knights in what looked like a mob.

They pointed fingers mostly at Hammerhand, who seemed unperturbed by the less than warm welcome and simply led his team on.

When the townsfolk reached them, a leader stepped

forward from their ranks—likely the man they had elected as their mayor from the look of his clothes—and advanced directly on Hammerhand himself. It was as if he had scant regard for the fact that the man who stood in front of him piloted a massive mech designed for large-scale warfare against ships in the sky from space. His apparent assurance seemed more incongruous given that he wore only fancy-looking clothes that were a little too big for him.

"What happened to our neighboring town?" he asked and spoke loudly to make sure all the people behind him could hear as well. "Did you attack them as you did us?"

The Knights leader made no answer, possibly because he wanted to give him the opportunity to have his say before he responded.

"You took the town in an attack that was unprecedented," the man shouted and looked around in a way that suggested he was actually addressing the people. It seemed fairly obvious that he attempted to rouse the crowd of Auburn citizens for his own purposes. "Your people came into our town in the dead of night to take what wasn't yours and intercede in events you had nothing to do with. You interfered without the consent of the people of Auburn."

Jessica13 leaned forward to study him more closely. "Wait, I think I recognize him. Yes…he was in the town when I infiltrated as a peddler. He was one of Athena's agents and actually approached me. I was talking to one of the younger women and he was her stepfather—Barrios, I think his name was."

"Well, that explains why he's trying to turn the townsfolk against us," Tinker said and scowled at the group of citizens that grew steadily angrier with every word from their new mayor. "He is Athena's man and is therefore trying to work for her while he maintains his own anonymity."

"Why don't we tell them that?" she asked.

He shook his head. "Even if we manage to present them with proof of it—which I doubt we could—he would be able to say it is only a ploy to remove him. Mobs like this cannot be swayed by logic, especially when they are whipped into a frenzy."

"What can we do?" She sensed the growing hostility take a turn for the worse when a group arrived and joined the rear of the crowd with comparatively small improvised weapons. Others, seeing this, began to return to their homes and places of work to collect weapons of their own. Pitchforks and plowshares obviously wouldn't do much damage against the mechs they tried to threaten, but she could tell that the end this careened inevitably toward was not a happy one.

"Nothing, really," Tinker said. "Hold your ground, try not to get involved if they decide to fight, and protect yourself without hurting anyone around you. They'll eventually take our lack of hostility and their inability to disable the mechs on their own to mean that it is an effort in futility and be more open to calm, rational debate. Of course, the time lost will be to Athena's benefit, and we can only hope they run out of heat quickly and allow us sufficient opportunity to deal with her when we have to."

Jessica13 nodded. There would be no need for the rifle on her back, but Mini had shown her there would be some use for the grappler if they used it correctly.

"Mini," she said and called up the controls for the grappler, "do you think there might be some way to temporarily reduce the power in the air gun for the grappler when we disengage it from the dart?"

"Yes, the settings are adjustable," he confirmed. "It would likely have to be done manually if you didn't have an AI to operate it, but thankfully, you do, and so—"

"Yes, I do, and I'm eternally grateful for that," she said briskly. "So there's no need to remind me constantly of how useful you are. Well, it might be a good idea to make sure I don't take you for granted, but at the same time, choose your moments, yes?"

"Understood. I will only remind you of how useful I am to you when we are not in some form of danger," he agreed.

"That is appreciated," she replied with a small smile. "Now, get it ready."

Mini did as he was told and pulled the grappler around and away from the dart it usually fired to give them space to operate from as she backed away slowly.

Unfortunately, that action on its own was enough to call the attention of Barrios, who still attempted to whip the citizens into a violent mob.

"That one!" he shouted, almost frothing at the lips. "She was in our town under false pretenses while she studied our defenses in preparation for the attack her people were planning. Now, she presents herself in our town like some kind of hero and not the infiltrating spy she is."

Jessica13 scowled and fought the urge to smack the man across the mouth, mech and all. Like Tinker said, they needed to hold off on anything they might do unless they had to protect themselves. Maybe not allowing them to damage their mechs and keep them from injuring themselves, but aside from that, there was to be no attack on them. Not only that, but speaking would only serve to rile the townsfolk further, as he had also mentioned.

"I'm glad Windchime isn't here to see this," she said softly as the group of townsfolk pushed closer and the mood seemed to escalate toward a peak that definitely suggested violence.

"Why do you say that?" Tinker asked.

"You remember how he struggled with his guilt over what we'd done in Auburn," she said. "It might not have been a problem on its own, but to him, it caused the town to be destroyed and the people killed."

"It was a shared guilt, lassie. We all had a part to play in it, and you know I believe that as the leader of the group, I had more responsibility—"

"I know," she interrupted impatiently. "But maybe because you're older or have more experience, you were…okay, a little more practical about it. We both know Windchime took it much worse and it still bothers him. It was all Hammerhand could do to convince him to take that guilt and use it to fuel his actions to protect others from a similar fate. If he were here and forced to do nothing while the locals accused him of the same thing he accuses himself of…well, I can't imagine what that would do to the man. I'm glad he's off doing something that's actually useful."

"Do you think what we're doing here isn't useful?" he countered. "Sure, in our current position, we can't take any action at this point without risking losing everything, so the best thing to do in this moment is nothing. Well, aside from protecting ourselves and making sure they don't damage our mechs. Aside from that, nothing at all."

"Could I use the air gun on my grappler?" Jessica13 asked. "It's not lethal, at least not the strike itself. I used it when I broke away from Sanctuary. There might have been some injuries I didn't know about, but he wasn't killed."

"Maybe keep it on hand in case we need it, but only use it

as a last resort," Tinker said. "Once again, we don't want to push them into committing further violence."

She nodded. In all honesty, she'd half-believed he would forbid the use of it, but at least he'd agreed it was something to keep in mind. She grasped the controls a little tighter as the people milled toward her. Barrios still pointed at her while he ranted about how she had betrayed their trust. She wondered if she could possibly have misremembered what had happened. While she had entered the town under false pretenses, she had done so with their best interests at heart and not only that, she had put considerable time and effort into repairing and rebuilding their town.

The Knights had also worked hard to do what they could to restore everything while they were content to wait for them to decide if they wanted to offer any kind of reward for their work.

"Maybe that's why," Jessica13 said to Mini. "Maybe they don't want to give us any reward for our work for them."

"It is unlikely, given that Hammerhand told them to decide what kind of reward they wanted to give, if any at all," he replied. "Although I suppose the reward element could have played a part. They don't have much to give and that could make them feel guilty. If they convince themselves we are not entitled to a reward, they no longer have to feel guilty if they don't give us anything."

That made no sense to her, but maybe people in general didn't always make sense. She wasn't sure why anyone would feel guilty about not rewarding someone for helping them. If they couldn't spare anything, the Knights would have understood. They were fighting to end that kind of shortage of supplies in the area, after all, since Athena bled the towns dry of resources to support her regime.

In that case, why would they want to remove them as the only chance that they had to get rid of Athena and her ilk?

She fiddled with her controls and took a deep breath. Understanding the kind of thought processes these people operated on—that made them make so many odd, illogical choices—was more difficult than understanding Mini's AI. She wasn't sure how much it would help to tell them the error of their ways, but like Tinker said, maybe saying anything at this point would only make them angrier.

Machines were so much easier to understand.

Reluctantly, she decided it was best to simply wait for them to get it all out and hope it passed.

"Mini, what do you think we can do to keep them away without hurting them?" Jessica13 asked because she did see sense in being prepared.

He had no time to answer as the group appeared to reach the peak of their anger and surged forward at the group of mechs. They held weapons in their hands and tried to attack in a rage. The instinct to fight back rose in her stomach and pushed her to take some kind of action that would prevent them from inflicting injury on her or her mech.

Tinker's words rang in her brain and helped to calm her as the crowd battered the outside of the mechs or tried to pry the armor plates loose to find something they could strike at and disable them. Most had targeted the combat mechs, perhaps because they were the greater threat, but a small group with pitchforks turned their attention to her.

"You're not welcome here," one shouted, stepped closer, and brandished his weapon. It seemed ludicrous that he could act like he wasn't trying to intimidate a young girl in a mech that was taller, larger, and heavier than he was.

"Maybe they know we won't attack them and that is where their courage comes from," Mini commented.

"If we don't give them any reason to continue attacking, they'll eventually stop," she said. "I hope."

"Enough!"

The voice was unmistakable and far louder than normal, and her cockpit actually shook with the reverberations. Hammerhand had decided to speak and there would be no interruption.

Most of the townsfolk fell silent and some covered their ears, but a small group surrounding Barrios tried to continue their ruckus.

The Knights' leader raised the hammer and brought the haft down hard enough to make the earth shudder around him. It had the desired effect and brought the pocket of unrest to a standstill. As one, the people of Auburn stared in silence at the massive mech that towered over them.

Their caution was understandable given that it looked even more threatening than it had only seconds before.

"You were pulled out from under the yoke of Athena's violence, and what have you become in her absence?" Hammerhand demanded and cowed everyone around him by the sheer volume of his voice. "I see before me the same devastating, horrifying kind of monsters you were delivered from. Rather than learn from Athena's cruelty, you attack a young woman who has worked to restore your town."

Mini hastily adjusted the sound filter in the mech to make the words a little less painful to listen to, but she could still feel the vibrations of the Excalibur speaking through the mech itself. It was possible that the man could use the speakers themselves as some kind of weapon against attackers.

"She had no reason to help you other than the goodness in her heart and the will and desire to help those in need," Hammerhand continued and took a step forward. Jessica13 couldn't help a small smile when Barrios and his men took an instinctive step back. "Outnumbered and possibly outgunned, she still came in alone to help to restore your town to functionality. Yet you have the nerve—the audacity—to accuse her of harming you?"

Her smile broadened and a hint of warmth settled in her chest and stomach when she heard what Hammerhand had to say about it. She had thought he didn't approve of what they had done. A moment's reflection reminded her that maybe he still didn't.

But he likely didn't like what the townsfolk did either. She wasn't sure why he said she had only the goodness in her heart and the will and desire to help those in need, but it was a nice thought.

"She's come from a bunker, exactly like all of you," he said, a little more subdued now that the people around him had settled into a far less aggressive mood. A couple even seemed to realize that he was right and turned to look at Barrios instead. They had to know he was actually one of Athena's men and that was the only reason why he tried to stir them to action against the Knights.

Now that the heat from their anger had begun to diminish, logic seemed to reassert itself. Jessica13 suddenly realized that these people were what the pirates liked to call bunker rats— folks who had only recently withdrawn from a bunker to live Outside. Whatever had prompted them to leave had made them start their lives in the area as well.

"I know there are those who suffered under Athena's regime," Hammerhand said with a sweeping gesture at the townsfolk around him. Barrios and his supporters attempted to shuffle away in an inconspicuous retreat but were stopped by the locals, who seemed to have rediscovered where their loyalties lay. "Loved ones were taken from you. Injuries were sustained and you suffered injustices and indignities. Those cannot be forgiven or forgotten but, in the end, you were set free from that. You fought back and took control of your town. Don't fall into the same traps that led you to rely on that kind of monster."

Jessica13 nodded as the people stared at Hammerhand with expressions of growing realization. She had seen the kind of injustices and indignities they had suffered—or at least had seen the video footage of how they had been forced to accept those while going through the checkpoints. That was only a small portion of what the oppressors had done. There was also the woman who had lost her father and whose mother was forced to marry Barrios.

It seemed there were considerably more than the few she was aware of. The words made a strong impact and people began to recall what had happened under Athena's reign—or, rather, experienced them more keenly when they considered them— and the tone of the crowd began to change.

It made her wonder how they had allowed Barrios to talk them into an attempt at action against the Knights. Maybe it was because he was a good father to the little girl and possibly a good husband. The knowledge of that and the fact that he had been some kind of admin for the town might have been enough to help the people decide that his experience was enough to qualify him.

Jessica13 could see how that could happen, but in the end, he had shown that his loyalties lay with Athena. If he had played a part in the horrors inflicted on the people of Auburn and other neighboring towns, they would ultimately remember that most of all.

"We stand at a crossroads, people of Auburn," Hammerhand said. "You live in a time of change in which your freedom has been restored to you. But this is also your time to choose. What will you do with that freedom? Will you fight to keep it, or will you stand back and let this Lady Hoot grind you under her heel once more?"

The consensus of the people gathered before him was a resounding no and they shook their heads and muttered agreement.

"This freedom is a beautiful thing and should not be squandered," he continued.

The crowd appeared to agree again, and Jessica13 looked at the people around her with both surprise and curiosity. Where there had been fear and impending violence, all that remained was a little confusion mingled with both determination and hope. She knew she couldn't inspire people like that, which was the reason why Hammerhand led the Knights and she was merely a mechanic who worked for him and was similarly inspired by him.

It was the result of his enormous charisma that was powerful, even through his mech, to touch the minds and hearts of the people around him. He could encourage them to take actions they never thought they could simply because he inspired them.

And maybe because they didn't want to disappoint his expectations of them. This was certainly something that played a role in her interaction with him, so it was a likely possibility.

It was, she realized, a dangerous kind of power to have over people. Athena probably had something similar—the ability to speak and put the people around her under what she assumed was a kind of hypnotic spell that made them do what she wanted them to. Unlike Hammerhand, she abused that ability. While it was pure assumption, it seemed to be a logical deduction when she considered the issue of the woman's power over people.

The Knights' leader moved forward again and made it seem like he joined them in looking forward to their future.

"I understand that the concept might feel a little foreign at first," he said. His voice remained calm and measured but carried a depth and strength that could not be ignored. "The thought that you can choose your own destiny might cause fear, but that is simply part of the beauty of it. None will have a say in how you run your lives—not even the Knights Mechanica. When I ask what you will do with your newfound freedom, you need not answer to me but rather to yourselves. What is that freedom worth to you? Will you fight for it? What would you do to keep it?"

The fear, the excitement, and the tension were almost palpable around them. These people finally realized what they had and the reality of what threatened it. Hammerhand's words showed them the way and they were following through.

"How easy it would be," Jessica13 said in response to her thoughts that vacillated between awe and alarm.

"What was that?" Mini asked. "Do you want me to connect you with someone?"

"No... I was thinking," she replied and shook her head. "How easy it would be for someone to use Hammerhand's ability to influence people for evil. Or bad things, anyway."

"His oratory skills are a little antiquated but very effective," the AI conceded. "I suppose it's possible that he practices his speeches in his mech where only he can hear them and so improves them before he actually speaks. But aside from that and a few other tricks, it is something some people are simply born with. They know instinctually how to speak in a manner that would help others see their point of view. There are a few genetic components, according to my records, but it is mostly due to upbringing and skills that are learned while very young and improved upon over time."

"I don't think I'd be any good at it," she grumbled.

"You have a great many other skills that make you invaluable," he said. "Your obvious knowledge and passion for those are what make people listen to you when you talk."

She smiled. "Well, you have a pleasant quality to your voice that makes it nice to listen to you as well."

"Your compliment is noted and appreciated," Mini said.

They turned their attention to Hammerhand, who pointed his hammer at the sky in the direction of the balloons that approached the town slowly. They had made noticeable progress and would soon hang over them, but even from a distance, they were an impressive sight—like a very real harbinger of the possible doom they would inevitably face.

"That is what is coming to take this newfound freedom from you," he stated. "They would fight to put you under their control again or, failing that, burn Auburn to the ground to meet their perverse need for retribution. There is only one way to hold them at bay and that is to fight them!"

The people roared in response. Where Barrios had roused them based on deeper, fouler emotions, Hammerhand brought out the best in them. He reminded them of who and what they wanted to protect and what they could do to accomplish it.

They were inspired. There was no other explanation for it.

The clouds rolled closer, hard behind the balloons, and Jessica13 pulled her rifle from her back and attempted to look more closely through the scope.

"I really do need to get a proper holster for this," she reminded herself. "The mag clamp can't have a very good effect on the metal. It could even warp it if I leave it on long enough."

"That is possible," Mini agreed as she adjusted her view to the plains around Auburn.

The scope still worked well and the software quickly corrected and zoomed into an area where she could see movement. It had simply looked like the grass moving at first and she'd almost moved on. But as the visibility settled and the cloud shielded any glare from the sun, she was able to determine that the movement actually came from a group of mechs that headed in their direction.

"Tinker!" she shouted into the comms. "You might want to take a look at this."

He moved hurriedly to where she stood and took the rifle she offered him.

"You might want to think about getting one of these for yourself," Jessica13 pointed out.

"I don't like firearms or weapons in general," the man said. "Of course, I know they're necessary, but I chose the role of support mech precisely for the reason that I handle weapons only rarely and mostly only to keep them in shape for others to use."

"We'll have to talk more about that later," she said. "But due south…maybe more southwest…there is movement on the hills. I'd say between forty and fifty klicks away."

Tinker peered through the scope in the direction she indicated.

"It looks like they're a way out still," he commented. "They could get here faster, but my guess is they're pacing themselves by those balloons, which probably means they won't push ahead. It might give us about half a day or maybe a little more. Alert Hammerhand and he'll know we should start to put defenses in place and get the village folk who don't want to be involved in the imminent violence as far away as possible."

"Understood." She reclaimed her weapon from him. "You could always simply find yourself a scope, you know. There's no need to have a weapon in your hands."

"That might work," Tinker said. "I expect there will be one I can scavenge should we live out the night."

Barrios and his supporters were jostled and shoved away from the bunker and toward the town. She wondered what was in store for them but decided it didn't concern her. They had betrayed their community, and the community would rightfully decide their fates. "We have friends with us," she reminded Tinker, relieved that Auburn had embraced the freedom and the challenge.

"Let's hope they live out the night too." He chuckled but it sounded grim rather than amused. "Run along, lassie."

CHAPTER THIRTEEN

It proved to be far more difficult to prepare for an attack than Jessica13 had imagined. There were enough points of entry to make it a nightmare to defend the town itself and Hammerhand finally decided they would remove the fighting from the streets.

It was a wise decision, as there was too much risk that Athena would simply order her men to set fire to whatever they could reach during the battle.

Moving out of the town presented even more difficulties. With even three of their Knights away to defend the other town and the numbers that appeared to advance on them, they would be heavily outnumbered.

Hammerhand could hold the center of a line but he was vulnerable to being flanked. After discussion, they decided to find a ravine or small defile into which they could draw Athena's people and contain them. Hammerhand and the flawless efficiency of the Knights he commanded would be more than able to wear the enemy down until they were left with nothing and no one to fall back on.

That would only happen if they weren't flanked and surrounded, however. Still, this plan would mean they only needed to worry about rocket-powered mechs that would be able to break free and move over them to position themselves to attack their vulnerable points.

The forest around Auburn gave them the kind of cover that would help them to a degree, and a few dips in the landscape in the area would be the best places from which to defend the town.

Most of Jessica13's time was used to locate places where they could move easier and put barriers up that would keep all but the most agile or rocket-powered mechs controlled. Hedgehogs were placed all over the area to funnel any attack through the shallow ravine they would guide the enemy forces to.

A few might be able to get over them and a few others would be able to destroy the obstacles, but either necessity would take time and expose them to the kind of attacks the Knights were ordered to perform should anyone try to get around the funnel Hammerhand attempted to create.

The townsfolk were enthusiastic enough to find ways to help as well. A few had willingly learned, assisted by Tinker, how to operate the mechs of the three Lancers, whose pilots had volunteered to man those Athena's people had left as they knew their way around such volatile mechs. The townsfolk elected to join the combat effort in the safer mechs while the commandeered Cinders would be positioned in line with Hammerhand as they were useful to prevent the attacks of their similar counterparts.

She thought it was a little ironic that the biggest weakness that plagued Cinders was other Cinders since they were vulnerable from the same close distances they needed to be in for their attacks to do any damage.

They were interesting mechs, which required very interesting pilots. Not many Knights used them as their main mechs but there were those that knew how.

Surprisingly, a number of the local people also opted to join the battle lines as support, using the mechs they used in the field. It was a brave decision given that none of them had any battle experience, but they at least knew their mechs and should be able to adapt to the role demanded of them. They gathered around Tinker and listened attentively as he instructed them as best he could in the time they had.

It wasn't long before the sky above them began to darken, even though it was barely midday and should have been the brightest time of day. The clouds gathered like a dense blanket that blocked the light and made it difficult to see what was around them. Oddly enough, even with the clouds and the filters in her HUD, the glare was intense and it was difficult to look at the sky without shielding her eyes.

The balloons were still a fair distance away, but those who monitored the advancing mechs were quick to note that they pushed ahead of their airborne guides once they were within twenty klicks of Auburn. It wasn't long before Jessica13 could confirm that the vanguards had entered the forest and shortly after, they encountered the first barriers that had been set up.

It was interesting to watch them attempt to navigate through the obstacles that had been positioned in a tight enough pattern that any mech would need to sidle sideways to get through. Very few were actually built to move sideways and certainly none of the larger, combat-oriented ones. Those that could were the smaller, lighter versions that were invariably support and would not be able to mount an assault on their own.

For the moment, it appeared as though they would move into the funnel the Knights had built for them, but there was no guarantee that it would remain that way. Once the fighting started, things would get messy and Athena's fighters would inevitably take chances and try to push through the barriers.

To counter this, any Knights who could deal precise damage from a distance positioned themselves in the formation in such a way that they could focus on the barrier line. Until the combat became close-quarters and demanded their full attention, they would attempt to eliminate any who might try to sneak in behind their team.

At the front and center, predictably enough, Hammerhand stood his ground beside his hammer that he'd planted in the earth. He knelt for a moment—she assumed to say a word of private prayer—before he settled his gaze on the seemingly endless lines of Athena's men in mechs that marched inexorably forward.

He stood slowly, then turned to face the men and women who followed him and seemed to sense the growing unease in them. When he lifted his hammer to catch their attention, even the Auburn townsfolk focused on him with bated breath and waited for him to speak.

All those gathered need his words to revive the inspiration he'd given them now that they actually faced the invaders that had previously been a concept rather than a reality.

"Be not afraid." His first declaration resounded through the forest to the point where Athena's men could probably hear him too. "Freedom is your goal and fighting for it is noble. Know that those who stand with you will not falter and will not be afraid. Take heart, my warriors."

Jessica13's heart pounded loudly in her chest.

Hammerhand arced his hammer into the soil with a thunderous thud that shook the earth around him. "As long as the people do not care to exercise their freedom, those who wish to tyrannize will do so. Tyrants are active and ardent and will devote themselves to their cause in the name of any number of gods, religious or otherwise. They will readily place shackles upon sleeping men."

She thought she'd heard the words before, possibly in one of the instructional vids. They sounded vaguely familiar but for the life of her, she couldn't remember where she'd heard them.

Hammerhand looked at the townsfolk and nodded at a few more who had chosen to join the battle. Some had mechs that had been improved somewhat with weapons to make them useful in defending their current position since they weren't overly mobile. Others had no mechs but were ready to fight regardless. There was little they could do in actual combat between the heavy, powerful mechs, but they had a valuable role to play. A handful of them had put work into laying improvised mines and others had offered to sneak in with tools that would help to disable some mechs and weapons to kill the pilots.

They had finished those tasks and now gathered on the battlefield itself, grim but determined. It was very clear that they were afraid, but Auburn was their home. While fear was evident in their eyes, they stood their ground with clenched fists and set jaws.

"Auburn has slept long enough, collar-bound to the bed and left in a hellish nightmare," Hammerhand declared and cut the air around him with a sweeping gesture of his hand. "No more. You've broken the shackles of Lady Hoot. Now, break the backs of the oppressors. Sleep no longer but dream as waking men and women and see your dreams realized."

The roar from Knights and citizens alike was deafening as he raised his weapon and swung it again. His team beat a rhythm on their armor and the citizens joined in as well as they could as the first lines of the familiar-looking Lancers became clearly visible through the dense foliage. They felled trees as they advanced to create as much space to attack as possible, although they avoided the tactic of burning their way through.

Jessica13 could only imagine that it was because of the unpredictability of a forest fire that could as easily turn on them.

She joined the two Sherlocks who had positioned themselves at the back in marksmen roles and they raised their rifles, aimed quickly, and selected their targets. They were in a group commlink that would allow them to see which mech the others had highlighted as a target so there would be no wasted round between them. A good shooter only needed one shot to kill the pilot in a Lancer, and while the mech would still pose something of a threat, it would not be as effective as it was with a human to guide it.

There didn't appear to be any kind of caution or assessment on the part of Athena's men, who pushed forward almost as soon as they had a clear shot at the Knights. They allowed themselves no grace period to study their opponent and no sign that quarter would be asked or given.

Their purpose was to kill, burn, and destroy. Auburn, in their minds, would be another example of the power Athena wielded and a statement of what she was willing to do with that power.

Jessica13 took a deep breath to calm her suddenly frayed

nerves, looked down her scope to choose her target, and together with the other Knights, opened fire.

The front line of Lancers shuddered and stuttered in place when they suddenly lost the control of their pilots and the AIs began to take over. It looked like upgrades had been installed since it only took a few seconds to achieve full control and they simply continued their advance.

"Tinker, let the loose townsfolk know how to identify the mechs that have lost their pilots," she called over the comms. "They should be able to take control of them and attack Athena's people from within their own ranks."

"Loose townsfolk?" he asked.

"The ones who don't have any mechs," she clarified and selected another target quickly while she spoke. "If they plan to go in there, they should be able to deal with those that don't have living pilots easier than the ones that do, right?"

"That's a good point. I'll pass it on." He moved among the group of folks who waited for their chance to strike and issued instructions and advice for what to do. The AIs were likely programmed to take the orders of any pilot who accessed them since they did appear to have been manufactured en masse. She wondered if Athena's power and resources enabled her to manufacture mechs—something that had occurred to her when they faced the Golem—or had simply managed to acquire them in good condition.

Perhaps they had been abandoned in the manufacturing facilities in the Cities-That-Were and she had been lucky or clever enough to find them. Irritated by the distraction, she pushed the thought aside. Irrespective of where they came from, their uniformity and basic design made them simple and easy to operate so those who were crammed inside needed as little training as possible.

Hammerhand threw his shield up to block an incoming volley from the line of Athena's Lancers that surged forward. Even those without pilots continued the charge since it was a simple enough task, although the fire from them was slower than it should have been.

While not as effective as she would have liked, she and her fellow sharp-shooters had made something of a difference anyway. Jessica13 grimaced when her thoughts led her toward an image of how the men inside were skewered by the hellebore rounds as well as whatever pieces of armor it cut through to reach them. It wasn't pleasant to imagine them tearing through the pilot and likely causing damage to the controls as well.

To balance this, she reminded herself of the nature of Athena's followers. They were the kind who would tattoo their leader's sigil onto their skin and when presented with the choice between living and dying, chose dying for the woman. It would have been nice to leave them alive, but it wasn't an option. They needed quick results since the battle lines had already begun to close.

Hammerhand's shield dropped for a moment, which was well-timed as the Raptor behind it had already launched a volley of missiles toward the enemy's front lines. The rockets tilted downward, however, and didn't impact the vanguard but rather showered the mechs behind them with as much damage as possible. A handful of Lancers dropped immediately, quickly disabled, while a few others fell and were slow to climb to their feet again.

More managed to get through, though, and some even trampled their fallen comrades to do so. Jessica13 and the two Sherlocks responded with alacrity to target the few that were ahead and eliminated the pilots with pinpoint accuracy. The enemy retaliated with a combined volley seconds before Hammerhand raised his shield again. He leaned forward and buried the barrier almost a full meter into the ground in anticipation of the press that was to come.

The clash was audible when two Lancers drove into his shield. The electric charge to maintain it had to be immense but he stood his ground and refused to allow any of those he resisted to pass.

A few managed to skirt the shield but were faced with the sudden challenge of the three Knights ranged behind their leader, who ached for a fight, and the enemy were quickly cut down.

With a bellowed roar, Hammerhand thrust his barrier forward and shoved the mechs back a few steps before he dropped his defense. Once again, the timing was perfect as the Raptor dispatched another battery of rockets. This time, they struck the mechs that led the assault and delivered significant damage to their ranks.

Those that survived the onslaught by using their own comrades and shields were quick to look up when a heavy hammer suddenly ignited from the back. It swung into a violent descent with a ground-shaking boom to crush one of them and destabilize one on each side of the target.

The shield came up again quickly. The Lancers weren't deterred by their sudden losses and instead, seemed to have been whipped into a frenzied blood-lust. They appeared all too happy to barrel into the teeth of the defense the Knights and Auburn citizens had established.

A crack of an explosion suddenly drew Jessica13's attention away from the center of the battle and she turned swiftly. A handful of Athena's mechs at the rear and some distance away from the actual engagement had likely been ordered to find some kind of way around the funnel. A couple of Watsons had managed to get around the first line of hedgehogs and began to make their way to the second.

One of them quickly ran into the makeshift mines that had been set up for such an eventuality. The mech itself wasn't destroyed but most of its left leg lay near it in a smoking mess. The pilot appeared to be dead or at least unconscious from the way the mech wobbled uncertainly on one leg before it finally sprawled and tripped another mine.

This time, the blast shredded the cockpit and left it mostly in pieces. There probably wasn't enough of it left for repairs and certainly not enough for anyone to take control. They would be lucky if they could pick up scrap pieces at the end of the day.

The other Watson appeared to try to pull away and retreat from the perceived minefield it had entered. There was little the Knights could do as they were still engaged with Athena's men and had to focus their attention on the group that attacked head-on.

Jessica13 swung her rifle and acquired her new target as he tried to circle the minefield. The Watson was likely equipped with the kind of sensors that would be able to pick up the locations of the mines it attempted to avoid but unlike the Lancers, the AI that would work the Watsons would be less intelligent than those that could operate a combat mech in battle. They wouldn't need that kind of technology.

She positioned her rifle and looked down the scope, located the cockpit fairly easily, and pulled the trigger. The round drilled through the armor like it was paper and the mech suddenly froze in place and settled into standby mode, possibly waiting for some kind of input from the pilot to allow the AI to take the controls.

"Tinker, there's a disabled Watson out in the minefield if you want to send someone over to take it," she called over the comms and immediately had his attention.

"Will do," he replied. "And if you have helping in mind, the mechs at the front lines need to be resupplied."

"I'm on it," she shouted. "Well, Mini, it's time to get this Minato to do what she was designed to do."

"Do you think the mech identifies as female?" Mini asked and settled it onto all fours to increase speed to reach the place where they had stored most of their ammunition.

"I don't think it's sentient enough," she responded. "Although all the pilots I knew thought of their mechs as ladies. I think it's some kind of tradition from before in the Cities-That-Were."

She held on tightly as Mini rushed to the ammo. It looked like a couple of the Auburn mechs that had been designated for support were already making bulletfoot runs.

Jessica13 paused and thought about what they could do next since she would not be able to carry the rifle and the crates on her back at the same time while running on all fours.

"What are you thinking?" Mini asked as they pulled to a halt.

"I wonder if we should sacrifice speed in favor of being able to handle the rifle while we deliver," she told him and moved them closer to the mechs that picked up the ammo crates the combat mechs were waiting for.

"I would suggest being armed as much as possible," he agreed. "Even in close quarters, the rifle can be used to help you to push into places other mechs might not be able to reach."

She nodded, decided to keep the rifle, and used her free

hand to quickly load the mag clamp on her back with a couple of the rocket crates the Raptor would be able to use. It was clear that it would be the basis for their current defense, but it wouldn't be much good to anyone if it had no rockets to fire when Hammerhand dropped his shield.

"Let's go," Mini said.

"Why don't you take the controls?" She highlighted the Raptor for him to take them to.

"What will you do?"

"Well, all things considered, I think we might want to keep a weapon at the ready to hold any potential enemies at bay, yes?"

"That does make sense, yes," he replied, took over the mech's legs and balancing systems, and left her control on the arms intact to allow her to maintain a ready defense against possible action by the enemy.

The earth shuddered when Hammerhand brought his hammer down once more to keep the Lancers at bay, although a handful of them was able to slip around before the shield came up again. The repetitive chatter of their assault rifles attempted to find any weak place on the Excalibur that they might be able to exploit.

She didn't think it was a tactically sound choice since the Raptor actually inflicted the most damage to them while they attempted to push the Knights' leader back and away. He was essentially the distraction while the others were responsible for the most devastating strikes.

Maybe they simply had no other option. The cornerstones of the Knights' defense were the Raptor and the shield, but there would be a couple more surprises in store for them if they made it through the first line of defense.

Hammerhand liked to say he would hope for the best and

plan for the worst, and they had gone through an intense few stages of planning for the attack they knew was coming.

Jessica13 raised her rifle and aimed down the sights while Mini moved them quickly and erratically. He seemed to have a way to calculate the rounds that might be fired at them and avoid those that would be able to punch through the Minato's armor.

It would take a fair amount of power to hit them at precisely the right angle, and the AI used all his algorithms that would keep them safe while they raced into the heart of the battle.

A handful of rounds did manage to catch their armor but ricocheted away. There was the chance that they would strike someone else, but they would be left deformed after they bounced off the Minato and would lose most of their piercing power. While any of them might be lucky, the chances were, with the reduced speed and piercing power, they wouldn't actually do much damage.

Mini kept them moving at a steady pace but not in a direct trajectory that would take them directly into the firing line. While the intention to use the weapon in tandem with their support function was a good one, she missed her first few shots as she tried to keep herself stable inside the mech.

"Would you like me to take over the shooting capabilities as well?" Mini asked and it sounded like he was a little sarcastic.

"Do you think you can keep us steady?" She growled her irritation and managed not to snap at the AI as they traversed the battlefield. Athena's warriors appeared to have determined the timing the Knights used and a couple of the larger, turret-based mechs began to line up at the rear. From this position, they coordinated their flurries of rockets perfectly to take advantage of the moments when Hammerhand's shield was down.

"I thought you might want to avoid being shot as a priority," Mini replied.

"Are you being sarcastic with me?" she demanded, her good intentions forgotten. "Right now? Really?"

"My apologies. I thought you might want some humor to defuse the tension of our current situation," he replied. "That can be postponed if preferred."

She felt a little bad about telling him to not engage his human-understanding software since it was exactly what made him such a unique AI. But honestly, there were times for experimental study and times for him to get his combat subroutines up and running.

Jessica13 chose to simply not reply and focused to place her shots a little more carefully. The rifle had a fifteen-round mag that took about three seconds to reload and a few quick alterations to the Minato allowed her to carry five more mags that were automatically reloaded from their slot in the arm.

It seemed she'd subconsciously adjusted to Mini's erratic movements as she fired a couple of rounds that both found their targets. She wasn't able to see if they managed to do any significant damage as Hammerhand's shield was restored and the Knights surged to attack the few of Athena's forces that had managed to get through. Their numbers increased now that they had improved their timing, and they would begin to push in harder.

It wouldn't be long before the defenders would have to begin a retreat from their current position and fall back to the secondary defense points. She didn't have much personal experience but if any of her somewhat random reading on how battle structures worked could be relied on, retreats were bound to be the point in battles where the most could go wrong. Positions needed to be adjusted effectively so those who retreated could be covered by people who were hopefully already in position.

Hammerhand would be the last one to withdraw, of course. That was the job he had taken by assuming the forward position and there was no indication from the man that he was anything other than ready for it. Jessica13 wouldn't tell him about the dangers, obviously, since he probably knew them better than she did, but she would try to help and cover him if she needed to.

She moved in beside the Raptor while Mini kept them low so they wouldn't be accidentally targeted by one of the enemy. Quickly, she inserted the new rockets into the slot that would take them into the firing mechanism of the mech.

A quick ping from the pilot expressed his thanks as he fired another volley.

Hammerhand's shield was down, and the rockets turned five of the mechs that attempted to pass him into scrap metal. She counted at least a dozen coming through, however. Most of them were Lancers, but two Cinders followed quickly and moved uncharacteristically subtly to avoid being targeted first.

Their ploy seemed to work. Most of the shooting was directed at the Lancers, which left the two Cinders unhindered. They took advantage of their position near Hammerhand's ankles to fire a couple of flechettes into the legs of the massive Excalibur, hoping to find a weakness they could exploit.

There was none, and they immediately proceeded to spark their throwers.

"We need to help him!" she shouted, not sure who would

be able to hear her over the cacophony of the battle around them. She couldn't even hear herself, and the Knights were busy holding the Lancers back while the flames crept up to Hammerhand's knees.

"Shit." She hissed her frustration. Mini had already anticipated her needs and quickly shifted onto all fours as she slapped the rifle onto her back again.

Jessica13 knew the AI would take control and put them in motion now, and all she could really do was brace herself since the damn inertia dampeners were still out of sync with the rest of the mech.

The Minato moved smoothly and sidled around the combat to keep them out of it. They evaded the Lancers that began to push toward the Raptor in an attempt to prevent it from being able to eliminate the front ranks that drove forward.

Mini took them quickly to the other side. Hammerhand was intent on keeping the shield up and pushing back despite the fact that he was attacked from below. None of the other Knights were able to reach him to help.

Except her, she reminded herself. It was odd how she still had difficulty thinking of herself as one of the Knights.

"Do you have any idea what we can do against two Cinder mechs?" the AI asked as they came out of Bulletfoot mode.

"Keep us moving," she said.

"I can't help but note that you haven't answered the question," he persisted.

She didn't know what she would do, which was why she hadn't answered the question, but she did have a basic idea of how to destroy the mechs. The only issue was that if she blew them up so close to Hammerhand's position, she wouldn't be able to contain it. They might cause damage to the Excalibur that they hadn't been able to accomplish in their attack.

"We'll have to be creative," Jessica13 said, yanked her rifle clear of the mag clamp on her back, and looked around for an opening for her to shoot. Hammerhand moved his feet in an effort to knock the Cinders away, which didn't do any damage. It was, however, enough to keep them occupied and they barely noticed her.

She pulled her grappler up, kept it connected to the dart, and pulled the trigger to fire it quickly while still on the move.

The dart embedded itself in the back of one of the Cinders' shoulders and she braced as the retractor began to pull. The first tug drew her closer instead of hauling the mech away, but when she leaned back and put the full weight of the Minato behind it, the Cinder finally began to tip and lost its balance while the AI inside tried to compensate. There wasn't much it could do, however, and she held her breath until it finally toppled heavily onto its back.

The other Cinder turned to see what had happened and swung the thrower and the flechette gun to aim at her while it maintained the same position. Its feet were set for maximum balance against the power of the weapons it fired.

"Engaging evasive maneuvers," Mini announced and shifted rapidly in place. The first round of flechettes hammered into the side of the Minato. None of them pierced the armor but a few were embedded and pushed Mini's balance off a little until he managed to engage the rest of the mech. A tongue of flame lashed out at them as he crouched but she could still feel the heat of it, even from inside.

It was instinct more than anything that made her pull the trigger on her rifle and she was almost surprised by the kick as the round fired. Pure luck or her recently discovered instinct delivered a round inside the Cinder's armor, where it caught one of the large gas tanks on its back.

A second ticked by as a series of chain reactions sparked after the round broke the containment of the fuel for the thrower. Then, in a bright flash of white light, it erupted across the mech and the force hurled Jessica13 onto her back.

"Shit!" she shouted and struggled to pull the Minato onto its feet.

The Excalibur reacted quickly to the sudden heat around it and released a cloud of steam from its cooling vents. The explosion did far more damage than Jessica13 had thought it would, especially to the fallen Cinder, and while the armor kept Hammerhand mostly intact, there appeared to be enough damage for him to finally have to address it. Sections of his armor were still ablaze, even with the steam rushing around it.

She managed to stand although she still struggled some-what with the off-kilter balancing systems, disengaged the air gun from the dart, and used the blasts to put the fire on Hammerhand's armor out.

It worked, even though she needed to try it a couple of times before the flames around his legs and ankles were finally extinguished, although it had spread slightly into the trees and shrubbery around them.

"Are you all right?" she asked over the comms. "I don't see much external damage from here, but you might want to run some diagnostics."

A moment of silence followed over the line.

"I have some heating problems," Hammerhand finally answered and sounded strained. "The shield won't hold like this for much longer. We need to get back to the secondary position. Prepare to fall back. Repeat, all Knights, prepare to fall back."

Jessica13 didn't want to leave the man alone but it was an order. She could see that Athena's fighters had been dealt with and the Knights hastily gathered what could be snatched in an instant before the Raptor uprooted from its defensive position and began to move back.

"Now, Jessie!" Hammerhand roared and startled her into action. She gave the nearby fires another hasty blast of air before she jogged away to join the others.

CHAPTER FOURTEEN

As she had anticipated, Hammerhand was the last to withdraw. His shield was overheating and there was more internal damage than she had actually realized, which meant he suddenly struggled to hold Athena's men back. A few of them began to attack the hedgehogs that protected his flanks rather than the shield itself. He held his position for as long as he dared before he dropped the shield and pulled away.

He wasn't about to retreat without a parting gift, however. A small group of invaders rushed forward, expecting some kind of victory, but the Excalibur stopped suddenly and drew all eyes to the hammer that arced lethally from above. Two of the Lancers weren't able to pull away when the others scrambled to do so.

They were conveniently positioned one directly behind one another and the weapon crushed them both with ease to leave nothing but scrap metal where they had stood.

Thin trails of pale white smoke issued when the Raptor launched a series of rockets once it was set up again for combat. The small group of Knights stood around it for protection. The two long-distance shooters from the Knights opened fire. It didn't take much to acquire a good target as Athena's men were thoroughly bunched in the confined space.

The hope had been that they could plug the hole with broken mechs, but while the strategy was sound, it made no allowance for the determination of the enemy. They simply plowed through and over the fallen and while their passage was temporarily slowed, it wasn't delayed sufficiently. Jessica13 fell back and reloaded her rifle quickly before she did what she could to hinder them a little more.

As had been the case with the earlier battle, the Raptor dealt most of the damage and fired volley after volley of rockets to destroy as many of the mechs that surged toward them as possible.

Once the enemy were out of the funnel, however, it became more and more difficult to target them in larger numbers. They were able to spread out and take proper combat positions to advance on the town of Auburn.

Jessica13 glanced briefly at the Knights, who stood their ground despite the fact that they were outnumbered. It seemed almost ludicrous that they could stand and wait so calmly for their attackers. That kind of courage wouldn't be found anywhere else, especially since they rallied in defense of someone else's home.

She had no idea what would happen to them, but at least they were fighting for something that mattered.

Their courage helped to quell her fear as she grasped the weapon in her hand and tried to steel herself against the sight of the advancing army. Rather than dwell on the overwhelming odds, she focused on identifying the more vulnerable mechs and continued to fire as many rounds as she could to keep up with the advance of their attackers.

"You have to be careful or you'll run out of bullets," Mini pointed out.

"What the hell else would you have me do?" she snapped.

"Maybe play the role this mech was meant to," the AI suggested.

She sighed because she knew he was right but didn't want to admit it as she peeled away from the Knight's line and one of the Sherlocks stepped into the hole she left behind. The enlisted support mechs worked to keep the combat mechs around them supplied, and Jessica13 was surprised to see that large groups of the Auburn townsfolk did the same. A couple had even taken control of any enemy mechs they could once the pilots were killed and had prepared for combat.

The enemy Lancers closed the distance quickly and opened fire both on the Knights and the buildings around them. It appeared that they wanted to cause as much damage and destruction as possible and pushed forward so violently that the fighting devolved into something of a perverse melee.

Hammerhand's shield came up here or there to intercept the heavier attacks, but he was soon involved in the battle. He took a step away from the Knights to gain the space he needed to allow him to swing his hammer without fear of catching any of his people.

The invaders took heavy losses but continued relentlessly and attacked with a kind of recklessness that showed a determination for victory that was no doubt motivated by thoughts of Athena's wrath and displeasure should they fail.

They outnumbered the Knights significantly and even with the losses, there were simply too many of them.

Jessica13 did as Mini suggested. Her instincts told her to be in the middle of the fighting to help where she could, but Windchime's warnings still rang in her head. If she charged head-first into a fight like this, they would literally be torn to pieces.

No, the best she could do was let them disregard her as a support mech for the moment, take her shots when she could, and always stay on the move to help others to maintain their higher rate of firepower.

It was painful to watch, especially when the Lancers attempted to swarm onto the Raptor. The rockets continued to fire, found their targets, and annihilated them, but they were close enough to climb without being in range of the missiles.

A Predator stepped among them and she gasped, certain that it was one of Athena's that had come to finish what the enemy mechs had started with its chainsword. The attacking mechs obviously thought the same, as they stepped back to give it space to work. Instead, however, it swung the weapon at the closest Lancer, thrust the blade into the cockpit, and carved through the armor until she could hear the screams from inside. The weapon found the pilot and was suddenly covered in red.

Her initial fear dissolved into a slightly hysterical laugh when she realized that the Predator was piloted by what was most likely an Auburn resident. The mech had obviously been one of those retrieved during the battle and thankfully, was still in good enough condition to do its lethal work.

It swung toward the next Lancer and one of the Cinders moved alongside. Between them, they managed to deliver a concerted attack that either destroyed the enemy or drove them back and away from the Raptor, which had barely noticed the mayhem and its close call.

"Shit!" she shouted with a brief surge of exultation and used the moment of confusion to fire at the scattered invaders. She managed to land a couple of effective shots and kill two of the pilots and the mechs jerked and staggered as the AIs tried to take control.

A small group of townsfolk raced from one of the nearby buildings and she gaped as they ducked and dodged toward the mechs she had partially disabled. Their appearance was both sudden and unexpected as she would have thought that any that had elected not to join the battle initially would be hunkered in the assumed protection of their homes.

It was the kind of action that usually went unnoticed in a fight like this, where most of the attention was drawn to the larger mechs shooting at each other and tiny, squishy humans who weren't in mechs were mostly ignored. The assumption was that they would be killed by stray fire or explosions that hurled shrapnel everywhere and so needed no real attention.

While that was a real danger, these people seemed not to care. With no apparent thought to the danger they might be in, they scrambled hastily onto the mechs, worked together to pry them open, and climbed inside before they closed it again.

The mech fell silent and didn't move at all now, despite having a new pilot. Unfortunately, Jessica13 couldn't remain where she was to watch the saga unfold and turned her attention to the battle around her. Maybe they were trying to work out how to operate it or possibly find a way to remove the dead body. Sure enough, when she turned once again to glance hastily in that direction, the hatch opened and a mangled corpse was shoved out.

She smiled as she continued to move through the battle-field to deliver ammo and supplies to those Knights who called for it. The unusual incident remained in her mind, though, and she realized that a number of other mechs merely stood unmoving while the combat ebbed and flowed around them. She had claimed a few of them and others showed signs that the pilot had been killed either through a hard external impact or by a bullet from another long-distance shooter.

But instead of an AI having taken control where the pilot was no longer capable of it, they remained absolutely still like they were powered down. She wondered how many of them had an Auburn pilot inside.

"Tinker, I think something's happening," she said over the comms as she collected ammo from his stockpile.

"Well, if you haven't noticed yet, lassie, we're in the middle of a fucking battle!" the man shouted.

"No, I've seen the locals taking over the mechs I and others have left without a pilot," she said, picked up a couple of the crates, and put them on the mag clamp on her back. "They're climbing into the mechs and not doing anything with them."

He paused in his work to look at her. "Maybe they simply don't know how?"

"But then why did they climb in at all?"

It seemed impossible for a mech to look confused, but Tinker's did for a moment before it shrugged its shoulders exaggeratedly. "There's no time to think about that. We need to keep fighting. I think the folks out in the eastern quadrant are in the most need. Get these rounds to them quickly."

She nodded and remained on two feet for the moment since it allowed her to fire from her rifle if she had the opportunity and on occasion, even use her grappler to bring a couple of the unsuspecting Lancers down.

Mini was still able to move them far more quickly than any other bulletfoot would be able to and she managed to eliminate a few targets she felt they could get away with. The Cinders that had begun to stream into the town were the easiest since most of their fuel lines were at least partially exposed and Mini could easily highlight the weak points for her to fire into.

Those tended to explode in a bright fireball, but some had only their pilots killed. Every time the latter occurred, people rushed in to remove the dead pilot and climb in.

Jessica13 had no idea what they were doing, but she was curious to see if they could make some difference. Even moving the mechs out of the way of combat would be a massive help.

Sending her into the eastern quadrant was a good suggestion, she realized, as it became apparent that this was the area in which most of their opponents now focused their attacks, thanks to Hammerhand's presence. He still used his rocket-powered hammer to deal all kinds of damage with every swing. Tinker had devoted himself to hasty repairs to the Excalibur so the Knights' leader was once again able to bring his shield up when needed without fear that it would fail, although it might only be temporary. She had no idea what the full extent of the damage had been.

This was the first time she'd seen Hammerhand actually fight alone rather than as a part of a coordinated formation. There were other Knights around him, of course, and they worked well in tandem to avoid being crushed themselves. A couple of Lancers stood beside him, as well as Taylor's Sherlock with a Watson in support.

Having a Watson around always tended to keep their attackers honest, she'd learned as she rushed in with the ammo they needed.

She pulled one of the crates from her back and made sure not to fully turn off the mag clamp to keep the second crate in place. The Minato bounded and darted through the battle and a couple of rounds dinged off their armor as Mini continued with the evasion algorithm he had worked out.

Once she was close enough, she pinged one of the Lancers on the comms to catch his attention before she threw the crate over the ten meters or so between them.

He caught it deftly and his AI loaded the ammo quickly as the other called for a reload as well. She moved over to the man and almost froze when she realized that Athena's men had begun to renew their assault. They filled the narrow street they were in and rushed forward.

"There are so many of them," Jessica13 muttered and shivered, although that could have been from the sweat that slowly seeped into her clothes as the heat of the mech began to affect her body. Unfortunately, she couldn't stop yet. They were a long way from victory.

Movement at the top of a building caught her attention and she turned her rifle to see if someone had perhaps thought to try to attack from above. Instead, all she could see were the residents.

Curious, she zoomed in and frowned as she tried to identify a heavy mechanism that they moved across the flat roof. It looked like a fuel tank mounted on wheels, and they pushed it across the top of the building to the side where Athena's forces had regrouped and now drove forward into a concerted assault.

Once the townsfolk reached the correct position, a mechanism lifted the tank, tilted it over the edge, and hurled it over the mechs that advanced on the Knights.

"Shield!" Jessica13 shouted to Hammerhand as she realized what was happening a moment before the tank fell free of the building.

The man in the Excalibur didn't question her call and

hastily brought the shield up as the other knights hunkered behind it.

The tank impacted the street and the contents suddenly ignited and exploded powerfully in bright orange flame that spread swiftly to envelop Athena's men in a bright, hot blaze. They seemed unaffected at first until the fire grew in intensity. A couple of Cinders couldn't resist the heat and their eruption annihilated a few others. Those who managed to survive the blast didn't last long as their mechs were engulfed in flames.

While the fire wouldn't reach inside a mech, the air filters would quickly run out of oxygen and the heat would cook whatever was inside in minutes.

In that instant—as if dropping the jellified fuel from one of the roofs was some kind of signal—those mechs that now had Auburn residents as pilots suddenly came to life. They were a little uncoordinated at first, but once the AIs that were supposed to operate them kicked in, they began to move a little faster.

Astonished, Jessica13 could only stare. There were almost fifty, she thought, but made no real effort to count them as they began to attack Athena's forces. The enemy was caught entirely unawares as they hadn't suspected that the mechs of their fallen comrades would turn against them.

The numbers added so suddenly to the defense made Athena's men falter, especially as these new mechs carried their own colors. Confusion in the ranks allowed the Knights that had virtually been pinned down to rally, rise up, and retaliate.

It took a while for the tide to turn fully as even with the added mechs on their side, the Knights needed to find a way to identify which were their allies. The enemy were rapidly outnumbered when other captured mechs joined the ranks and they settled into an organized formation that allowed them to drive forward together. Hammerhand took the lead and the defenders gradually edged the invaders out of the town and engaged them in the open fields outside Auburn.

Some very soon realized that they would lose this particular battle and slunk into the woods behind them. They would no doubt try to regroup and meet with whatever was left of Athena's troops to attack again.

Those who remained were quickly defeated by the now bold townsfolk. Jessica13 and the two other sharpshooters killed the pilots they could while Hammerhand crushed those that were left.

It seemed almost surreal when combat ceased. There were still a few pops and explosions in the distance, evidence of smaller skirmishes to weed the last of Athena's men out, but for the moment, it appeared that victory was theirs.

There were no cheers or celebrations, however. It almost felt disrespectful to stand where hundreds had been killed and cheer. Besides, there was no sense of finality.

While no one actually voiced it, there was a pervasive awareness among all of them that Athena herself hadn't been present at the battle, which meant that more would come. All they could do was pull back, regroup, replenish, and prepare for the next wave, whenever that was.

Hammerhand immediately took control and issued orders. A few were sent into the hills to keep an eye out for any more approaching mechs. Others were directed to help the people of Auburn repair the damage that had been done to their town, and the remainder were given the task of clearing the battlefield of any loot that could be gleaned from those who had fallen.

Jessica13 looked at the sky when the clouds above them began to release rain that fell steadily and extinguished the fires around the town. A few of the Auburn folk cheered briefly for the welcome downpour, but the sight of the balloons that continued to approach diminished their enthusiasm fairly quickly.

She scowled at them and shook her head at the flickers of lightning that sliced through the clouds. A few of them arced and sizzled into the ground below. It seemed almost impossible to contemplate, but if Athena had some way to control the lightning over them or even to weaponize it, they needed to be prepared for that eventuality as well. Tinker hadn't seemed convinced that it was possible and she'd agreed with him, but instinct told her that this new threat was real despite how impossible it seemed

"What are you thinking?" Mini asked.

Trapped in her thoughts for a moment, she didn't reply and instead, picked her rifle up and moved quickly to where their leader issued orders to those who still waited for tasks to be assigned to them.

"Hammerhand," she called over the commlink and drew his attention. He turned to look at her.

"What's the problem, Jessie?"

"It's not a problem, not yet anyway," she replied and pointed at the sky. "Do you think Athena will be able to create or harness the lightning in those clouds to strike us?"

He studied the clouds for a long moment before he turned to where Tinker stood beside him in his patchwork mech.

"I suppose," the older man replied, pushed his head out from inside his mech, and scowled when water landed in his eyes. "I didn't think so earlier, but the way that lightning's behaving…well, I'm inclined to change my mind now. And if she can do that, it will be a problem."

"I hope that problem has a solution," Hammerhand said and turned quickly to her.

"They dealt with lightning problems in Sanctuary by putting grounding rods at the top of the mountain. The rods made sure the electric charge didn't strike anything but dirt," Jessica13 said. "I could take those townsfolk who aren't already working to start putting those up around town on top of buildings and the like. They should keep them from being able to hit us."

Hammerhand turned to Tinker to confer with the man in private for a few moments before he faced her again. "Do it. Take what materials you need and get it done. We can't worry about an attack from the sky as well as the ground."

CHAPTER FIFTEEN

Under any other circumstances, Jessica13 would have thought an entire town working together to bring life to an idea she had based on what had worked in her own past was completely insane. She wasn't used to people actually listening to her or following her advice since her role tended to have her taking orders and making them happen using her expertise instead.

These were different circumstances, however. The knowledge of what was coming and the results of what had happened during the battle they had all fought were too fresh in their minds. Merely the thought that more was on its way was enough to spur them into the kind of action that accomplished things, no matter who it was who gave the orders.

Hundreds of people coming to watch as she pulled together the pieces she needed to build the lightning rods simply felt natural. There was no power to it in her mind, only the knowledge that the rain that fell was a small indication of what would happen once those balloons reached them.

The lightning crackled across the sky, a strong enough

incentive to unify the townsfolk in the task to rob the fallen mechs of the copper cables, strip them, and mount them on improvised towers across the town. It wasn't long before even the Knights helped as well and took apart the pieces they could use to mount the lightning rods securely on the rooftops.

Athena was coming, if not in person then at least in the form of her followers, and that meant they needed to be prepared for every eventuality.

The rain quickly transformed most of the ground to mud, which made it difficult to slog through it while carrying heavy chunks of metal but none of them lacked incentive. No one wanted to be caught by lightning while having to deal with the next wave of attacks.

They covered most of the town in an impressively short time thanks to the number of people who had committed to the project. The section farthest from where the battle had ended was left for last since it took longer to carry all the parts and pieces required through the mud and the rain.

"There's a visual!" a man shouted. She assumed it was one of those who had been sent to work as scouts and wondered why the comms crackled with interference.

"Visual of what?" Jessica13 asked.

"Maybe you should guess?" Mini retorted.

She scowled and could have sworn she heard a sarcastic undertone in the AI's voice. When she thought about it, though, there was nothing in his programming that suggested he was treating her sarcastically. She would have to run a few diagnostics to get a better idea of it later.

For the moment, however, they needed to deal with whatever it was that approached.

The Knights, now joined by those who had piloted the

fallen mechs, began to gather toward the edge of town on the side where the balloons advanced and loomed ominously overhead.

"Is it them?" she asked and looked at her teammates.

"Who the fuck else would it be?" one of the Knights snapped.

Jessica13 knew better than to take what the man said personally. They were all under a great deal of stress, after all.

She turned to the townsfolk who stood and stared at the balloons that continued their slow yet inexorable journey toward Auburn.

"Get those generators running," she said. "Now!"

They had almost seemed in a trance until she snapped the last word and caught their attention firmly. She instructed them to head to the section of town where a large number of the power cores from the crushed mechs had been gathered and connected to the entire network of grounding towers they had erected.

It had been an idea from one of the locals, and she had agreed without hesitation. She had actually been surprised by their inventiveness, and the idea to store the grounded electricity from the lightning had been fairly brilliant and easy to incorporate. Given that they didn't know what to do with the stored electricity, she hadn't been sure about dedicating any resources to it but they would have to survive after this and having fully charged power cells would always be useful.

There would be time enough later to find a use for it once they had all survived Athena's attacks.

The generators they would turn on would set up the capacitors, which would make sure the power surges didn't short any of the cells out. Working on that would be enough to keep the townsfolk busy for the moment while the Knights determined what kind of attack they would face.

They had needed to abandon the outer defenses since they would be too far away from the rods and too close to the trees, which could end up destroying the mechs if they were struck by lightning. Unfortunately, this meant they would have to do any fighting that was necessary within the town itself. Hammerhand hadn't liked the idea, but at least the defenses would slow any ground invasion.

Jessica13 scowled as the lead balloon moved slowly across the final distance and entered the airspace of the town below. With it this close now, she could see it had a prow at the front with a crude owl carved into some kind of metal to display Athena's sigil proudly. None of the others had it, but even one seemed to be something of an announcement.

Obviously, it was intended to fill everyone who saw it with dread as they looked up and saw storm clouds, lightning, and her sigil watching over it all.

Lightning flickered through the clouds with new intensity and a few shafts even streaked toward them, caught the rods, and showered the ground around them with sparks.

Her fingers and muscles ached after all her effort and her entire body begged for some kind of rest before this next encounter. She knew that every other man and woman, Knight and civilian alike, felt the same way. They were all exhausted, drained, and on their last reserves, but none of them would simply lay down and die. They would fight to their last breath.

As Hammerhand moved in front of the group, they all felt the same dread and yet steady, firm attitude toward what approached. There was no need for heroic speeches this time. They knew what was coming and they knew what the likely end would be if they failed in their task. That was why they wouldn't fail.

"So it begins." His voice rumbled through their ranks as he raised his hammer and a cloud of steam erupted from his cooling vents. Lines of mechs were now visible as they moved through the trees and approached the line of hedgehogs that had managed to funnel the first wave into their kill zone.

It would still slow the bulk of their troops—and bulk did appear to be the best description for what advanced on the town—but a few lines appeared to approach the hedgehogs with no intention to find the easy way in.

Jessica13 looked down the scope of her rifle and scowled. They were mostly Predators and Balthazars that had been stripped to the bare minimum of parts to make them as light and mobile as possible for the attack. They would be able to advance much faster and ahead of the main force and already, the first few passed between the hedgehogs.

"Hold your fire," Hammerhand communicated to the Knights, who complied and held their fingers motionless on their triggers for the moment while the modified mechs marched toward the second line of hedgehogs.

Lightning crackled above them again and flared repeatedly as each bolt struck the towers instead of the ground. If there was any question as to whether it was directed intentionally at them, she only needed to look and see that none of the bolts touched the forest Athena's men pushed through.

A loud pop erupted as the first of the lighter mechs found the minefield that had been placed there earlier. It was no match even for the improvised explosive that had been set in its path and it fell in smoking pieces as the others came to a halt behind it. Surprisingly, it seemed the first wave hadn't communicated this the second, although common sense dictated that they should.

"Open fire," Hammerhand said, raised a hand, and gestured at the group that now attempted to find a way through the minefield.

Jessica13 and the Knights' two sharpshooters selected their targets and opened fire. There was no indication that the armor did anything to slow the hellebore rounds, and while the AIs were quick to take over, they were less careful to avoid the explosives that had been set out for them.

It took her a full minute and a handful of accurate shots to register the tactic they had quickly adopted. The men who piloted the mechs didn't want to be blown the hell up and neither did they want to run headlong into the rounds that eliminated them by the dozen. Those who were already dead, however, had no real use other than to clear a path through the explosives. It was both logical and inevitable, and all the Knights did was speed up the process.

The other defenders opened fire on the group that reached the clear path that had been made through the hedgehogs and pushed toward the town without delay. The lines were closing again, and she knew her role in it.

As much as she wanted to continue doing her part in the fighting, she knew her role as a bulletfoot was far more meaningful to the group as a whole. She wasn't in this for herself but was there to help others.

It was a difficult decision to come to but once made, it became easier to back away from the group that kept the lighter mechs at bay and she rushed to join the support team. The townsfolk in their commandeered mechs seemed to have settled into the role surprisingly well.

The lightning continued its staccato bursts with unnatural

regularity and each strike made the ground shudder with ear-shattering rumbles that could be felt even through the mech. Jessica13 scowled at the sky and wished the damn balloons were in range—although Athena had no doubt taken a ground attack into account. She pushed her frustration aside, grateful that they at least had protection in the form of the towers, and continued to move. There was a routine to her task that came easily, despite the challenges of having to carry the crates to the front where all the fighting took place and immediately return for more.

Trudging through the mud was slower than she was used to, but it at least appeared to slow the enemy mechs as well, which made them easier to target and eliminate or disable. A couple of Balthazars elevated to hover above the battlefield and fire on those below.

For the most part, she could tell that armor would be more relevant than mobility in a battle like this, and while they had the advantage of the Excalibur on their side, a few Guardians marched through the trees to join the front lines and their plasma rounds already impacted solidly with Hammerhand's shield.

Armor like that wouldn't be easy to pierce.

Jessica13 delivered the ammo she had collected and turned quickly to join the group that targeted the lighter mechs. These had finally navigated through the minefield and the hedgehogs and began to rush at the sharpshooters. The intention was clear, of course. Athena had likely noted the casualties that had been suffered thanks to them and had put the lighter mechs in place to engage them, keep them occupied, and kill them while the rest of the battle progressed without their help.

It was an excellent strategy, and there was little the

Knights could do to adjust for it. The Sherlocks moved quickly and maintained fire to slow their attackers, but it wasn't long before two Predators surged into their ranks with their chainswords ready to cut through the light armor and find the pilots beneath.

Jessica13 managed to shoot one before he could begin his assault and the mech suddenly slowed.

Surprisingly, a Watson lurched in front of the other and fired a series of electric filaments that quickly electrocuted it into submission. The wiring inside sizzled dramatically and left it a smoking husk that collapsed within moments.

The pilot of the Watson seemed almost surprised by the efficacy of its attack but hastily reloaded the filament shooter as it turned to find another target.

Lightning flashed suddenly and the booming roar of thunder reverberated across the battlefield. Jessica13 ducked and instinctively put her hands behind her neck.

When the flash faded and the roar moved away, a hasty check confirmed that she and the Minato were intact, although the light and sound filters still struggled to cope.

The Watson, however, had been flung aside by a bolt of lightning that blew its intended target to pieces. It was pure dumb luck that the enemy mech had surged forward and pushed the defender back to avoid its attack, effectively taking its place in the firing line. Only a few signs remained of the main chassis, and those she could identify were a smoking wreck, useless even as scrap metal.

"Shit!" Tinker shouted. "I thought that was supposed to be avoided with those towers that you put up."

That comment was directed at her, and Jessica13 turned to see why the towers now allowed bolts through. The cause was immediately apparent, and she couldn't believe she hadn't seen it before. A light emanated from the wiring that had been set up to connect the improvised towers and glowed bright white all the way down to the cores they had used to connect and ground them all.

It resembled a spider web stretched across the entire town and made it look like hundreds of different threads spread between them as arcs of electricity jumped from one wire to the other.

She wasn't sure what was happening, but it seemed like the power that was gathered by the towers somehow spread outward and fed into the rest of the wiring.

Her brain insisted it was impossible and yet, there it was, right in front of her. The whole town was illuminated by the power collected by what was supposed to attack them.

Either way, it seemed as though what was stored in the wiring directed itself back to the towers, which made them less viable to draw the lightning to them. A couple of bolts struck the ground as Hammerhand took advantage of a moment clear of fighting and looked at the balloons above him. They weren't as high as they had been earlier, and she wasn't sure if this was a good or a bad thing. Lower meant they might be within range, but it also meant they could have moved to be within range to attack.

The one in the lead was heavily armored, which accounted for the slow pace, but those that brought up the rear were less protected. She narrowed her eyes and focused, and was finally able to see a couple of weak places in the armor and even where the chambers themselves were exposed.

Hammerhand stared into the sky as a couple of bolts struck the Excalibur and made it shudder, but it looked like most of the energy was quickly transferred into the ground. Startled, she looked more closely and realized that he had pulled up a couple of grapplers on his right arm and aimed them skyward.

She realized that Tinker stood beside him and had worked to attach the weapons to his arm while the Knights' leader had defended them both. She doubted that raising his shield would have done much to suppress the high-energy attacks of the lightning and even though it looked like the suit was designed to transfer the energy into the ground as quickly as it struck, it was only a matter of time until a bolt burned something out and caused a short that impacted the rest of the mech.

The Knight continued to aim above his head while the mechanic worked frantically. It appeared as though he attempted to ground the Excalibur further to protect it from additional strikes as the first of the grapplers was launched. There was no cable attached to the dart, but the weapon fired quickly, soared above them, and pounded into the balloon that trailed far to the left.

The impact of the dart seemed to have no effect at first, but as the chamber ruptured, it began to lose altitude—slowly, at first, but it gained speed, drifting toward the ground, and dragged a couple of the others it was tethered to with it.

Hammerhand lowered his arm to let Tinker reload the darts since his mech appeared to have no reloading mechanism of its own. The two men seemed to work well together, and it was easy to discern that they had been forced to do so more than once in the past.

Jessica13 turned away suddenly as another flash seared into the ground, close enough to her that it made her sensors panic and throw red lights up as a warning before they settled. She blinked to ease a blind spot in her vision and focused on the area where the lightning had struck. Her heart sank and a sick feeling settled into her gut.

Tinker stumbled and finally fell on his back. Various sections of his mech were on fire. He was quick to eject once it was down and used an emergency booster to remove the cockpit from the chassis. It splattered through the mud and he climbed out, looking a little the worse for wear.

The most significant damage appeared to have been dealt to Hammerhand, however. The mech was frozen in place and she could only imagine that hundreds of malfunctions skittered through the mech's hardware and software as the man inside tried to cope with the damage the bolt had caused him.

After a few seconds of stillness, she noticed some movement. Not the kind that would come from the hydraulics of the massive mech but rather the result when gravity acted on it and tugged it almost in slow motion. In the next moment, it simply plummeted to land hard enough to make the earth shake beneath her feet.

Hammerhand, the invincible leader of the Knights Mechanica, was down.

For what seemed like forever, her brain seemed to freeze in a place where no thought was possible. The sight of the felled Excalibur made her feel numb somehow. It was impossible and yet she couldn't deny the evidence of her own eyes.

Jessica13 snapped out of her shocked immobility when one of the lightened Predators climbed onto the chest plate of the Excalibur and one of the Balthazars drifted down to land beside it. Together, they began to pry the armor open to gain access to the cockpit.

"Oh...fuck no." She growled an incoherent sound of quiet fury and raised her rifle.

"Jessica13, what are you doing?" Mini asked.

She didn't answer and simply strode over to where Hammerhand lay with the Predator already in her sights. With unnatural calm, she pulled the trigger and the shot hurled it clear of its perch.

The Balthazar turned, trained its twin assault rifles on her, and fired a few rounds before two of her shots drilled into the mech and ended its efforts. She took their place on top of the Excalibur, stood her ground, and glowered at their enemies that began to converge on them.

"Jessie," Hammerhand called over the comms, clearly strained, "what the fuck are you doing? Get the hell out of here!"

"You work on getting this fucking mech on its feet!" Jessica13 snapped. The fact that she had actually at cursed her commanding officer didn't even occur to her as she took calm, measured shots at the approaching forces. "Don't you worry about me."

"Jessie—"

"Was I fucking unclear?" she demanded. She intended to stand over him and protect him as long as he needed it and he would have no say in the matter until he could get his mech on his feet.

When he managed that, he could yell at her for disobeying a direct order. Not if. When.

She startled at an odd noise in the distance and turned her head toward the hills. The cloud parted a little to reveal a glimpse of the sun starting to set in the west and she frowned at the vivid image of mechs sky-lined in the distance but moving closer.

What sounded like a low, indistinct buzz grew louder as they approached and what she thought might be deep trombones announced their arrival.

"What is that?" Jessica13 asked but shook herself out of her stupor. She had to focus if she wanted to keep Hammerhand safe. While the enemy had, like her, been distracted, they had quickly recovered and now tried to take advantage of his fall and her divided concentration.

"Ride of the Valkyries by Richard Wagner," Mini replied.

"Who?"

"It was a song commonly used to indicate that the cavalry had arrived," the AI said and displayed an image of a long-haired woman riding on the back of a horse with wings.

"What cavalry?" she asked in bewilderment. No winged horses approached as far as she could see.

"One led by our friend Windchime."

Thankfully, her would-be attackers must have realized that the new arrivals might be cause for concern and were momentarily confused. They seemed a little confused as to whether they should continue their efforts to eliminate Hammerhand or regroup to meet what might be a new threat.

She used the opportunity to zoom into the mech that led the others. Sure enough, her teammate strode ahead as quickly as his mech would allow.

There was no mistaking the crazy-looking, four-armed machine of his.

CHAPTER SIXTEEN

Windchime marched at the head of the troop that hurried into the town to engage Athena's men who now quickly tried to form up again to repel this new and unexpected force. He had brought the two Knights he had taken with him to the neighboring town but had somehow acquired additional fighters.

Dozens of mechs flanked them and rushed into the fight with the same vigor as the Knights themselves. They were a patchwork force, put together hastily but surprisingly competently, no doubt the result of concerted effort to put as many of them in action in as short a time as possible.

Their leader was difficult to miss as he was the first to reach the line of Athena's men. His assault rifles spoke first and delivered a consistent barrage that forced the enemy back inch by inch before he finally attacked them with his blades. It looked like a whirlwind of vibroswords and each strike released a shower of sparks. They began to focus their attacks on him as he sliced into their ranks and almost completely ignored the group of mechs that assaulted them from the side.

The lines crashed together, and the surge of energy that rushed through the other members of the Knights Mechanica was almost visible. A feral kind of violence raced through their veins as their numbers were boosted by their returning comrades and what she could only guess were the members of the nearest town who were willing to help.

She raised her rifle and relished the surge of power in her veins as she continued to target those mechs that tried to attack the Excalibur while their comrades drew the attention of the defenders.

Finally, the massive mech's systems began to reboot and she turned as Tinker, still alive and well, scrambled up beside her.

"I'll take care of Hammerhand, lassie," the man shouted and immediately opened a couple of panels to help with the repairs. "You get on down there and help them in the battle. They need you."

With a nod, she clambered off to rejoin the combat and rush to the side of her comrades. With Hammerhand in Tinker's capable hands, she could fight alongside them while still running support.

One of the Balthazars turned and noticed her—and that she was alone and her teammates engaged in the battle. Almost lazily, it fired its assault rifle at her.

Jessica13 paused when she felt the pings as the rounds struck their armor and bounced away.

"Mini, I'll need a little help here," she called and struggled to keep the mech in motion.

"Understood," the AI said and immediately took control of the left arm and the grappler attached to it as reached the outer edge of the fight. They stayed away from the worst of it while he aimed the grappler at the Balthazar and, after a moment of swift calculation, fired it.

The dart with the cable attached flew quick and true and it planted itself firmly and remained rooted in the boot of the Balthazar.

"What the hell was that supposed to do?" she asked. The damage to the other mech was minimal and it continued to fire as if nothing had happened.

"One of the grounding towers is to the left there," Mini replied. "Run in and I'll release the cable into it."

It was risky as she could see the bolts of electricity still buzzing from the pole although it was connected to the rest of the spiderweb network, Still, with Mini manning and timing the grappler, she was more or less confident of success.

If not, she would have to deal with a similar amount of power entering her mech as had gone into Hammerhand's and with considerably less protection.

She turned and dragged the Balthazar, still in mid-air, toward the tower. At what seemed like the final second, the cable came free with a loud twang and whipped forward to wind itself around the base of the tower.

The reaction was less explosive than she thought it would be, but the rockets on the Balthazar instantly cut out, as did the rest of the movement, and all it could do was fly into one of the nearby buildings with a significant thump.

"Well played," Jessica13 conceded.

"Your compliment is noted and appreciated," the AI replied.

It was easy enough to quickly reload another dart into the grappler as Windchime came over to where she stood.

"Good afternoon there, Jessie," he said over comms and laughed.

"You have no idea how good it is to see your face again, Windchime," she replied with a broad smile. "Well, not your face, but you know what I mean."

"I do, and I have to say, it's good to see you alive and well too," he said. "I see you're still not taking my advice to stay far away from the fight."

"It's against every fiber in my being," she tried to explain but he raised a hand.

"Soon, you'll learn there are times to follow orders and times to follow your instincts," he said. "Let's get these fuckers out of here and we can talk more about it."

It sounded like the promise of something to look forward to, and as she settled in behind him and used her rifle to deliver what damage she could, it was impossible to miss the sight of Hammerhand rising from his prone position. It was a slow, difficult process, especially for a mech of that size, but a few Knights had assembled to help him with a combination of pushing as well as cables to pull him onto his feet again.

One of his teammates helped him grasp his hammer again, and the speakers came alive with a loud crackle.

"Knights Mechanica, to me!" His voice rolled across the clearing around them to draw their attention. The defenders gravitated toward him and he twisted a little in place, likely still dealing with a handful of difficulties with his mech.

But if there was ever someone who could power through it, Hammerhand could.

The shield came up with a crackle as the Knights fell in behind him. Not all had been Knights at the beginning of the day, but all had fallen under the same banner by the end. It wasn't long before they surged forward into Athena's fighters, who had managed to regroup as well.

While the enemy might have regained their battle-readiness, they were still unprepared for the reinvigorated and reinforced Knights. With Hammerhand at the tip of the spear, they powered into the fray.

Jessica13 fell into the back lines to provide support once more and fired at those she could while her teammates drove forward in a powerful assault that decimated the lines of Athena's men by half almost without effort. Their leader used his shield to push them back and his hammer to finish, while the others delivered killing blows to those adversaries not directly in his path.

Athena's men were separated by the wedge and shoved aside and into the streets of Auburn. Once they lost their group formation, the combat quickly devolved into a group of smaller skirmishes. One of the teams that still managed to find a way to resist was led by two Guardians that used their plasma cannons to keep the Knights at bay.

They seemed to reach a stalemate when the team was forced to take cover behind Hammerhand's shield.

"I have an idea," Mini said.

"I won't like it, will I?" Jessica13 responded cautiously.

"Well, you have been fairly reckless all day so I'm fairly certain you will," he told her.

The AI still had control of the grappler arm, and with a quick shot of the new dart, the cable was launched to the top of one of the taller buildings near them. The retractor was quickly engaged and the building was stable enough to allow them to climb the side of it without tipping it, which gave them a view over Hammerhand's shield.

They were exposed as well, but the Guardians below and the Lancers in the formation were too occupied with the Knights they confronted to care about a small support mech that overlooked their position.

"What are we doing here?" Jessica13 asked.

"There is a weak point on the cannons that can be exploited on the Guardian mechs," Mini explained and highlighted it. "If exposed to oxygen, the plasma slugs will overheat. They will either expand in the cannon and jam it or cause a backfire that damages the mech itself."

After a very brief moment of thought, she decided that either scenario was acceptable and took aim at the closest Guardian. Rather than rush it, she gave herself time to follow the weapon's motions carefully before she pulled the trigger.

There was no backfire but the stream of superheated plasma slugs came to a halt as the last round expanded and jammed the chamber shut.

Jessica13 adjusted her aim to the second Guardian, who realized they were under fire from above and scanned for targets. Her heart seemed to jump in her throat as the massive canon swiveled to aim at her and she squeezed the trigger almost without thinking and held her breath.

The bullet penetrated the weak place on the mech and the explosion that erupted was thunderous. It ripped the rifle free from a hand that was instantly transformed to mostly charred junk metal. The Guardian stepped back and the pilot almost instinctively knew they were in trouble.

Hammerhand, seeing their sudden advantage, pressed the Knights forward in a concerted attack and rapidly defeated those who still stood their ground.

A few realized the danger they were in and tried to make their way surreptitiously out of the twisting streets of Auburn, but they were quickly overtaken and eliminated. None of Athena's men thought to drop their weapons and beg for mercy. Surrender was no option for them. They would either run or die.

And die they did. As the last mech fell, the Knights turned their attention to the balloons and airships overhead. While the battle raged, no one had thought of the airborne threat and they had gradually descended—possibly, Jessica thought, to increase the effectiveness of the lightning bolts at a shorter range. It seemed, however, that Athena also knew that defeat was imminent and now attempted to withdraw them from the battle as the lightning they delivered was not enough to pass through the grounding towers.

"Tear them out of the sky," Hammerhand roared, and the Knights turned their fire upward to deliver volley after volley of rounds into the slow-moving airships and balloons.

The latter were easily punctured and perforated and immediately lost altitude, and even the armored airship was not built to sustain the kind of firepower the Knights released. Its nose inched earthward until it lost what held it in the sky and gained speed to careen toward a collision that was difficult to miss, even from a distance.

It was marked by a bright yellow explosion and pieces were flung hundreds of meters away, still in flames. Jessica13 raised her fist, unable to restrain a cheer as she realized that the sky now began to clear to display the brilliant reds and purples of the sunset.

Hammerhand raised his fist as well and bellowed something she couldn't understand in a language she had never heard before. The Knights swiftly took up his call.

The feeling of jubilation was exhilarating, and she didn't want to come down from her position at the top of the building from where she had a clear view of the flames of the last of Athena's attacks.

"Do not be afraid of them," Hammerhand roared to his followers as their voices quieted. "For they have been delivered into your hands. Your victory is your own. This is the victory that has overcome even the world and your faith has prevailed."

The Knights responded with another roar, echoed by the local townsfolk who had come to their aid. They'd had little to offer except their bravery and ingenuity, without which the victory would not have been possible.

As the sun slid beyond the far horizon, Jessica13 caught movement out of the corner of her eye. Flashes of light flickered in the distance, probably near the bunker where Athena had established her base.

"What—" She turned to the other Knights, some of whom had already noticed it and were equally as confused and a little alarmed, as she was.

As if by an unspoken agreement, the group moved toward the top of the hill for a better view. Suggestions of movement in the distance were caught in the somewhat distorted illumination provided by the still-burning airship and the light that flickered from the far tower.

Suddenly, the light solidified with a crack that resounded across the plains. It seemed to possess an unnatural power and visibly bent the grasslands away from it in a ring that spun and arced around the tower. Jessica13 recalled seeing a similar effect from Athena's spear when they had spied on her at the church. The light from it was blinding, almost like a second sun, and painted the increasing stream of motion vividly against what had been growing darkness. The scene held an eerie quality like the impossible had been birthed by the crackling, shuddering white illumination.

The sight took Jessica13's breath away. Athena's forces marched in what looked like synchronized formation. Entire companies of infantry to mechs were organized into square blocks and pushed across the open grasslands like legions of the Ancients.

It seemed impossible, yet there was no denying the evidence. Her mind immediately tried to find explanations, still in rebellion because she hadn't even considered the possibility that so many people could live Outside. Had the woman gathered them from farther afield? Had she recruited from the Cities-That-Were, or were these smaller communities she'd assimilated and bullied, coerced, or wooed to her cause? How far did her power stretch to create and sustain a force of that magnitude?

Hammerhand moved ahead of the Knights, who stared at the sheer numbers that marched inexorably toward them. Victory had seemed sweet for the few moments they'd had in which to enjoy it but now, it was a little bitter. It was as if a precious promise had been stolen from them before they could take hold of it, the approaching horde a mockery of their jubilation and achievement.

Their leader, however, seemed to look beyond the main army as if to discount the ranks of Lancer mechs led by dozens of Guardians, all armed to the teeth and ready for a fight.

His gaze sought and found the one thing that hadn't been a part of their previous battles. Jessica13 knew he had expected to face Athena from the moment they had decided to turn aside from their search for Citta del Mar toward the towns that needed their help. She had wondered about the woman's absence herself and now realized that for him, the victory must have been tainted by the knowledge that it was far from over. While the tyrant remained at large, victory would never be complete.

Her gaze finally located another massive, hulking Excalibur mech much like his, and yet not. A long, tattered cloak hung from its shoulders and a spear in its hands crackled with electricity in a mirrored replica of the tower behind it. The shimmering visage of an owl was carved into its helm.

Hammerhand stood motionless, his demeanor unreadable. It could have been either expectation or resignation and acceptance of the inevitable but either way, this was what he had waited for. He evidenced no surprise at the seemingly endless legions of Athena's men who came to a halt with one gesture from the woman herself. She stood well in advance of the rest of her army, supremely arrogant and sure of her invincibility.

"There's no way to defeat this," Jessica13 said softly.

"Do you want to hear the odds?" Mini asked.

She shook her head, her eyes irresistibly drawn to the Excalibur mech that stood on the hilltop almost three full klicks away. Her presence was such that even the distance couldn't obscure her and she somehow seemed much closer to the gathered Knights.

For a moment she stood in silence, the only sound in the air the distant crackle of thunder amidst the storm that approached. Her cloak whipped in the wind and she raised her spear in a challenge.

"So, Hammerhand," Athena called over the radio, "we meet again at last."

The story continues with At Athena's Gates, coming soon to Amazon and Kindle Unlimited.

ABOUT THE AUTHOR

Marshal Rust was born in Boulder, Colorado, where he still resides to this day. His parents - both hard-working blue-collar folk - made sure he got a good education and ensured that included reading as many books as he possibly could. And it's no surprise he came to absolutely love science fiction and fantasy. He cut his teeth on the works of Heinlein, Asimov, Tolkien, and more. He later progressed to the works of Robert Jordan, Terry Brooks, David Brin and Cormac McArthy, and many of their contemporaries through and over the years. He's worked in his father's trade as a welder, moonlighted as a delivery man, sold computer hardware, and done a brutal stint as an animal massage therapist (yes, it's a real job), and has even had to chase a goat that made off with his paper bagged lunch, but nothing makes him happier than clear skies and a blank sheet of paper to write on.

Bulletfoot Series

Origins (Book 1)

The Auburn Rebellion (Book 2)

At Athena's Gates (Book 3 coming soon)